The Lysander Passenger

Other novels by Peter Clements

The Fifth Agenda
The Third Temple
Russian Revenge
A Murder at Bletchley Park

The Lysander Passenger

Peter Clements

Strategic Book Publishing and Rights Co.

Strategic Book Publishing & Rights Co., LLC
USA | Singapore
www.sbpra.com

For information about special discounts for bulk purchases, please contact Strategic Book Publishing and Rights Co. Special Sales, at bookorder@sbpra.net.

ISBN: 978-1-948260-28-2

Disclaimer: 'All the characters in this novel are fictional and any likeness to persons alive or dead is coincidental.'

This is a story of treachery, betrayal, and duplicity, human failings of which all men and all governments are capable, and to which many succumb in war.

Preface

France, 1942

I am a traitor, a judgement that if known would bring universal condemnation. As to whom and what I have betrayed, the evidence exists, and if you look hard enough you will find it. Perhaps I should add that I have not been coerced or compelled in any way. My past duplicity and that which I continue to practice has been calculated to benefit only one person, me; that others may have gained from my anomic endeavours is neither here nor there and is anyway amply balanced by those whom I have betrayed.

It would be easy to excuse what I have done and continue to do, to hide, like so many others, behind some mistaken loyalty to an old man and a regime whose very legality is questionable. To pretend that the Christian roots of our country and the sanctity of the family are at risk is absurd. Save for a few fanatics, does anybody truly believe that? Can the occupation of one's country by a foreign army be so effortlessly explained away? Does the fear of one dogma, one 'ism, justify the toxic embrace of another? To replace 'Liberty, Fraternity, Equality' with 'Work, Family, and Fatherland,' the Third Republic with '*L'État français*' is nothing more than factitious pomp. If what I have done and continue to do solicits a moral question, then I hold out little hope for a satisfactory answer.

It's almost time for my meeting with the corpulent Major Speidel of the Abwehr. There is much to report. Three pickups in his zone were planned for the next full moon period, giving the Germans a lot of material to work through before I seal the packages and pass them on to London. Then I had to compile a list of names. Who should I expose? Over the course of the last few weeks I've been introduced into the *'Manet'* network. They had been so trusting. Should I run them for a while to see if I can net more agents? There's so much to consider. As with other networks I have penetrated, some names I would hold back, names that were of more value to the Gestapo and for which I would be better paid.

Speidel remains a tiresome individual, burdened with a conscience, a man in the wrong profession, a man who made no secret of his dislike for this humble servant, who was only doing his best to help end the war in Germany's favour and his own. During one exchange, he explained what he thought of *verräter*, those who were able to live, as I do, without the crutch of patriotism. It was all rather tedious, and were it not for the occasional benefit begrudgingly bestowed upon me by the Abwehr I would be done with Speidel's moralising and deal only with the unrelievedly menacing Otto Meuller of the Gestapo, a tall skeleton of a man who makes me shudder whenever I'm in his presence. His dead ice-blue eyes, sunk into a skull of almost albino complexion, disturb me more than I care to admit. But unlike Speidel, Meuller understands me, in spite of his own misguided commitment to a cause, National Socialism. About Meuller, there is no pretence and, above all, no righteousness.

There are, however, other matters to consider in my dealings with the Germans. My central philosophy is to look after self, and to that end I have to think of the future. A man would be a fool to believe that the outcome of the war was not now in doubt. Things have changed since those decisive days of 1940 when my duplicitous career blossomed. In truth, the bud of perfidy has always lived within me, even at school. But now the Russian bear has grown in strength and is pushing the Germans hard in the East. The Americans have landed in North Africa, initiating a countermove by the Germans to occupy the whole of France, a further drain on their already stretched forces in Russia. Then there's the stubborn English, a nation that admires the amateur over the professional, because that is what so many of their agents are, rank amateurs and, I have observed, an eccentric group. As for the pilots of the aircraft that drop off and pick up the agents, of those I have met both in France and in England, they seemed to be no more than overgrown schoolboys out for a lark, a lark that others refer to as war. And yet obdurate Albany, this nation of *boutiquiers,* has defied the might of the Third Reich.

I will be the first to admit that, as things stand, a victory for the Allies would leave me in an invidious position, so steps must be taken to ensure my survival, no matter which way the dice fall. When I'm next summoned to England for a meeting with SIS, there will be certain proposals I must put to them concerning my future.

* * *

England, 13 November 1942

He could not believe his luck. He could not have planned it better. It was almost too easy. The man had stepped out onto the patio for a smoke, closing the French doors behind him. He had studied the photograph assiduously, and there was no doubt in his mind as to who stood before him in the calm Bedfordshire winter evening air puffing on a cigarette, probably luxuriating in the mistaken belief that here, in England, he was safe.

The heavy drapes precluded anyone sitting in the lounge from observing the garden. There was the risk that the doors would suddenly open and another guest would step outside, but the opportunity was too good to miss. He had only a few minutes before the smoker's eyes would adjust to the night and the element of surprise would be missed. Less than eight metres separated them. To rush him, head-on, would run the risk of the victim crying out, either from astonishment or fear, and yet where he stood made it impossible to approach from behind. If only he were to leave the patio and walk down onto the lawn it would be so much easier, but it was asking a lot, and time was running out. Then, as if he had willed it, the man turned to his left and looked up at the night sky. It was a move that would cost him his life.

Noiselessly sprinting the short distance that separated them, making sure not to trip as he mounted the stone steps of the patio, he closed the distance, his left hand deftly covering the mouth at the same time pulling the head back as his right brought the knife in a slashing motion, from left to right, across his throat. The victim briefly struggled and, just for a split second, he wondered if a second strike was necessary. For all his violent past he had never cut a person's throat before and had wondered what it would be like, but to think is not to do, and the doing he found was quite another matter – so easy, so quick. He had no need to worry; a second slash wasn't necessary, and the victim slumped forward. Carefully he helped the bleeding body onto the ground. It was as if he had come across a stranger in the street, someone who had suddenly collapsed, so carefully did he rest the body down.

The Lysander Passenger

Chapter One

Tempsford, Bedfordshire

November 1942

Strapping himself into the cockpit, he adjusted the height of his seat using the wheel by his right leg and then slid the hood overhead forward, locking it into the top of the windscreen. Sergeant Ian Gifford of the Royal Air Force was on his third trip into occupied France. His aircraft, a Lysander, produced by Westland Aircraft, was originally designed as a spotter plane for the British Army. This modified version had a new role – to carry agents into occupied territory. Still, though, it was slow, unarmed, and no match against a Messerschmitt 109. When such an encounter occurred, thankfully not that often, its only defence was its manoeuvrability, which wasn't saying a lot. That was why, during his hurried conversion onto type, he had practiced extreme manoeuvres and recovery from unusual attitudes, being careful not to stall or spin the aircraft, since the Lysander wasn't built for such adventures, and all this at night, for that was when they worked, when the moon was full.

His acceptance into the squadron had come as something of a surprise to all concerned, including himself. When he had first applied for aircrew, at the RAF recruiting office in Plymouth, they had passed on his details to Air Ministry, but there was no response. At the time, he had the distinct impression that his licences and logbook were regarded as fraudulent documents. Also, they had never heard of the company for whom he had flown in Canada, which didn't surprise him. The recruiting sergeant who suspiciously leafed through his logbook would have had difficulty identifying Canada on a map. While waiting for their reply, he had written to White Waltham, Maidenhead, enquiring if the Air Transport Auxiliary (ATA), whose unofficial motto was, 'Anything to Anywhere,' along with the nickname 'Ancient and Tattered Airmen,' was interested in employing as a ferry pilot a thirty-two-year-old divorced Englishman who had spent the last six years as a bush pilot in Western Canada? He knew they took those either too old or medically unfit for the Royal Air Force or the Fleet Air Arm. Being 'sound in both wind and limb,' surely it would be churlish of them to regard his application unfavourably. By some bureaucratic route, unknown to the great unwashed, the ATA had contacted Air Ministry. The good folk at White Waltham, knowing something about civil aviation and having verified his flying experience, had contacted the RAF, saying, in effect, 'If you don't want him, we do.'

Nine months later, on being awarded his wings with the RAF, he was sent to RAF Silloth for a Hudson familiarisation course. After a spell at an operational training unit (OTU), he had been posted, as a sergeant pilot, to Coastal Command, in Cornwall, escorting Atlantic convoys from the seat of a draughty Hudson. But nothing had equipped him for the mind-numbing, not to mention bone-chilling hours spent flying over a vast expanse of ocean. Then, while on leave one evening, away from the Atlantic cold, he had visited a pub in Tangmere near Chichester and fell into talking with an aircraft maintenance sergeant who serviced Lysander aircraft at the local airfield. After a few pints of weak ale, he had introduced him to a flying officer, a fellow pilot, who showed an interest in his flying experience in Canada. It was not long after returning to his squadron in Cornwall that he was called into the office of his squadron commander.

"Gifford, you're leaving us and Coastal Command. Can't tell you more than that, but you're to report to RAF Tempsford as soon as we have a replacement. Some specialist squadron. Do you know something I don't?"

"No, sir."

"Very well. You had better start packing your bags. OTU informs me they can have your replacement here within a couple of days. You haven't been with us long, but I'm reliably informed that you have a good pair of hands when it comes to flying. Good luck at Tempsford."

"Thank you, sir. Just one thing."

"Yes?"

"Where is Tempsford?"

"How the hell should I know?"

* * *

His acceptance into the elite group of pilots at Tempsford was thrown into question when he was interviewed by the station commander, Wing Commander Farrington, a short well-built man in his fifties with a ramrod back, short, cropped, greying hair, and a walrus moustache, the colour of which had defied the aging process. Among the ribbons on the breast of his battle dress tunic, Gifford identified both the DFC and a DSO. Clearly the wing commander was no chair-born warrior.

"Coming to us poses something of a problem, Gifford."

"It does, sir?"

"Yes, it does, Gifford. We handpick our pilots, and although you are no exception, your rank is. We're not like Coastal or Bomber Command; all our chaps are commissioned. So you see the problem."

"I guess I do, sir." His years of living in Canada, among the freewheeling people of British Columbia, a far more egalitarian community than that of Great Britain, had given him a dislike for the social structure into which he had returned. Before taking up his new life in Canada he hadn't even noticed the deeply entrenched class system within his own country; it was something he had grown up with, accepted without question, a social order he had taken as the norm. Only when experiencing a very different society was he able to see Britain for what it was. The RAF was but an extension of that hierarchical system writ large.

Why his rank should be a problem for the wing commander he couldn't imagine. Within the air force there were hundreds if not thousands of pilots who, for one reason or another, the powers that be had considered not suitable for a commission, men who in some cases had been given command of four-engine bombers and a crew of eight, many of whom were commissioned. Had he not been flying for Coastal Command with the esteemed rank of an NCO? It was possible, of course, that moving into the small mess set aside for non-commissioned officers at Tempsford might disturb matters in the dovecote. With him being the only pilot, he would be viewed as something of an oddity.

"You're also older than most of our chaps," the wing commander continued, "but we're short of suitably experienced pilots, Gifford, otherwise you wouldn't be with us. Under peacetime conditions I wouldn't have a civilian-trained pilot on my squadron. That's the way of it, just so you understand. It would have been a damn sight easier to have left you in Coastal Command, but you're here now, and, damn it all, we need you. Your experience on the Hudson and this flying you've been doing in Canada may be useful. Our immediate need is for Lysander pilots, so we'll get you checked out on the old 'Lizzie' as soon as possible. But this matter of your rank is a problem, and I'll have to sort it out. Leave it with me." All things considered, there was not a lot Gifford could do about it anyway. "I see from your logbook," he said, carefully handling the civilian document as if he might catch some virulent disease from its pages, "until you joined Coastal Command you had little or no night time. Well, as you now know, we are bats. We only fly at night. You know what they say, Gifford, 'Only birds and fools fly by day; only bats and bloody fools by night.' I assume you speak French?"

"Pardon, sir?"

"Do you speak French?"

"No, sir."

"Funny, I thought they spoke French as well as English in Canada."

"Not in British Columbia, sir."

"Oh." He paused and looked out of his office window as if seeking inspiration. "Now that you know what we're about at Tempsford, no doubt you'll try to fit in. By the by, something is puzzling me. Why did you return to home shores? I would have thought, with the Dominions being part of this war, you would have joined their team and gone into the Canadian Air Force instead of coming back here."

"My parents, sir. My mother is not well, and my father thought I should visit her before . . . After arriving in England, Hitler marches into Poland, and I'm stuck in Devon. I tried to return to Canada but couldn't get a berth due to the evacuation of so many . . ."

"I see, I see. Well, any troubles, you know who to go to. I hope you find your time with us rewarding. You'll find the Lizzie a bit of a dray, but it does the job. It's not a kite for beginners, but no doubt you'll handle it."

"Thank you, sir." It was Gifford's opinion that, rewarding or not, his time with the squadron, if the wing commander had anything to do with it, would be short-lived, and his stay would last only until pilot numbers could be brought up to strength. It was not something that bothered him. He might even enjoy flying the Lysander, if not the social order in which he found himself. Flying a Lysander at night over occupied France seemed preferable to hours spent in an incommodious Hudson over the Atlantic.

Unlike most of the pilots who had joined the squadron, he was familiar with short, rough field landing techniques, something for which the Lysander had proved ideal. Some of the landing strips he had flown into in British Columbia, particularly around Prince Rupert and Kitimat, were even shorter and rougher than those the squadron used in occupied France.

For his conversion onto type he was issued with loose-leaf pilot's notes that had been reproduced from typescripts, along with ten pages of descriptions, photographs, and handling notes. The rest was up to him. The Lysander proved to be an aircraft he would grow to like, but the wing commander was right, it definitely wasn't a machine for beginners.

No matter how often he carried out his pre-flight checks, he took his time. They had to be done correctly, both for his own safety and that of his Joes (agents). Pull the engine through, then, once in the cockpit, check prop pitch is set to COURSE, prime the engine, first the carburettor bowl, and then turn the lever and direct six good hard pumps to the cylinders. Press both boost-coil and start buttons simultaneously. When the prop turns, after three blades, put mags to ON. Let the engine tick over until the oil temperature reaches 5 degrees C, move pitch to FINE for take-off once oil pressure is confirmed. Meanwhile, test the flight controls and brake pressure, running the engine up to 1,800 rpm against the brakes and chocks. Then, at cruising throttle, check the alternate magneto switches.

Satisfied that all was well, he waved the chocks away. By having the mixture to max rich and with slow movement of the throttle he found he could have the engine running smoothly on the ground. Leaving the Carb Heat to HOT further helped for smooth running by richening the mixture. The Lysander was not the easiest aircraft to control on the ground, having a long wheelbase, with the two main wheels close together and a heavy tail. Its turning-moment, he had quickly discovered, was restricted. The brake lever on the spade grip, plus the differential on the pedals, had to be treated with care. At the end of the runway, while waiting for take-off clearance, he checked that the tail actuator was set for TAKE-OFF. It had been impressed upon him during his conversion how important it was to have the trim control in the correct position, whether for take-off or for landing. It was a powerful control, and it was impossible to overcome it by pressure on the stick if he had opened up to take-off power with the tail adjusted for landing. In truth, there wasn't enough elevator authority to control the aircraft in all phases of flight. He had got into the habit of setting the trim halfway between the TAKE-OFF mark and FULL-UP, giving him the best chance of recovering from engine failure at the critical point. However, if he carried two or more passengers he found it best with three bites of down trim for take-off in order to have the aircraft correctly trimmed, with the mixture control set to NORMAL, and the pitch control pushed in for fine pitch. Recheck the fuel – he needed full tanks with what could be eight hours of flying ahead of him. Next check that the gills on the engine cowling were open to increase airflow over the engine. A green light flashed from the tower. Having obtained take-off clearance, he turned onto the long flare path, carefully eased the throttle open, and commenced his short take-off. Unlike most tail-wheelers, the Lizzie took off in the three-point configuration, getting airborne at about 80 mph. Such was its performance that, if necessary, the Lizzie could be airborne in 200 yards with a speed of just 65 mph.

Once airborne he accelerated to 110 mph for the flaps and slats to automatically retract. Another peculiarity of the Lizzie was its automatically operated flap and slat system, over which the pilot had no control. He moved the prop to COURSE to stop the engine from over speeding beyond 2650 rpm, the max climb limit being 2,400 rpm. To keep the engine cool he kept the gills fully open.

The weather for most of the flight had been bad, with layered cloud up to 15,000 feet. He had climbed up to 9,000 feet between layers for the crossing. The winds had been such that he never exceeded 120 mph, which meant that it took him an hour to cross the Channel. However, at that speed, and by putting the mixture to weak and the power at 2,200 rpm, fuel consumption was reduced to 30 gal/hr, and the Lysander could stay aloft for hours and had a range of over 1,600 miles.

"Let me know if you see land," he asked his passenger. "We should be crossing the coast about now." He had faith in his navigation but not in the weather. If they could get a fix on the point at which they crossed the coast he would know how far, if at all, he was off course. The wind was right on the nose, so time would be more of a problem than drift. Conditions, he reasoned, were no worse than those he had experienced flying off the coast of British Columbia, and there he had to contend with mountains.

He had just one Joe (agent) for the outbound trip, a young woman, possibly no more than twenty. In briefing her he had made sure she knew how to put on and take off her parachute harness, how to fit the chest-type parachute, how her flying helmet plugged into the intercom, how to use the intercom switch, along with what to expect throughout the flight and what to do upon landing. She seemed intelligent and well trained as well as determined – that she was also courageous was a given. The thought of such a creature falling into the hands of the Germans was not something he wanted to dwell upon.

"There is land beneath us," she said over the intercom. "I think I saw some fields through the clouds."

"Thanks, we'll start letting down. We don't want to stay up here all night. Keep your eyes open for German aircraft." He had planned to cross the coast at Cabourg, near Caen. If his navigation was correct they had approximately seventy minutes to run to the target area, but the farther they penetrated into France the worse the weather became. At 1,500 feet cloud obscured any chance they had of seeing the landing zone. By 01.30, working off his compass and airspeed they should be approaching the target area. Letting down to 800 feet he at last caught sight of the ground and, to his relief, two landmarks that confirmed his position, a river and a railway line. He was only ten or twelve miles port of track. Turning to starboard he maintained altitude. A few minutes later he began to circle, looking for the field.

"There is a light flashing to our right," came the soft voice from the rear. Dash dot dash dot, the letter C for Charley. Swinging the aircraft around to starboard and using his signalling key, he replied with the letter B for Bravo from a small lamp below the fuselage. Almost immediately three lights appeared, forming the letter L for the landing direction and flair path.

He configured the aircraft for the approach – mixture to NORMAL, pitch to FINE – and when on final approach he opened the cowl flaps (the gills) for more drag and set up for the go-around. Speed back to 100 mph.

With a little power still on, the aircraft skimmed over the boundary hedge at 70 mph, with slats out and flaps having automatically extended. Seconds later they were on the ground bumping along on the undulating surface. Closing the throttle, he at first applied minimum braking before putting more pressure on the brake pedals but not so much that he didn't have enough momentum to swing the aircraft through 180 degrees. They taxied back to the first light and the waiting reception committee. As the aircraft came to rest, her last words to him over the intercom were, "Thank you, I hope you have a safe trip home." Having passed down the luggage and load, she climbed down the ladder and left the aircraft. The last he saw was of her slight figure disappearing into the night, clutching a small suitcase. What sort of war was it, he wondered, that sent such young women behind enemy lines? Suddenly he had an almost overwhelming need to protect her, but it was not why he had come to France.

The changeover was seamless, with the outbound passenger and load aboard, the cockpit roof shut, the thumbs-up given for taxi, and the shout "okay," all within four minutes.

Space aboard all SOE/SIS flights was at a premium, so it was unusual to have had only one inbound passenger, but even more so to have just one for the return flight. If he had thought about it, the answer to that oddity lay back at Tempsford, in his briefing folder for the flight. There was not one but two Air Transport Forms. One was printed in black for the outbound, indicating it was an SOE operation, the other printed in mauve, which meant that his return flight was for the SIS (Secret Intelligence Service).

Once airborne, he set course for the coast, retracing his outward-bound route to cross at Cabourg. There was no improvement in the weather. If anything, it had deteriorated, and he was forced to fly at 600 feet to maintain visual contact with the ground. He knew that at some stage he would have to climb, at which time he could expect icing. Carb icing was a problem with the Mercury engine, so he would need to keep a watch on the carb temperature gauge. Because of German air defences he had no choice but to climb. It was tempting fate to cross the coast at low level.

An accurate fix of his position before crossing the Channel was essential, something that looked increasingly unlikely the further north he flew. By Saint-Calais he could see that the cloud ahead, towards Bertey and Vibraye, was right down on the deck, forcing him into either climbing early, up into the 'clag' and deadheading for the coast, or return south to look for a better route. The weather briefing he had received prior to leaving Tempsford made the first option more appealing, not that either held much promise. He didn't envy meteorologists their job. England's maritime climate made their briefings speculative at best. It was said that, 'Meteorology was an inexact science practiced by exact people.'

Shortly after commencing the climb it began to rain, and at 8,000 feet the aircraft started to take on ice. The cockpit in the Lizzie was sufficiently forward that the pilot had a good view of both wings' leading edges. Shining his torch along the starboard wing leading edge, he could see the speed at which the ice was building up; attempting to climb any higher would very soon be impossible. The four tons of aircraft that held them aloft was about to become a lot heavier. Soon the engine coughed. Jazzing the throttles restored power, but for how much longer? Applying heat to the carburettor helped solve the problem but did nothing for the build-up on the wings. Being in 10/10th cloud meant that he was unable to fly around the cumulus clouds embedded within the layers of altostratus. The clouds of vertical development tossed them about, with the updrafts and downdrafts becoming more violent. He had not spoken to his passenger since take-off, being first preoccupied with the flight and now with trying to control the aircraft in turbulence. He presumed that the poor chap was by now beginning to wish he hadn't come along for the flight.

"You okay down the back?" he asked.

"Yes. I am Henri, a friend of Squadron Leader Huntington-Brown. I often stay with him in England."

Huntington-Brown was Gifford's flight commander, a man who, from the first time they had met, exhibited a certain disdain towards a pilot who was not only a sergeant but one who had learnt to fly outside of the air force and, to add insult to injury, in the colonies.

"Good for you. Have you found the thermos and sandwiches?"

"Yes, but it is not easy to drink or eat in such conditions. Will we be in cloud all the way to England?" His English reminded Gifford of a second-rate actor putting on a French accent.

"Pea soup all the way, I think. Sorry about the bumps. I can't promise when we'll be free of them, I'm afraid. With luck it'll be better once we're over the sea." It was something he could only hope for but did not for one moment believe would happen. "One thing, this weather means we won't be bothered by the Luftwaffe tonight."

They soldiered on for the next hour, by which time he estimated that they should be crossing the coast, if they hadn't already done so. With nothing other than his compass to steer by it was impossible to know how much drift he had on. The forecast was for north-westerly winds. He had laid off ten degrees of port drift, hoping that that would be enough. If not, they could be crossing the coast as far east as Le Havre or even farther. Then, through a small break in the cloud, he saw water beneath them. But now the weight of the ice on the aircraft had become such that they started to lose altitude. Not until they were down to

1,500 feet could he maintain height, by which time they had shed most of the ice and were flying in smoother air.

The rest of the flight was trouble free, and when they landed at Tangmere, Gifford's flight commander and a man in civilian clothes drove up in a large American car and whisked his passenger away without a word.

Chapter Two

<u>Milton Ernest, Bedfordshire</u>

Sergeant Alan Hodges of the Metropolitan Police would never know what had occupied Inspector Sim of Special Branch since the previous year when they had last met. He had received the summons to report for duty as soon as possible to the local police station at Milton Ernest, where he would meet with the inspector and receive his briefing. In a curious sort of way, he was looking forward to the experience.

Having the previous year failed to solve the murder of Chief Wren, Sally Evans, in the grounds of Bletchley Park, one of Britain's most secure establishments, he had not expected to hear from Special Branch ever again. It had taken a few months for him to become reconciled to the fact that they had failed to find the murderer and that he was destined to continue to serve the people of the East End, along with what the Luftwaffe had left of dockland. But it was a community where he was comfortable, where he was at home, known and respected, even among those who had little or no regard for the law. He knew them all, the prostitutes, spivs, and the ex-jailbirds who had been rejected for military service, many of whom had gravitated to his patch, along with those poor souls whom fate and an imbedded social structure had decreed would remain at the bottom of the heap. They were his people, and yet . . . He looked back on the short time he had spent in Buckinghamshire, working with Inspector

Sim from Special Branch, as an interesting time in his career, enjoyable almost, away from the bombing with its sleepless nights and continual exhaustion, along with the responsibility of being a station sergeant on one of the Met's roughest patches. But, given his position in the grand scheme of things, he was dreaming if he thought that his time with Special Branch had been anything more than anomalous, yet here he was, summoned to Milton Ernest.

"Good afternoon, Sergeant," said Inspector Sim, extending his hand from across the small counter. He was wearing the same crumpled dark grey double-breasted three-piece suit from when they last met. No doubt he was still living with his aunt in Hampstead, or was it Belsize Park? Behind him a rotund uniformed senior constable hovered inquisitively. It wasn't every day they had a visit from the Met. The police station was small and typical of its type, built of red brick during the reign of Queen Victoria at a time when the establishment saw the need to keep the good rural folk of Milton Ernest in order, along with those of the surrounding countryside. And now, with the food shortages, poaching was again in vogue, the prevention of which had been the main reason for the station's creation in 1880.

"Afternoon, sir. I didn't expect to meet you again."

"There's no discharge in the war, Sergeant, and in war all things are possible. Let's leave the constable here to get on with his job. There's a tea room right next door. We can talk there. Bring your bag. You're to board with a Mrs. Hall in the village. No room at the inn this time, I'm afraid."

Minutes later, as he poured them both a cup of tea, the inspector said, "I'm pleased the Met could spare you, Sergeant. How's the war been treating you since we last met?"

"A bit better now that Jerry isn't visitin' every night. Other than that, much the same, sir, no shortage of crime, you might say. Good of you to think of me, I mean, workin' again for Special Branch." He particularly liked the fact that wherever Inspector Sim was, a cup of tea was never far away. Sergeant Alan Hodges was one of those Englishmen for whom tea was more than a drink; it was a way of life.

"I'm glad you were able to make it to Bedfordshire, Sergeant. The criminals of the East End will probably welcome the rest. We're here following another untimely death, I'm afraid. That's if any death in wartime can be termed timely." Taking a sip of his tea, he continued. "It's not the sort of crime you would normally associate with rural England, even in wartime. Two days ago, a man was found by his host, in a house just outside the village, with his throat cut."

"A bit brutal. Who was 'e, and why bring in Special Branch, sir?"

"I was coming to that. It seems the deceased was a foreign gentleman. Special Branch has been called in because he was someone of importance to the war effort. I've always found that phrase condescending, haven't you, Sergeant? Are the rest of us unimportant to the war effort? He arrived in the country a few days ago, on the tenth, to be precise. Apparently, his presence in the country and subsequent death poses a security problem for His Majesty's Government and also, I suspect, something of an embarrassment. The office of the Free French in London is also taking an interest in the case, which I think we may assume is a lead as to the nationality of the deceased. We are to have a briefing from SOE."

"And who are they when they're at 'ome?"

"I understand it's an acronym for Special Operations Executive. Some quasi-military organisation. All rather hush-hush."

"Bit like last year, Bletchley Park, sir. What was the foreign gent doin' 'ere?"

"You might well ask, Sergeant, but that particular morsel of information remains off-limits to us, at least for the present. He was meant to leave the country yesterday."

"The day after 'e was killed. Well, 'e won't be doin' that."

"Exactly. He met his end at the home of one of the RAF pilots stationed at Tempsford, which is a place that appears to be not unlike Bletchley Park, maximum security. We're fishing in dark waters again, I'm afraid. You now know as much as I do. Perhaps the good folk at SOE will be able to enlighten us further. Have you noticed the marked increase in acronyms since the beginning of the war?"

"Now you mention it, I suppose there 'as been. It's probably somethin' to do with the military mind, wouldn't you say?"

"You may be right. This all has to be kept under wraps, you understand, Sergeant."

"Of course, sir. Not your normal sort of crime, though, is it? I mean, I can't see the folks of Milton Ernest goin' around slittin' each other's throats, can you, sir?"

"Quite. I would say it's more the work of a professional killer."

"My thoughts exactly, sir."

"I think we can assume it has something to do with whatever the man was up to in this country and whatever is going on at Tempsford, otherwise, why would we have been called in? First, we have to identify the deceased and then his connection, if any, with Tempsford. Who knows, we might then find the killer this time. Whoever he is, let's hope he's left a lot of little things behind him to point us in the right direction."

"Right, sir. When do we meet with these people at, SOE, was it?"

"That has yet to be decided." Pouring himself and the sergeant another cup of tea, he asked, "How is your daughter? She's in Canada, isn't she?"

Throughout their time while working together at Bletchley Park, never once had the inspector shown any interest in his personal life. But then, theirs had been a professional relationship, with neither trespassing on the private life of the other. War throws together those who in more peaceful times would not normally meet, let alone spend day after day working together. The chances of Inspector Sim's orbit and that of Sergeant Hodges coalescing would, under normal circumstances, be remote. But the megalomaniacal ambition of a little Austrian paperhanger had changed everything, both for them and for the whole of Europe. And so the melancholic Gerald Sim, late of the Indian Police Force's Special Branch, once retired and now back in harness for the duration, a bachelor with a middle-class background, was, upon request, once again working with the widowed Alan Hodges, father of one, a man whose daily working environment among the working class of the East End mirrored his origin.

"She's fine, sir. Lives with 'er uncle in Toronto, 'avin' a great time of it. Ice cream and chicken, you might say. It's goin' to be a bit tough on 'er when she comes back 'ere, whenever that's goin' to be."

"Let's hope it won't be too long, Sergeant. A lot has happened since last year."

"You mean America comin' in to the war, at last? If you recall, sir, that Mr. Pettit we spoke to at the King's Head in Aspley Guise last year, didn't 'e say they would be in within the year?"

"Yes, he did, quite prophetic, really, although things don't seem to be going our way in the Pacific, at present."

"Singapore and all. Wasn't it supposed to be impregnable?"

"I think that's what they said. Military hubris, wouldn't you say?"

"What 'appened to those big guns that were meant to defend the place?"

"I understand, Sergeant, that they were facing the wrong way. Something of an oversight."

"Nobody told them Japs to come by sea, then?"

"It seems not."

"I've got a young cousin who was sent there with 'is regiment. They arrived the day before it fell. God knows what's 'appened to 'im."

Although the threat of invasion had passed for Britain and the heavy blitz was history, the country was far from secure. He was about to mention a beer lunch he had shared recently with Ian McCleod, a ships officer, but thought better of it. McLeod was someone he had befriended two years previously, having fished him out of Surry Commercial Docks following the massive raid by the Luftwaffe on the 11th September 1940. He had given his word to the sailor that he wouldn't repeat the substance of their conversation. The raid on Surry Commercial Docks had gone on for twelve hours without relief, during which McCleod's ship, along with a number of others, had been sunk under him while birthed at King's Wharf. It had been a point of annoyance to the man that he had survived a crossing of the U-boat-infested waters of the Atlantic only to end up swimming for his life in the Surry Commercial. Their most recent meeting, however, had produced an even more harrowing tale. McCleod's ship had been torpedoed in mid-Atlantic en route to Halifax, Nova Scotia, and he had, after two days adrift in an open boat, been rescued by the Royal Navy. The convoy had been ripped apart by a wolf pack. Up to seven U-boats had attacked at night, scattering the ships and then picking them off one at a time. It had been the worst month McCleod had known for losses by the British Merchant Navy. He had then rattled off a list of ships that he had seen sent to the bottom, including his own and others that he had heard of that had recently suffered a similar fate. November 1942 proved to be one of the worst months of the war for ships lost, over 117 in 30 days.

"At least we're winnin' in the desert. Rommel's got 'is marchin' orders, thanks to Monty and 'is Desert Rats, and those Russians appear to be givin' the Germans a run for their money." There had been precious few victories in the beginning; it had been one defeat and one retreat after another. Now the mood was changing.

"They say that our gallant Russian allies are about to encircle the Germans at Stalingrad. That's something, I suppose. I've arranged a meeting with a local inspector, at the house, after we've got you established in your digs. I would like to look the crime scene over before it gets too dark. I managed to book the last room at the Queen's Head. We'll make that our centre of operations. I understand that your landlady, Mrs. Hall, is quite accommodating."

"Right you are, sir. 'Ow are we off for transport?"

"Tempsford has supplied us with a car and driver. In fact, there it is."

A Humber had driven past the tea room and parked outside the adjacent police station.

"Come on, Sergeant, let's go and meet our driver. You don't suppose it could be another like that mad girl at Bletchley? What was her name?"

"LACW Adler, sir."

"That was it. I remember you mentioned at the time that she may have been working for the Germans. Do you think she might still be driving?"

"I shouldn't think so. Killin' a civilian cyclist like that isn't something the air force could sweep under the carpet. I wonder what they did with 'er."

While Inspector Sim waited in the car, Sergeant Hodges introduced himself to his landlady, Mrs. Hall, a stocky woman in her mid-forties, with short grey hair and a swarthy complexion. The upstairs room to which he was led was minute, even by London standards. It was at the back of the house, facing east, and overlooked a small walled vegetable garden. Although the day was mild for November, the room had a damp chill about it. If the sun ever penetrated its confines it was probably for no more than for a few hours first thing in the morning and only then in summer.

"Breakfast is at eight, after that you'll have to fend for yourself. I've got a job to do in the village. I locks the door at ten p.m. sharp. If you want a key, there's a deposit. There'll be no visitors, if you know what I mean, and I expect my guests to strictly observe the blackout, and no smoking in the room. I'll be requiring your ration book if you're staying long." There existed something of the theatrical about her affected accent and exaggerated hand movements. Maybe, at some time in her life, Mrs. Hall had trodden the boards. A pity some of them had not been loose, he thought. That such a harridan should be running a boarding house said much for the shortage of accommodations in Milton Ernest.

It was not the welcome he had hoped for. With luck, they would quickly solve the case, enabling a swift return to 'the smoke' and the house that he and Mavis had bought before the war. It had been his intention to sell it upon returning from Bletchley Park, but one thing after another had got in the way, and, he reasoned, it was doubtful he would find a buyer while the bombing continued. The house reminded him of a wife whose death he didn't mourn, something for which he knew he should feel guilty but did not, and, for reasons he could not explain, the hours he spent in the house remained free of remorse.

They arrived at the detached, two-storied mock-Tudor edifice, with a manicured front lawn and a walled rear garden that included a small orchard, with both men impressed at the driving skill of their WRAF driver. An inspector of the Bedfordshire constabulary led them to a patio at the rear, from which there was access through French windows to a large well-furnished lounge. In the fast-fading light, a young constable was desultorily searching that part of the rear lawn that led to the orchard.

"This was where the body was found. As you can see, there was a fair amount of blood," the local inspector commented, pointing to stains on the stone paving. "We haven't found the murder weapon. We're still searching the grounds, but we haven't found much yet. We don't often get this sort of murder in Bedfordshire." He was tall, in his fifties, but with a stoop that aged him. He didn't attempt to hide his displeasure at the incursion of Special Branch onto his patch.

"I don't know why they called you people in. This isn't the first homicide we've had to deal with in the county. But obviously someone up there thinks we're not up to it."

Sim ignored his pronouncement. "Who found him and what time of day was it?"

"After dinner, about eight or nine. He was found by his host, a Squadron Leader Glen Huntington-Brown, the owner of the house. Come to think of it, he might even rent it, for all I know. I've already spoken to him, but I didn't get very far. A bit up himself, if you ask me. It's all very hush-hush, which is why they brought you lot in, I suppose," he added sarcastically. "The deceased had stepped outside for a smoke. There was a bit of a party going on. The curtains prevented anybody seeing what happened. The squadron leader found him after he went out to investigate why his guest hadn't returned."

"Is the squadron leader around?"

"No. He's back with his squadron."

"That's unfortunate."

"Yes, well, there's a war on. It's a couple of days since the murder, and life goes on. You can speak to his wife. You'll find her in the kitchen, but I don't think you'll get much out of her, either. As I said, I've spoken to the squadron leader, but, shortly after, it was made quite clear to me, by no less a person that the chief constable, that I was not to get involved with the case and that it would be handled by Special Branch. I can't say I'm happy with the state of affairs. I mean, this should be a local matter. Quite why your lot have become involved I don't know. But then, I'm only the inspector around here"

"So you said. No doubt, the reason will become clearer with time, Inspector, when we know more. I don't suppose there is any doubt that it was murder?" Inspector Sim could not explain, even to himself, why he had asked such a fruitless question.

"Not unless he cut his own throat, which I think you'll agree is unlikely."

"Just a thought. Any idea who the deceased was?"

"Some foreigner, a houseguest of the squadron leader. He hadn't been in the country long, I understand. As I've said, all very bloody hush-hush. We've already spoken to the neighbours. They saw and heard nothing, so we've saved you that much legwork." Patting the sides of his coat as if in search of something, he added, "No doubt, you'll get to the bottom of it. I'm off home. If you want to contact me I'm at the central Bedford station. I've arranged for a constable to remain on duty here until you've seen all you want to see, which I hope won't be long. We're short-staffed. I can't afford to waste my manpower on dead foreigners, even if it is all hush-hush." With that, he strode purposefully away, out of sight around the corner of the house. It began to drizzle.

"Do you get the impression we're not welcome, Sergeant?"

"Looks like it, sir. Do we know where they've taken the body of the foreign gent?"

"To the morgue at Bedford, I presume. We'll have to check on that. You would think the squadron leader would have made himself available."

"You 'eard the inspector, sir. 'There's a war on.' Maybe 'e didn't know we were comin', then again, maybe 'e did and 'e doesn't want to talk to us."

"If so, why? Let's go and meet the wife, shall we?"

They entered a spacious kitchen with dark oak beams, cottage furnishings, including a large coal range, and a long pine table at which sat a woman in her late thirties dressed in a tweed suit and wearing sensible shoes, her fair hair done up in a loose bun. A single strand of pearls adorned her pale neck. She was nursing an empty sherry glass. A half-empty crystal decanter sat resting expectantly on an otherwise bare table. In spite of the hour, there was no evidence of an evening meal being prepared.

"Mrs. Huntington-Brown?"

"Yes. You are?"

"Inspector Sim, and this is Sergeant Hodges. We're from London to investigate the death of your houseguest."

"You're a bit late, Inspector. I've already spoken to that other policeman. Take a seat, if you like." Her speech was slurred.

"Thank you. We won't keep you long. This must all be very disturbing for you."

"Not at all, Inspector. I was brought up in East Africa during the last war. Death holds no surprises for me."

"I see. Your husband isn't available?"

"Do you see him? I think not. He was called back to his precious squadron. He doesn't know it yet, but when he eventually returns we're going out for dinner. With Henri's death I have no desire to stay in this damn house a minute longer than is necessary."

"I see. Henri?"

"Oh. I wasn't supposed to tell you that. My husband said it was all terribly hush-hush. 'Be like dad, keep mum,' isn't that what they say?" More than a note of mockery had entered her voice.

"I believe so, but that's all right, we'll find out eventually. There was a party the evening he was murdered, is that correct?"

"A party? I wouldn't call it that. We had a few friends from the squadron around for dinner – Glen's colleagues, fellow officers and their wives. But I've told all this to that other inspector fellow."

"I'm afraid we'll have to go through it all again. I would like a list of their names and where I can find them."

"You'll have to ask my husband about that. Squadron business. But they all live in the village, except for the two single chaps, Roy and Basil. Oops, there I go again. Anyway, they live in the mess."

"And you were all in the room when your guest stepped out onto the patio, is that correct?"

"Not exactly. I was helping in the kitchen at the time when … I won't allow smoking in the house, you see, that is why Henri stepped outside."

"You say you were helping in the kitchen. Was there someone in there with you?"

"Yes. Roy. Actually, I'm not sure who was helping who, but anyway, we were both preparing supper."

"Roy?"

"Really, Inspector, I do believe you're trying to trick me up. It's not gentlemanly," she replied coquettishly while pouring herself another sherry. "A few of the chaps had something else on, so we all had an early dinner."

"I see. So you didn't actually see Henri leave the lounge and step outside."

"Well, no. As I said, I was in the kitchen. Rather hard to see him from the kitchen through the blackout curtains, wouldn't you say? When I came back into the lounge, I noticed he wasn't there but . . ."

"Quite. Can you remember what the time was when your husband went outside to look for his guest?"

"Between eight and nine. I remember the clock in the hall chiming, but . . ."

"Thank you. And all the time you were in the kitchen, you heard nothing untoward?"

"No, nothing, nothing," she said, gazing into the bottom of her almost-empty sherry glass.

"I understand that it was your husband who phoned the police."

"That's correct. Glen always knows what to do."

"When do you think the squadron leader will be available to talk to us?"

"I couldn't say," she replied in an offhanded manner. "He said he wouldn't be long." With that she downed her drink and reached for the decanter. Sergeant Hodges speculated on the lonely evening the squadron leader could expect if he delayed his return.

"Thank you. Would you tell him to contact me as soon as possible? I'm at the Queen's Head. We'll see ourselves out."

Leaving his inspector to ruminate on their interview with the squadron leader's wife, once outside Sergeant Hodges embarked on a reconnaissance of the grounds. If the murderer was not among those in the house that evening, then whoever killed poor old Henri had either entered by climbing the six-foot brick wall that surrounded the garden or entered via the side gate. A careful inspection of the brick work revealed nothing. He had been hoping for some disturbance of the moss on the surface of the top portion of the wall. In all probability he had entered via the side gate, which would have exposed the perpetrator to anyone passing by the house, and yet the neighbours claimed to have seen nothing. Whatever the method of entry, how did he know that his victim was a guest at the house, let alone the exact time he would step outside onto the patio for a smoke? Or was he just lucky? In Sergeant Hodge's experience, the crime precluded any thought that they were looking for a female. It wasn't the sort of illicit act a woman would carry out. Now, if he had been poisoned ... But then he remembered reading somewhere that women can be just as cold-blooded as men, if not more so. They just don't know it until after they have passed their menopause, so possibly he was wrong to restrict his thinking only to the males of the species. But one thing was clear. They could limit the suspects to those who knew he was staying with the squadron leader. He was convinced it was not a random attack.

The drizzle had changed to rain as they returned to the car. They found their driver sheltering under the eaves of the house, deep in conversation with the young constable who had been searching the grounds.

On their way back to the village, Sergeant Hodges couldn't contain his curiosity any longer regarding the fate of the late LACW Adler of Bletchley Park.

"Been drivin' long, miss?" he asked their WRAF driver, who looked young enough to still be at school.

"I joined up in May, sir, as a Craft GD, general duties, but then the air force taught me to drive. Tempsford's my first posting."

"Interestin'. Your name, miss?"

"Jane Little. ACW, sir."

"So you won't have known a driver at Bletchley Park, LACW Adler?"

"No, sir, I don't think so. I've been to Bletchley a couple of times, but I don't remember meeting an LACW Adler. The FANYs do most of the driving from Bletchley."

"You wouldn't by any chance have driven a foreign gentleman to the house we just visited? It would have been within the last few days," the inspector asked.

"I don't think so, sir. No, in fact I know I haven't. I would remember driving to that house if I had."

"Just a thought. Are there many WRAF drivers stationed at Tempsford?"

"No, sir. As I said, most of the drivers are FANYs stationed at Bletchley." After a pause, she added, "I understand there's been a murder at the house, sir. Is that correct?"

"Is that so? I wouldn't believe all you hear, ACW Little," the inspector cautioned.

"Right, sir," she replied.

As they pulled up outside the Queen's Head, ACW Little looked in the rear-view mirror. "What time do you want me in the morning, sir?"

"Eight will be quite early enough, thank you."

The area around Milton Ernest has played host to the human race since Saxon times, although the Queen's Head could only claim residency since the seventeenth century. The lounge bar was small, and, to their surprise, it offered a welcoming coal fire, something Sergeant Hodges thought he would like to take back to his room at Mrs. Hall's shabby establishment. Each clutching his beer, they retired to a table by the fire. They were the only occupants. Judging by the noise emanating from the public bar, it was clear which of the two saloons was the more popular.

"We'll eat here this evening, if that's okay, Sergeant."

"Of course. What do you 'ave planned for the mornin', sir?"

"Well, I thought we might meet with Squadron Leader Huntington-Brown, assuming he makes himself available. We need to find out the identity of the foreigner. That's our starting point. Also, we have to be available for our briefing with SOE."

"Don't you think it funny that London didn't feel fit to tell you the identity of the foreign gent, before comin' up 'ere, I mean? I would be surprised if they didn't know who 'e is, or was."

"I'm sure London is perfectly aware as to the identity of the victim. They just chose not to tell me, for some reason. Perhaps SOE will be more forthcoming."

Dinner, served in the bar, consisted of bubble and squeak followed by bread pudding, a meal on which Inspector Sim offered a qualified opinion. "Not at all bad, Sergeant, perhaps not up to the standard of the Shoulder of Mutton, but still ..."

"There's a war on, right? I think you'll be well looked after 'ere, sir," the sergeant replied, while ruminating on his own misfortune.

"I hope so, Sergeant." Pausing until a sullen-faced youth removed their plates, he continued. "Thinking about it, there might be a connection between whatever is going on at Bletchley Park and RAF Tempsford. Why not? Two top-secret establishments so close together, they must be connected in some way, wouldn't you say, Sergeant?"

"But what would that be, sir? What's the connection?"

"If we knew that, Sergeant, we would know what our foreign guest was doing in the country. 'I keep six honest-serving men. They taught me all I know. Their names are What and Why and When, and How and Where and Who.'"

"That's rather good, sir. Your friend Kipling, I presume?"

"Yes, but I'll be damned if I can remember where it's from. The key to this murder, Sergeant, is who knew that the man was in England and staying at Milton Ernest? It wasn't a random killing."

"My thoughts exactly, sir."

"Either of you two gents Inspector Sim?" the barmaid called out from behind the bar.

"Yes."

"There's a phone call for you. You can take it in reception."

A few minutes later the inspector returned to his seat.

"That was the squadron leader. He'll make himself available to us tomorrow morning, after nine."

"That's very good of 'im. Though I wouldn't think the missis will be on deck at that time, judgin' by the way she was knockin' back the sherry."

Chapter Three

Scapa, Orkneys, Scotland

October 1942

Wilhelm Milch (real name: Karl Oberhümer) stepped ashore in Scotland believing that his luck had changed. The voyage from Archangel to Scotland via Reykjavik, where they had been forbidden to leave ship, had been one of the most uncomfortable and fearful experiences he had ever had the misfortune to endure. Their convoy had been harassed by U-boats for most of the voyage, with two ships lost off Svalbard. The sea temperature was such that any chance the survivors might have had quickly died with them in the frozen waters.

The cramped living conditions aboard the SS *Hunbury*, along with the monotonous diet, were bearable, not that he felt like eating. It was the sea. He was not a sailor. When they set sail from Archangel, the Barents Sea had been like a mill pond, but not long after entering the Norwegian Sea a deep low moved in over the area, and their little ship, along with the others in the convoy, were hit by monstrous waves twenty metres high. It remained rough for the rest of the voyage, but it hadn't stopped the U-boats.

Wilhelm Milch was one of four Austrians aboard, Soviet agents of 'Operation Pickaxe.' Following the German invasion of the Soviet Union, in a radio broadcast to the nation, Winston Churchill, the British Prime Minister, said, 'It follows that we shall give whatever help we can to Russia and the Russian people. . . . We have offered to the Government of Soviet Russia any technical or economic assistance which is in our power and which is likely to be of service to them.' What the great man neglected to tell the British public was that he had entered into a secret agreement with the tyrant Stalin and that the help his government would extend to the communist regime in Moscow would include assisting the NKVD (*Norondny Kommissariat Vnuyrennich Dyel*), the People's Commissariat for Internal Affairs, to infiltrate their agents into Western Europe. If the British public were to be kept in the dark, so also were the governments in exile of the Low Countries, and in particular Charles de Gaulle's Free French. Neither was the United States to be made party to the information. And what Stalin did not tell Churchill, a man naturally inclined to the clandestine, was that his 'gang of five,' British spies – Philby, Blunt, Burgess, Maclean, and Cairncross – were busy doing their level best to undermine the British establishment that was offering to help him fight the Germans by flying his agents into occupied Europe.

Milch's journey had begun eight years earlier when, having fought against his own government in Austria, he, along with several hundred other Socialists, members of the *Schutzbund*, a paramilitary organisation, had sought refuge in Moscow after fleeing their homeland through Czechoslovakia. It seemed the whole of Moscow had turned out to welcome them on the 30th April 1934. However, it wasn't long before the suspicions the Soviet regime reserved for all foreigners began to affect his life in Russia. Each factory he was assigned to work in was located farther away from Moscow than the last, and, with each move, living and working conditions became more primitive and his fellow Russian workers less educated, to the point where many were almost illiterate. Then, in 1936, relief came when, like many fellow members of the *Schutzbund*, he went to fight with the International Brigade in Spain, first with the XXIst (German) International Brigade in the defence of Madrid, then with the Multinational XIII (Chapayev) Brigade. Finally, after recovering from a prolonged bout of dysentery, he was back with the XXIst Brigade but with the Austrian '12 Feber' Battalion. It was while he was with the Feber Battalion that he first met Hans, a Marxist and a member of the Austrian Communist Party, the KPO.

Upon his return to Russia in 1939, at the end of the Spanish Civil War, they had kept in touch. Hans, the committed Marxist, had contacts and, following the invasion of the Soviet Union in 1941, he, on behalf of the NKVD, was charged with recruiting men and women of the *Schutzbund* and the KPO as agents to be dropped into Western Europe. It was for Wilhelm Milch a second reprieve from the bone-breaking tedium of life in the 'worker's paradise.'

After training at Military Detachment 113 – the Bykovo espionage school near Moscow, where agents learned how to work with explosives, various weapons, and of conditions in their target countries – he moved to Kuibyshev to study parachuting and improved shooting. From there he went first to Moscow and then Archangel to board the SS *Hunbury*. The party of four was forwarded to the United Kingdom by the Fourth Directorate for Special Tasks and Guerrilla Warfare, headed by Pavel Sudoplatov. A representative of that directorate accompanied them on the train before passing them over to the paternalistic care of the British SOE at Archangel.

On landing at Scapa, they were transferred to the mainland and then by train to Inverness, where they met a Corporal Claridge, their conducting officer, who issued each with a false Swiss passport in the event that Scotland Yard should take an unhealthy interest in them. He escorted them to London and the Rhodesia Hotel, 20 Harrington Gardens. It was there that they were introduced to the head of the Soviet Mission, DPR, attached to the SOE, a Colonel Ivan Dekanozov, to whom Milch took an instant dislike. Milch had been trained to operate in his native Austria, and since the other three were also Austrian he assumed that they too would be heading home. But at their first meeting, Dekanozov hinted that there might be a change of plan but would not elucidate further.

Conditions in Britain were not as he had expected. Milch, along with the others in his group, had in Moscow been led to believe that England was on the cusp of a revolution, that the workers were about to rise up and overthrow the ruling class along with their corrupt leader, Churchill. They were also told that the British would then join the International and wage war against fascism as never before. But on his journey and when out walking the streets of London he could see no sign of impending revolt, quite the reverse, and the reverence held for the British Royal family by the average man and woman in the street had, along with so much else, been something of a revelation.

During their training, on the sickening voyage from Russia, and on the journey south to London, he had come to know very little about the other two members of the group, Karl and Freda, but they were not stupid. What was the point of Moscow feeding them such obviously wrong information about conditions in Britain, or did the functionaries in Russia believe the rubbish they had been espousing? And if they had been wrong about conditions in England, what else had they been wrong about? Dekanozov, being based in London, knew the truth, at least as it related to England. Had he not informed Moscow, or was he, along with the others at the Soviet Embassy, simply telling Moscow what it wanted to hear? Hans, the committed Marxist in the group, engaged in motivated reasoning and would only see that which enforced his ideological belief, but Karl and Freda were, like himself, socialists and less extreme in their thinking, less ideological, more pragmatic.

He first met Karl Wenninger (real name Josef Kuebler), aged twenty-eight, at their briefing by the Fourth Directorate in Moscow just before leaving for Archangel. Of average height and weight, with fair hair and a face you could easily forget, he looked to be the ideal agent. Mistrust and suspicion of everyone being the norm in the Soviet Union, it was not until they had boarded the SS *Hunbury* that Milch felt he could sound out his fellow agents as to their past and their motivation. It took the entire voyage for him to learn that Karl, a tram driver, had been a member of the Social Democrats (SPO) in Vienna and, in February 1934, had, rather belatedly, joined the Schutzbund to fight against the Fascist Heumwehr militia. When the uprising failed, the result of dithering on behalf of the SPO's chairman, Otto Bauer, along with the rest of the party's leadership, Karl had fled to France, where he spent a year before moving on to Czechoslovakia and then Russia. As to whether he still had family in Vienna, Milch would remain in ignorance. As far as he knew, Karl had sat out the Spanish conflict.

Freda Volkmann, (real name Gertrude Eisner) originally from Graz, with a French mother and Austrian father and in her late twenties, had moved to Vienna in 1932 to work for the SPO. If Karl was economical with his past, Freda was even less forthcoming. A singularly unattractive woman with few physically redeeming features, she discouraged any attempt at conversation. If she had family still in Austria or France, he would never know. She did, however, wear a wedding ring, so someone had loved her, once. If her husband was alive it was not something Freda felt inclined to talk about.

Then there was Hans Kotze, who he had known as Hans Heidegger, the Marxist he had met in Spain and had periodically corresponded with during their exile in Russia, the man who had recruited him into working for the NKVD. He had revealed little of his past over the years. Milch had always found him elusive, diffident almost, but very assertive when defending communism. He gave the impression of someone who would do whatever was asked of him by the Party. Only once did he come close to revealing more about himself. It was while they were incarcerated by the French in Perpignan, having escaped the collapse of the Republic six months before Franco took power. They were awaiting repatriation to Russia. Having bribed a guard, they had a night on the town. Hans had got drunk and started a brawl in a brothel. They had run from the police, finding refuge under a railway bridge with two bottles of *vin ordinaire*. Milch was suffering a return of the dysentery that had plagued him for most of his time in Spain and let Hans, who was already intoxicated, empty the two bottles down his receptive gullet. It was only when both bottles had been drained of their contents that Hans, after a period of silence, began to talk a little about himself and yet, even with all that wine in him he still managed to control the flow of personal information about Hans Heidegger. Much of what he said solicited more questions than answers.

After what turned out to be a prolonged stay in London, all due to Moscow failing to provide the four agents with proper documentation for life in occupied Europe, they were moved to a country house near RAF Tempsford to await aircraft availability and acceptable weather. Throughout their stay in Britain much care had been taken to keep them apart from other agents. Shepherded around the country in their own little bubble, they had only each other for company.

Chapter Four

<u>Azay-sur-Cher, Tours, France</u>

They took her to a farmhouse a little beyond the village. It was small and poorly furnished, but the welcome from the farmer and his wife, if not effusive, was warm, though cautious. One thing she would remember of her short stay at the farm was that after her arrival, in the shadowy interior, beyond the candle light, a retarded boy in a red nightshirt had suddenly appeared, only to vanish just as quickly, his presence ignored by all.

After the tension of the pre-mission hours, arriving back in France had been something of an anti-climax: the flight in the Lysander, seated in the rear cockpit, facing aft and told by the pilot through a microphone to keep an eye open for night fighters, then the bumpy landing, the reception committee's organised evacuation of the landing zone, taking with them the containers of arms and propaganda material. It was all so rehearsed that she felt like a novice actor in a long-running play. But she could feel and smell France, the exhilaration of which almost consumed her; she was home.

It had been the third attempt to drop her into France. The first two, aboard a twin-engine Hudson, had been aborted, the first because of unexpected low cloud over the area, the second when the pilot failed to receive the correct identifying signal from the ground. At one stage, even the third attempt looked in doubt when, shortly after leaving Tempsford, the pilot diverted to Tangmere.

On landing she was told to stay in the aircraft. After a few minutes on the ground they resumed their flight. No explanation was forthcoming as to why they had been diverted into Tangmere.

Grace Harris had returned to England just days before the German invasion of her mother's country. Born in Bristol to an English father and a French mother, she had been brought up in Saintes, in the Saintonge, following the death of her father in a flying accident. In spite of this loss, her childhood had been a happy time. Unlike most young French women in pre-war France, who were generally not granted much independence, Grace had been allowed a measure of freedom and encouraged to make her own choices, but, even so, it hadn't been an easy decision to leave those she loved and France. Once in England she had followed the shameful capitulation of Pétain and the setting up of a treacherous government of collaboration. She knew then that she had been right to leave. She returned to her birthplace, Bristol, where her father's sister ran a small hotel. To earn her keep Grace helped out at the reception desk and cleaned rooms. It was not what she had hoped for when returning to England. It didn't seem to be a very productive way of helping defeat the Germans, which was now her main aim in life.

Throughout England, April of 1941 was dry, dull, and rather cold, with an excess of north-easterly and easterly winds. An anticyclone was moving slowly south-eastward from Iceland, bringing mainly dry weather, apart from a few scattered showers, with Bristol enjoying rather more than its fair share of sunshine for the month. Earlier that day she had taken advantage of the sunshine for a quick walk down to the bridge. Upon returning to the hotel, she helped make the beds with Maureen, a troublesome Irish girl who had been taken on a few days earlier. Then she went down to reception when a short, balding man in a smart suit entered the hotel. He looked familiar, but she couldn't remember from where.

"Can I help you, sir?" she offered.

"I hope you can, Miss Grace Harris."

His knowing her name caught her by surprise.

"Perhaps there is somewhere we could talk?" he suggested.

"What about?"

He didn't reply but continued looking at her expectantly.

Capitulating, she said, "I'm meant to be looking after reception. If you care to come through to the office, I can keep an eye on the desk while we talk. We're full, if you're after a room."

The windowless office next to reception was no bigger than a broom cupboard, forcing her guest to sit on the only chair available at a desk piled with old newspapers, a few roles of much-in-demand toilet paper, and cleaning fluids. An ancient typewriter sat to one side. Wooden shelves covered the walls holding files and binders, some of which could have been there since the turn of the century. Grace stood in the doorway with one foot in the office, the other in reception.

"Who are you, and what did you want to talk to me about?" she asked politely.

"My name is Graham Sutton. We've already met, last year, although you may not remember. You had just arrived here from France, and I was a guest at the hotel. At the time, I thought that you were French. The accented English, you see, but I have since learnt that you were born here in Bristol and that your father was English."

"That's right, but—"

"Let me finish, if I may. How would you like to do something more for your country than working in your aunt's hotel? Not that I'm in anyway denigrating your employment or, for that matter, your aunt."

"What did you have in mind?" she asked.

"Let's just keep to the principle for the moment. Are you interested?"

"Well, yes." After a short pause, she continued, "The thought of spending the entire war here doesn't fill me with joy, although I'm very grateful to my aunt for taking me in when she did, but I can't see how working here is going to help defeat the Germans in any appreciable way."

"And you would like to do that, to help defeat the Germans?"

"Wouldn't we all? Yes, of course I want to see them defeated. They have invaded France. My mother is still there."

"Quite so. Are you a fit person, Miss. Harris? You look healthy."

"Yes, I think so."

"Well, that's a start. There are some people who would like to meet you. Can you come up to London next week? Let us say on Wednesday? Your fair will be paid."

* * *

After the selection process and having been chosen for F Section of the SOE, Grace was sent for three weeks to Wanborough Manor, near Guildford, for her introductory training and assessment course and from there to Arisaig, in Scotland, for five weeks paramilitary training, where she was taught how to kill. The unreliable Sten gun, the Bren gun, and the Thompson submachine gun, all had to be mastered to the point where she could strip them down and put them together in her sleep. She was also expected to learn how to use handheld revolvers, among them the Colt .32 and .45, Browning, Luger, Mouser, and the Walther P38. Never having held a firearm before, let alone fired such a thing, she was surprised to find that she was a better-than-average shot, although she did find the Bren gun intimidating. What had been especially hard was learning to kill with a knife. The closeness of the violence, the experience, even the thought of creeping up on an opponent from behind and slitting their throat or plunging the knife into someone's chest repulsed her. She could only hope that such a need would never eventuate. The forced marches across boggy Scottish moors in the pouring rain carrying a heavy pack, sleeping rough, and living off emergency rations had all taken her bodily responses to places they had never been before. Passed as being an above-average student, she then moved to Ringway, near Manchester, for parachute training. She completed five practice jumps, the last at night. She had never thought of herself as a brave or courageous woman but was surprised to find herself less scared of leaping out through a hole in the aircraft in mid-flight than many of the others. One trainee would not leave the aircraft, in spite of the 'encouragement' levelled at him by the flight sergeant in charge. With Wanborough, Arisaig, and Ringway behind her, it was on to Beaulieu, in the New Forest, for training in clandestinity and as a courier, all under the tutorage of a Mr. Kim Philby. For her final training she moved to Tempsford, where, at a satellite field close by in Somersham, she and another student, a tall Frenchman with a pronounced limp, were taught how, with three lamps, to lay out a flare path into the wind, how to select a landing site, taking into account tree clearances and the firmness of the ground, along with avoiding ditches and other ground hazards. It was at Somersham that Grace first met a Lysander. In order to effect a three-minute turnaround, it was necessary for agents to practice climbing into and out of the aircraft using the ladder attached to the rear cockpit, load and unload the aircraft, as well as clear it for take-off. It was also the first and only time she was required to wear a uniform, that of an army officer.

When it was issued to her at Tempsford, she was told to take care of it as it was on loan and would be required for another agent in training after she had moved on.

The need for a full moon, aircraft, and available crew had conspired to delay her third attempt at returning to France. Weeks turned to months before she eventually found herself again at Gibraltar Farm, the nerve centre of RAF Tempsford. There she was escorted by a kind young officer into a barn where she donned a 'striptease' suit– a baggy jumping suit equipped with many pockets into which she put a dagger, hard rations, a flashlight, first-aid equipment, secret maps and papers. Would this be the real thing? Was she really on her way at last?

* * *

Somewhere close by a cock was crowing. She would have to leave the warmth of her bed and face her first morning in France. The window that she had left slightly open in the night had slammed shut with the wind, and as a result condensation had formed on the small panes of glass, obscuring her view of the frozen farmyard beneath her room. She had been told in England that on no account was she to try and contact her mother while in France. Her life and that of others in her network, not to mention that of her mother, depended on it. To be so close and yet unable to see her would be one of the hardest parts of her mission.

Her first task was to contact the man for whom she would be working, her wireless operator Gilbert, someone who had defied the odds and remained in the field for over three months without being detected. The average time was six weeks before an operator was caught. *Gonios* – German radio-detection vans operated by the *Funkhorchdienst* – had become more prolific and efficient since the beginning of the occupation in 1940 and were not always easy to spot, being disguised as anything from a butcher's van to that of the local plasterer. Gilbert, having been notified of her arrival, would be at a safe house in a neighbouring village to which she would cycle, after breakfast, on a machine borrowed from someone from her reception committee.

As she rode into the village she had her first encounter with the German army. A lorry full of soldiers was blocking the narrow, cobbled road outside a *pâtisserie*. Dismounting, she pushed her bicycle along the pavement past the lorry, attracting whistles and vulgar catcalls from its occupants. Drawing level with the shop doorway, she almost dropped her bicycle when a young soldier, no more than a boy, carrying a bag of bread suddenly stepped out onto the pavement, bumping into her.

"Entschuldigen Sie bitte," he said, stepping back, allowing her to pass.

Was this the enemy she was expected to kill?

Holding her breath and ignoring the young soldier, she walked on, telling her body not to run, an impulse she almost surrendered to. Seconds later the lorry drove past with another chorus of ribald comments and catcalls from the soldiers. Barely had the sound of their voices died away before she turned right into a lane on both sides of which stood terraced houses that opened onto the lane. If the directions she had been given were correct, the safe house was the third on the left. The lane was deserted as she stood before a red door and knocked.

The old woman who opened the door looked frail and worn, her bent body a testament to years of hard physical labour, but her eyes sparkled with life and just a hint of mischief.

"Yes, how may I help you?" she asked in a voice the strength of which belied the frame in which it resided.

"Madam Carré?" Grace asked.

"Yes."

"My name is Simone, may I come in?" Of all the code names she had been given, it was Simone that best suited her, she thought.

"Of course, my dear, come in."

The old lady slowly led her through the house to a small kitchen. The décor and heavy hangings were those of a bygone age, reminiscent of the *Belle Époque*. A level of dust lay over everything save that which was in daily use.

"How may I help you?" she repeated.

It had been forcefully instilled into her and the others, throughout her training, that nobody was to be trusted. Collaborators were everywhere, and they came in all shapes and sizes. That so many Frenchmen and women could turn on their own country was to her a complete mystery. Many networks had been infiltrated by double agents, with many good people lost to the treacherous activities of those who worked for the Germans, and all for their own selfish ends.

Sensing Simone's reluctance to divulge her reason for coming, Madam Carré sat down at the small round table covered by thick green velvet and, waving her arms in the air, said, "We are alone. There is nobody else in the house."

"I am looking for Gilbert. We were to meet here."

The woman did not reply immediately but sat looking at her, all the time playing with the numerous rings on her fingers. Eventually she spoke.

"Really, Gilbert you say. I am sorry, Simone, I know nothing of any meeting, and I do not think I know anybody by that name. Of course, I am old and ..."

"I see. There seems to have been some king of mistake. You are Madam Carré?"

"Yes, indeed."

"Thank you, madam."

As the old lady followed her to the front door, Grace could feel those sparkling eyes boring into her back. It had been a wasted journey; how could she have got it so wrong? Just as she opened the red door, Madam Carré suggested, "A nice day for a walk through the park, Simone."

With that, the door behind her closed and she stood alone in the lane. To her horror she found that the bicycle she had left outside leaning against the house was gone. A bicycle in occupied France was to be valued, and she would now have to explain away the loss. It also meant that she would have to walk back to the farm while making sure she was not out and about after the curfew. It was a less-than-auspicious start to her mission. There was, however, something in the old lady's parting words that she could not ignore. On her way into the village she had noticed a small park adjacent to a school. What had she to lose?

In the summer, when the chestnut trees spread their welcoming shade across the grass and the narrow flowerbeds were a riot of colour, the park would have appeared inviting; now it was drab, the trees barren, and the beds uncared for. It was as if the park were in mourning for a nation that had shamefully capitulated. There were, however, a number of elderly people and young children out walking their dogs in the weak November sun. One had even brought out into the winter air a cat, complete with collar and lead. Traversing the park was a shingle path scattered along which were wooden benches, and on one sat a thin, nondescript man wearing an old raincoat and cloth cap. Leaning up against the back of the bench on which he sat was a bicycle. As Grace approached him he rose and, taking the bicycle, walked slowly away. Grace followed.

He led her to a church surrounded by a walled cemetery where in front of a recently dug grave he knelt after first leaning the bicycle against a tree. Extending his right hand, he gently patted the ground beside him. It was an imperceptible gesture, one she almost missed, her attention having been taken at that moment by a large crow that had chosen to settle on the ground close by. The earth was hard to her knees. When was the last time she had knelt beside a grave, if ever? She had been too young to remember her father's funeral, but even then such an act of veneration would have been unlikely, given her mother's dislike of graveyards. The few funerals she had attended excluded the internments.

She could smell his closeness; his clothes and body were unclean. Whatever else was included in his life, personal hygiene was not high on his list of priorities. Working with such a man would not be without its problems, she concluded.

"Monsieur Gilbert?"

"You would be wise to look after your property a little better, mademoiselle." His accent surprised her. She knew that he was English; this much had been disclosed to her before leaving England, but she had not expected the Bretagne dialect in which he addressed her.

"I will try to be more careful in the future, monsieur."

"That would be advisable for both our sakes. You must not return to the farm. It isn't safe. Someone has talked. The whole network may have been compromised."

"But my clothes, monsieur and – everything is at the farm."

"Are they worth your life? You have a job to do. Your clothes are not important. The job you have been sent to do is. I need a courier. Do you have money with you?"

In truth, everything was not at the farm. She had, beneath her light cotton summer dress, her money belt, with sufficient funds to keep her for a month. "Yes, monsieur, money will not be a problem."

"You must go to Montsoreau. It is not far. It's where the Loire meets the Vienne. There is a safe house in the village. Go to the café Brion in Montsoreau and ask to speak to Claude. Tell him I sent you. Have you got that? On no account go back to the farm." As he rose to leave he added, "I will contact you. Remain in Montsoreau and trust no one, mademoiselle."

"Not even you?" she parried.

"Especially me."

Chapter Five

SIS HQ, Broadway Buildings, St. James Park, London

Adrian J. Padmore sat at his desk looking at the latest edition of the War Cabinet's protocols, a weekly digest put out by his betters. It was something he had no intention of reading, but it was something upon which he could focus his gaze while he thought about his beloved Lagonda, now parked up for the duration. He had bought it from a friend four years previously, when war looked some way off. Now, petrol, like most other things, was in short supply and when it was available, even via the black market, he couldn't afford it. The Lagonda had become too much of a luxury.

But he was no stranger to parsimony; it was something he had been forced to practice for at least half his life, particularly in his formative years. It was a cross he had born stoically among friends and acquaintances alike, most of whom had private incomes. The education he had received from his second-tier public school had been sufficient to earn him a place at Oxford, where he rubbed shoulders with those whom his mother would always refer to as 'top drawer.' But there was never enough money for him to take his place alongside their noble frames. Needless to say, he had not been invited to join the Bullingdon Club. There were a few, a very few, undergraduates from state schools who had won scholarships, but he had little in common with them, and, anyway, they worked fiendishly hard at their studies. What had been missing from his life was a rich benefactor, someone who could have helped him when help was most needed. Losing his father in Russia while serving with the 236th infantry Brigade had created within him an abiding hatred for communism. He never questioned the illogicality of his loathing, it being equally valid to blame the Minister of War, Winston Churchill, for sending his father, along with thousands of others, on such a fruitless and futile mission.

On June 20th, 1918, primarily to hold back German forces in the east and protect two million tons of military stores from falling into hostile hands, Winston Churchill, Minister of War, dispatched British troops, part of an Allied force, to Murmansk. On August 2nd they moved on to occupy Archangel. It was during the fighting the following spring, between Allies and Bolshevik forces, that his father was killed. Six months later, on 30th September, the Allies abandoned Archangel, then, on October 12th, Murmansk. The evacuation of the Allied troops in the face of superior Bolshevik numbers was only effected through a diversion of 8,000 more British soldiers, an escalation for which the minister received a great deal of adverse criticism.

The death of his father, a man he never had the chance to know, created financial hardship for the family that was to last for years. And his going up to Oxford had put a further strain on the already stretched family budget, only somewhat relieved after coming down and his passing the Foreign Office entrance exam, following considerable coaching, and becoming, if not gainfully employed, at least earning.

If Oxford required a private income to live a tolerable existence, then the FO was even more demanding. However, with a level of frugality that would have impressed Scrooge, he managed. Quite how he had ended up some years later in the opaque world of intelligence would remain a mystery, as was his selection for service abroad, in spite of possessing only modest linguistic ability. There seemed little doubt that he had a natural flair for 'the game,' something someone somewhere within the labyrinth of power had recognised. Serving in foreign countries, later known as the Third World, had at last allowed him to live the life he aspired to. Throughout, when serving abroad, the service had been blissfully unaware of his backstreet financial dealings, though it was something he never practiced when stationed back in the UK. He had traded copra in Malaya and precious stones in India. The stones had proved particularly profitable and had enabled him to marry and start a family upon his return to England. Emma came from a Scots family of the cloth and had attended St Leonards. Her financial position when he first met her, and that of her family, had mirrored his own financially distressed background. Now it could be said, thanks to his 'out of house' enterprises, they were comfortably well-off, though still not sufficiently flush to run the Lagonda in war-torn Britain.

"What ho, Squeegee. Reading the right stuff, I see. I'm impressed. Talking of being impressed, have you seen that new redhead in the typing pool downstairs? Second row, third desk in, on the left. What a cracker! Don't suppose you know her name? No, I don't suppose you do." Enter Titan Fairweather without knocking, a colleague fifteen years his junior. Since his first appearance in the office, three months earlier, Padmore had wondered how Fairweather had uncovered his nickname from school. It grated on him. As yet, only Fairweather used the sobriquet, but how long before it caught on?

"What do you want, Fairweather?" In the short time he had known the man he had found it best to cut to the chase when conversing with him. Besides, he was coming to the conclusion that he didn't much care for Titan Fairweather. Personal feelings aside, Old Etonians, as with those who attended Harrow, invoked within him that all too familiar feeling of inferiority. The less he was in their company the better.

"It's this Pickaxe business. What the dickens are we doing bringing Reds into the country and then dropping them on the poor unsuspecting Frogs? I take it you know about SOE's latest exploit?"

"Yes, I had heard. But I didn't know you cared that much about the French."

"I don't, old boy. Wouldn't trust them any further than I would trust SOE! Did you know that three quarters of the French troops rescued off the beaches at Dunkirk, at great risk to our valiant seamen, I might add, asked to be repatriated once they reached Blighty! And, in our darkest hour, only twelve French pilots volunteered to join the RAF, compared to a hundred and forty Poles. And now the Frogs are blaming us for their defeat. Best thing we ever did, sinking their mangy old fleet at Mers-el-Kebir." Fairweather was a man for whom Crécy and Agincourt were as yesterday. He was also prone to repeating himself, as per his current diatribe, one that Padmore had heard a number of times. No doubt he would next move on to mention, as he had done previously, the mammoth French submarine *Surcouf* and the demands of all her crew, bar the captain, to return to France after birthing at Plymouth and the shooting of a British sailor by the sub's doctor. Fortunately, the Old Etonian held back on retelling the story of the *Surcouf*.

"C is not pleased. He only learnt about it from a leaked SOE memo. It really is too much. It seems the SOE have agreed to assist their people, the NKVD, with intelligence training, as if the SOE would know anything about that! They will also provide training facilities, radio, and small arms, that sort of thing, and documents, although I think Five is going to supply those. The

RAF is supplying aircraft and crews to drop them behind enemy lines, and it's not only France. The Low Countries, even Austria!" He had parked himself on the edge of Padmore's desk, after first moving his in tray before helping himself to a cigarette. "Got a light, old boy?"

"How do you know all this, Fairweather?"

"It's top gen, old boy, take it from me. In fact, four more of the blighters stepped ashore in Scotland earlier this month, so I'm led to believe. If *mon Général* gets to hear about this there'll be a frightful brouhaha."

"What makes you think he doesn't already know?"

"Because if he did the whole thing would have been scuppered. Believe me, de Gaulle is as much in the dark about the Reds as the rest of the nation. Trust me, Duke Street (the base for France's Secret Service in England) has been kept ignorant of what's happening. Mark you, Colonel Passy is having his own problems with SOE's F Section. They still take their orders direct from London and are completely run by us British, so it's not surprising they don't know what's going on. While the Free French run their own show and there's no liaison between them. It's all a bit of a dog's breakfast over there. What I think the Frogs call a *panier de crabs.* Gaullists, anti-Gaullists, conservatives, communists, Vichyists, and none of them talking to each other. No wonder they're in such a mess. On this Pickaxe business, apparently C has written to SOE reminding them that they're obliged to have prior FO clearance for such proposals, and they're supposed to consult us before going ahead."

"What about our American friends? Are they in the know?"

"I wouldn't think so. I'm sure they're not. And neither are the Dutch or Belgium governments. It's all hush-hush. Those wallies in SOE are just not up to our professional standard, that's all there is to it. They're inefficient and wasteful, blundering amateurs, if you ask me. Do you remember last year, before my time actual? West Africa, because of the mess they were making of things, they had the temerity to suggest we join forces with them! C soon put them right about that. Then there was Norway last year. Another cock-up by SOE at our expense. Now the latest news is that the chiefs of staff have come up with yet another mad idea to amalgamate us with them."

"Hadn't heard that one," Padmore replied.

"Oh, yes. We would come under the 'general direction of the Chiefs of Staff Committee."

"What? Prise us away from the FO?"

"That's what it would mean. C wouldn't have a bar of that either. In fact, if you look inside that copy of the protocols you're holding, you'll see C's reply to the chiefs. His old dictum, 'Intelligence is the mainspring of action.' He also goes on to say that, 'Intelligence should always be given priority over special operations.' That's clear enough, even to the parvenu of the SOE, wouldn't you say?"

"I presume Five is keeping a close watch on this Pickaxe business?"

"One would presume so, old boy. After all, they're part of it if they're supplying documentation for these fellows. I mean, what are they going to do if one or more of these Reds decides he's had enough of Uncle Joe's way of running things and asks HMG for asylum, while passing through, as it were? On the other hand, what if the whole thing is some Machiavellian plot? That these Reds are in fact double agents sent to infiltrate SOE or to set up communist cells for when the war ends. Has Five thought of that, I wonder?"

"Do we know who's running their show here in England? Is it the DPR at the Soviet Mission."

"Five would know for sure, but I think it's some colonel at their mission. That's the extent of my knowledge. Outside my purview, old boy."

"These Pickaxe agents, I assume they're being flown into France or wherever by Special Squadron at Tempsford?"

"Correct. We have our own show with those chaps, don't we?"

"Couldn't say. Well, Fairweather, if that's all you have to offer, or was there something else?"

"No, just passing by, Squeegee. Just thought I would drop in. But you've got to admit this Pickaxe business is a rum show. It's really beyond the pale. Try and find out who that cute little number is down in typing, will you? Toodle-pip."

The cultural hegemony of the upper class was not something Padmore would ever question. After all, was he not himself a product of it? He may not have gone to Eton or Harrow, nor did he have the lineage that would take him to the top ranks of the FO, but he hadn't felt at all fraudulent embracing the mores, habits, and political attitudes that were part and parcel of the Service. Although not particularly well-read in political philosophy, he had enough knowledge and bigotry to know that communism threatened the correct order of things, if not the downfall of civilization. Operation Pickaxe was an insidious evil and not something he could tolerate, particularly since those at the top were clearly unable to see the threat it presented to democratic societies. It was of course Five's job along with Special Branch to root communists out from within British society, but could they be trusted with the task? He felt it was his bounden duty to expose the whole operation. There and then he resolved to do something about Operation Pickaxe. It was personal.

Chapter Six

Milton Ernest, Bedfordshire

The homely middle-aged woman wearing a green apron who admitted them to the house led them through to the lounge where Squadron Leader Glen Huntington-Brown was waiting, in uniform. He was standing by the tiled fireplace with one foot resting on the hearth. Short, with boyish good looks, he could have walked out of an air force recruiting poster, except for his greying hair, a lock of which hung low over his right temple. From his right hand a cigarette hung limply between extended fingers, and his left was thrust deep in his tunic pocket. He exuded a certain cavalier confidence. It immediately struck Sergeant Hodges that here was someone with an inflated sense of his social position.

"Inspector Sim? Sorry about yesterday. How may I help?" His manner was on the edge of being imperious.

"Good morning. Squadron Leader Huntington-Brown?"

"I am he. And . . . ?"

"This is Sergeant Hodges. We're from the Metropolitan Police. We're looking into the death of your houseguest, Henri?" At which point both policemen showed their warrant card.

"I thought as much. Perhaps I should explain. Henri's death presents us, meaning the squadron, with something of a security problem. Yesterday I obtained instructions from my superiors on what I was permitted to tell you. We're running something of a special show here at Tempsford, you see."

"So, everything in order now, is it Squadron Leader? What you're permitted to tell us, I mean?"

"To a certain extent."

"I can assure you both the sergeant and I have been cleared by the Home Office, at the highest level. So, shall we proceed?"

"By all means."

Sergeant Hodges took out his notebook. "The full name of your guest."

"Henri Bonoteaux." He then went on to spell the name.

"French, I assume."

"I believe so."

"And who was this Henri Bonoteaux and the reason for his being in the country?"

"You may ask, Inspector, but in doing so you have hit upon the very nub of our problem. I can tell you that he is a friend and was staying with us for a few days. As for his reasons for being here, well, who knows?"

"I'm sure *you* do, Squadron Leader. This is going to be a lengthy business unless you become more forthcoming. I'll ask you again. Why was this Henri Bonoteaux in England and, just for good measure, why do you think he was murdered?"

"Look, Inspector, there are matters going on here at Tempsford that are not for public consumption – security, matters of importance that even those at the highest level in London are unaware of. As to why he was murdered, well, your guess is as good as mine. I appreciate that you have a job to do, but there it is. Your next question?"

"Perhaps I haven't made myself sufficiently clear. Firstly, the sergeant and I are not, as you put it, members of the consuming public. Secondly, it is an offence, even in wartime, to impede the investigation of a murder. And thirdly, we are not leaving until you have answered my questions. I should add that we have all day."

Silence ensued that was only broken by the appearance in the room of the housekeeper with a tray of tea, at which point the three men sat. Tea was something Sergeant Hodges had been hoping for.

"I'm off 'ome now, Squadron Leader. I'll be back later on. Mrs. Barrington-Brown says she don't want to be disturbed."

"Thank you, Mrs. Fletcher, make sure the back door is properly closed when you leave." After the woman had left, he continued. "Now, Inspector, I can sympathise with your position. You have to find whoever it was who murdered poor old Henri. But really, I don't see how—"

"I should point out at this stage that you, along with everybody else who was in the house at the time, is a suspect and unless you can tell me—"

"Really, Inspector! I don't think we're going to get anywhere if you start bandying accusations of that type around."

"Really? I want a list of all the people who were in the house at the time of the murder, and I still want answers to my questions. Who was the deceased, and what was he doing in England?"

A further silence followed as the squadron leader examined his position. His instructions from on high were sufficiently vague to allow him room to hold back as much information as possible.

"We're a special operations unit here at Tempsford. We have two squadrons, not that that should concern you. You'll find no mention of our work anywhere because what we do is top secret. Even some of those who work on the station don't know what is going on at Tempspsford.

"And that is . . ."

"By now I'm sure you must have put two and two together, Inspector. Henri was on official business while visiting England. We are, as I have already said, a special operations squadron. In our own way we are a travel agent. You can work out for yourself how he got here from France, and while visiting England he has been my guest. Does that satisfy you?"

"We're to have a briefing from SOE. No doubt they will be more responsive. But just to make sure I have got this right, you, or someone from your squadron, flies to France, picks up Henri and brings him back to England where, before he can return, he gets himself murdered."

The inspector received no confirmation of this, instead, his host studiously poured himself and those of his guests a cup of Mrs. Fletcher's tea.

"And, just as a matter of interest, was Henri's reason for being here, whatever it was, successfully concluded before he was killed?"

"That I can't tell you. Not within my sphere of ops, I'm afraid. Possibly SOE will be able to enlighten you on that point. But whenever he is in the country, my wife and I or one of the other pilots acts as host. That is or was the extent of our relationship with the man."

"While he was with you, did he receive any visitors? Someone from outside of Tempsford?"

"Not to my knowledge."

"So, Henri was a regular visitor?"

"Let's just say that this was not his first visit."

Inspector Sim shot a glance at his sergeant.

They hadn't worked together for some time, almost a year, and yet they picked up where they had left off; they were a well-oiled team. However, since the outbreak of the war, with the exception of his short time at Bletchley Park, Sergeant Hodges had had little to do with the military, unless you count the time spent with Military Police who came onto his patch searching for deserters. Working with other units such as the ARP (Air

Raid Protection services) and the fire service, something he had done throughout the blitz, had been a much more relaxed affair, if any operational relationship could be so described among the chaos and mayhem of a burning city. With the military it was different. Certain protocols had to be observed, and then there was the military mind-set, something he would never understand. Whether it was his time with the Indian Police or with Special Branch, the inspector seemed able to accommodate their world in a way he found hard. He remembered something rather comforting on the matter, something his father had said from the first show, 'War is much too serious a thing to be left to military men.' What he found interesting was how quickly those who were in the forces, if only for the duration, succumbed to the highly singular military mind-set.

"Can we go back to the night 'e was murdered, sir. We understand that after dinner you were all in 'ere when your guest steps outside for a smoke, is that correct?"

The squadron leader did not immediately reply but looked at the sergeant as one might who was not accustomed to being questioned by someone of inferior rank. When he eventually responded, it was imperiously.

"I believe so," pause, "Sergeant."

"Except your wife, Mrs. Barrin'ton-Brown, and one other, they were in the kitchen when Henri went outside onto the patio for a smoke."

"What? They may have been. If she says that is where they were then . . . Does it matter?" The squadron leader didn't hide his annoyance at being corrected by an NCO.

"And you 'eard nothin' comin' from outside the French windows?"

"As I have already said, nothing. As I remember it, one of the chaps was 'shooting a line,' as it turned out, a rather long one. When he had finished, someone asked where Henri had got to. I went out onto the patio and there he was, the poor chap. The curtains are, as you can see, thick velvet, and that must have deadened any noise."

"Excluding those who were 'ere that evenin', who else knew that Henri was stayin' with you?"

"In the squadron, you mean?"

"Not necessarily. In general terms, say, 'ow many people knew Henri was in the country, for example?"

"There are two questions here, Sergeant," he corrected. "As for the squadron, only a few of the pilots and some of the FANY drivers knew he was staying here with us. As to who else, I really couldn't say. You would need to talk to London about that. I can tell you that his visits were always brief and discreetly managed."

"This Henri fellow, what did 'e do for a livin' in France?"

"Do you know, I never asked."

At this point Inspector Sim rose.

"We would like that list of all those who were in the house when Henri was murdered."

"I'm afraid, Inspector, I'll have to clear that with the station commanding officer."

"And he is?"

"Wing Commander Farrington."

"Very well. Will you please contact him on the matter and as soon as possible? We may need to speak with you again, Squadron Leader."

"Where to now, sir?" ACW Little asked.

"RAF Tempsford. It's time we met the wing commander. I dislike being messed about, don't you, Sergeant?"

"Indubitably, sir."

Although it took less than thirty minutes to drive to RAF Tempsford, it was almost lunchtime before they were eventually escorted into the office of the station's commander. Guards at the camp gate had not allowed them to pass until the wing commander's adjutant had first spoken with his superior and then with London.

"You are the people from Special Branch, I presume. My squadron leader said you might put in an appearance," the wing commander said as they entered. A short, square-set man of middle age, with an out-of-control moustache and a cropped head of hair, remained seated behind an enormous metal desk piled high with files.

Through the window an ancient tractor was rusting away amid a carpet of nettles, and beyond that a dilapidated barn that looked as though the smallest gust of wind would flatten it. Tempsford was like nothing they had seen before. The entire camp was camouflaged. When the station had been built, in 1940, the services of an illusionist, Jasper Maskelyne, had been employed to modify existing farm buildings so that overflying German aircraft would see what appeared to be a disused airfield set in farmland. Even the three concrete runways were painted so as to mislead the Hun.

"Take a seat, Inspector. Sorry you were kept waiting. We like to know who our visitors are, bona fides and all that. You're here about that business at Squadron Leader Barrington-Brown's house." That said, he deftly filled an old briar with tobacco from a leather pouch before sticking the unlit pipe purposefully into his mouth.

After Inspector Sim had introduced them both and confirmed the reason for their visit, the station commander eyed them warily.

"No, the squadron leader contacted me but didn't mention a list." He then seemed to loosen up and become more amenable. "I think we can accommodate you there. After all, it's in our interest as much as yours to find out who did the deed, so to speak. We can't have homicidal maniacs running around the Bedfordshire countryside."

"Quite. You think it possible that the murder is unrelated to Tempsford?"

"Do you have any reason to suppose otherwise, Inspector?"

"It seems to me more than probable that whatever Henri Bonoteaux was engaged in has something to do with his murder. In which case, Wing Commander, you would be better able to explain his death than either Sergeant Hodges or myself."

"That is supposition on your part, Inspector. I'm rather busy. There's a war on, and, whatever the reason for the poor man's demise, I have an operational station to run. I see no problem with you having access to the names of those who were there that evening, and no doubt you will want to interview them. Although you won't find your murderer among them, I can assure you. My adjutant will provide you with the list once he has spoken with Squadron Leader Barrington-Brown. You must understand, this is an active station, and as far as my chaps are concerned one or more of those who were at the house that evening may be otherwise engaged. You'll just have to grab them when you can. The adjutant will see you out."

"Thank you for your time, Wing Commander. Just one more thing. Are you able to tell me what it was that brought the deceased to England?"

"Even if I knew, which I do not, I wouldn't. Good day, Inspector."

The adjutant, a Flight Lieutenant Mortlock, took them to his office, where he asked if they would like tea. Their past experience with the military left them unprepared for this unexpected act of hospitality.

"Thank you, but no, Flight Lieutenant. The sergeant and I have work to do, and you have a war to run, as we have just been informed. The wing commander says you can provide us with a list of those who were at the house that evening."

"The list isn't a problem, Inspector."

"That would be most welcome. I didn't expect—"

Handing over an A4 sheet of paper, he said, "When the squadron leader was here yesterday he gave me the names in anticipation of your request. We simply required the CO's approval. The chaps on the list will, I am sure, be expecting a visit from you and the sergeant, as will the ladies. Good luck with your enquiries." Handing over the list, he added, "This affair with the Frenchman has thrown things out of gear around here. It's something we could have done without."

"I'm sure. Did you know him?" Sim enquired.

"The Frenchman? No. I haven't been with the squadron long. I've just finished my first tour of ops with Bomber Command."

"Congratulations, Flight Lieutenant. That's thirty missions, isn't it?" Sergeant Hodges asked admiringly.

"Yes. Being at Tempsford is like being on leave. It's funny, you look forward to making it through, you know, surviving, but at the end of your tour you feel as though you're deserting the squadron, leaving the chaps to face it without you, particularly the men in your crew. That's the hard part."

"I'm sure. I understand that the attrition rate has been unexpectedly high in Bomber Command, although I suppose we may never know just how bad it is. Perhaps we shouldn't be talking about such things."

"Why not? It's true. To say that our losses have been unexpectedly high would be something of an understatement. I suppose there's been a great deal about this war that was unexpected, Inspector. When it's all over somebody may have some questions to answer. On my last trip only fifty percent made it back. Fifty percent. Not something we can sustain for long, I would have thought. You know the Nissen huts we're billeted in? After each operation the MPs swiftly come through and empty the contents of the personal belongings of the poor sods who didn't make it. It's just so bloody clinical. It's as if they had never existed." This bitter observation by Flight Lieutenant Mortlock left the two policemen speechless.

The sound of an aircraft engine bursting into life broke the silence.

"There is a tide in the affairs of men which, taken any way you please, is bad."

"I would have to agree with you, Inspector."

"Thank you for your help, Flight Lieutenant. We may have to call on it again."

"Any time, Inspector. Sergeant."

They found ACW Little standing beside the car in humorous conversation with a corporal of the Military Police.

"I think it's time for a spot of lunch. The Queen's Head, please, Miss Little. And then, Sergeant, we'll start trying to contact some of the names on that list." Lowering his voice, he added, "We're still waiting on that briefing from SOE. Maybe I'll ring London."

Chapter Seven

<u>Montsoreau, Loire, France</u>

Grace Harris (alias Simone) considered herself the fittest she had ever been following her flight aboard the Lizzie into occupied France. Her training in England had seen to that, but, even so, the ride from Azay-sur-Cher to Montsoreau had been demanding. Montsoreau sits in the Loire Valley, with the River Loire fronting the length of the village. Evening civil twilight was not far off as she cycled the last few kilometres. It would not do to be caught out after curfew.

There had been few vehicles on the roads, although she had passed a German military convoy outside Bourgueil. Earlier she had stopped to buy a coffee and some bread at a café in Gizeux. A tired woman of her mother's age had served her. At first, she was suspicious of this stranger who did not offer her coupons and had chosen to land on her so late in the afternoon, but she quickly dropped whatever doubt she had for the visitor after they had chatted for a few minutes. The woman was lonely. Her husband, like thousands of other men of working age, had been taken off to Germany to work in their factories. There was a son whom she hadn't heard of since the start of the war when he left to join the army and had been posted to Indochina. All attempts at trying to find him through the army and the Red Cross had proved futile. It occurred to Grace that it was the women of France who had been left to carry much of the burden of defeat and occupation. The Vichy regime went so far as to partly blame the women of France for its defeat in 1940. On June 20th of that year, Pétain, that revered father figure, successor to Joan of Arc, Louis XIV, and Napoleon, but to others *traitre extraordinaire,* declared that there had been "too few children, too few arms, too few Allies." The women of France had "neglected" their duty to the state by failing to produce enough children. He failed to mention that at the time of its defeat, France had the largest army in the world and that, from the little Grace knew, most of its high command were useless.

The village of Montsoreau rests on gradually rising ground sandwiched between a high cliff and a river. On the higher ground runs the main street and between that and the cliff can be found the Hotel Bussy, a three-storied white-fronted building dating back almost as far as the decaying Château de Montsoreau itself, a sad but still impressive fifteenth century structure built on the riverfront. Three German officers sat drinking wine, enjoying the superb view of the river and the chateau from the hotel's terrace as Grace pushed her bicycle past the Bussy. She only glanced at them, but it was sufficient for her to notice the SS regimental flashes on their uniform. During her training in England she, along with others on her course, had been taught the various uniforms and insignia on the uniforms of the Third Reich. There they sat, loud, arrogant, and confident, with their legs outstretched and their jackboots shining in the weak winter evening light. Prime specimens of 'the master race.'

It didn't take long for her to locate the Café Brion once she had entered the village's main thoroughfare. It was just off the Place du Mail, a two-storied structure, vintage early eighteen hundreds, situated between two shops, both of which were boarded up. After her previous experience, she had been loath to leave her bicycle outside unobserved, but there seemed little alternative other than to trust in the honesty of the folks of Montsoreau. She felt a pressing need to get off the street. A dusty twilight infused the café interior as she entered. The few customers seated at small round wooden tables were preparing to leave. It was close to that time when it would not be prudent to be caught on the street unless you were prepared to answer to the occupation forces or the local police. Behind the small counter that ran almost the length of a mirrored wall to her right stood an elderly man so short that he was barely visible. Grace stood to one side until she and the small man behind the bar were alone.

"Monsieur Claude?"

"And you are, madam?"

"Simone. Monsieur Gilbert sent me."

"Monsieur Gilbert, you say. Do I know him?"

Here we go again, Grace thought. Is anybody to be trusted in France? Does trust even exist? She had heard stories of French families torn apart since the start of the occupation, confidence in each other destroyed, with doubt bringing into question the loyalty of its members. If such a breakdown can occur in families, how much easier was it for trust between strangers to be non-existent?

"I have come from Azay-sur-Cher. My bicycle is outside. Will it be safe?"

"I wouldn't think so, madam. Perhaps . . ." He paused, doing as he had done so many times since his country was defeated and the traitors had appeared among them, making a judgement on face value, one that, if wrong, could have disastrous consequences. "It will be safer off the street. Are you staying in Montsoreau?"

"I had hoped to, monsieur, at least for the night."

"I see. I take it you have not made arrangements?"

"No, monsieur."

"What is the world coming to when young women such as yourself go cycling around the country on their own with nowhere to stay the night and so close to curfew?"

"It was necessary for me to leave Azay, monsieur. I was not at liberty to choose my time of leaving."

"I can imagine, madam, or should I call you mademoiselle?"

"It is mademoiselle, monsieur."

"Very well." Monsieur 'Claude' had made up his mind; he would trust the young woman, at least for the present. "We must first get your bicycle off the street and then find you somewhere to sleep. Have you eaten?"

"I had some food at Gizeux, nothing since."

"I'm about to close. These days I don't stay open after curfew, there is no point. Before the end of demarcation the local police would look the other way, now it is different. Bring your bicycle in and we'll put it in the back. Then we'll find you something to eat."

Grace had barely finished her meal of bread, sausage, and a fine local cheese when her host excused himself, leaving her alone in the kitchen at the back of the property to ruminate on her position, the bicycle safely leaning against the large wooden sink. Just as it seemed he had chosen to trust her, so she had put her life in his hands. But, perhaps, instead of going to find her a bed for the night, if that indeed was what he was doing, he had gone to fetch the police. She had her bike; she could ride away before he returned and take her chances on the road, but where would she go? Anyway, he had locked both of the café's doors prior to leaving, taking the keys with him. Even if she could get out, how would she make contact with a network? And how long would she be free in what was now an occupied zone? Whom could she trust? Above all, if she left, how would Gilbert find her? She hadn't even begun her mission, and now here she was on the run, hiding like a criminal, after all that training, unable to carry out the simplest of tasks. It was an inauspicious beginning to her mission.

She had no choice other than to sit and wait for Claude's return. It was odd, since arriving in France she had not felt fear, something she had expected to experience the moment she stepped out of the aircraft. Surely now, waiting for him to return, she should be scared. During her training they had told her how to handle it, how to control fear and to stop it becoming all-consuming, to the point where paralysis could take over. In fact, fear was necessary, they had said, to keep agents alert to the hostile environment in which they worked and to the ever-present danger that went with being in the field.

"Fear is your friend," Sergeant Major Wilson, their instructor, had told them. "Fear is your friend. If you don't know him, you bloody well should! Fear will save your life. Fear will help you stay alive. Remember that!" So fear was good, but she didn't feel it. At a time when her brain should have been telling her body to activate various reactions, including the release of adrenalin, it seemed to produce only curiosity; what might happen, how does this or that event affect the outcome? It was as if her cognitive skills were operating outside of her body, observing.

He must have been away an hour, during which Grace had fallen asleep, her head resting on her arms across the table in the centre of the dimly lit kitchen. A combination of the food, the glass of wine he had served with her meal, and exhaustion from her cycling had left her unable to keep her eyes open. She didn't hear him enter and was thrown into shock when he gently touched her shoulder.

"Mademoiselle, you must wake up. You cannot sleep here. I have found a bed for you just a few streets away, but we must go now."

It took her a few minutes to realise where she was; she had been deep in sleep. As she rose slowly from the table there was a sudden banging on the front door of the café. They both froze. The banging continued.

"Open up, the police," the words coming through to the kitchen from the room beyond with electrifying clarity.

"Stay here, mademoiselle, stay quiet. I will go and see what they want.'"

Claude quickly left the room, closing the door to the café behind him.

Grace stood with her ear to the door, trying to hear what was being said in the next room. Would these be the last free moments of her life? Was it all going to end here? She was confident that the papers she carried would pass examination, but what possible reason could she have for being in Montsoreau and in the Café Brion? Her cover story had a backup, but her mind didn't seem to be moving quickly enough to adapt it to current circumstances. The minutes ticked by. Eventually she heard the front door close and the bolt pushed home.

"We are fortunate, mademoiselle. The policeman who came to the door is an old acquaintance. We knew each other as boys. He told me the Germans are looking for some resisters. There was a shooting in Saumur this morning. A German officer has been wounded. The streets will not be safe until they either find those responsible or they have taken hostages. Last year they shot eleven villagers in Beuxés after a similar incident."

"I'm aware, monsieur, that my presence in your café exposes you to danger. I apologise. There was nowhere else for me to go you see, and Gilbert—"

"Do not distress yourself, mademoiselle. But what is to be done? The police and the Germans have drafted more men into the area to search for the resisters. We have to be careful. You have papers?"

"Yes."

"Good." He stood with his head back, his small podgy hands by his side, staring at the ceiling, as if the answer to their situation would fall from the sky. Eventually he said, "Then this is what we will do. You will have to stay here, with me. I live upstairs, above the café. There is only one bedroom, but there is a box room that I now use as a storeroom. We will have to put you in there." He paused. "Before the war, my wife and I used to rent it out to a man who had been in the Legion, in Algiers. Then one day I came back from a trip to Tours and they were gone."

"Your wife and the legionnaire?"

"Exactly. It was all very difficult. She did most of the cooking, you see. I was left to run the place on my own. The café doesn't make enough for me to employ someone." Again he paused, this time his thoughts were no doubt caught up in the past, with his errant wife and the legionnaire. "There is a mattress in the loft, unfortunately I gave the bed away. Give me a few minutes and I will get it down." It was only then that she noticed, in a dark corner of the kitchen, the steep, narrow stairs leading to the upper floor.

What to make of this man in whom she had entrusted her future, her freedom? Clearly the departure of his wife with the legionnaire had come as a surprise to the owner of the Café Brion. Men can be so blind. However, he looked at his loss more in practical terms than to any emotional attachment he might have had for the poor woman. Was she tall, Grace wondered, or like Claude, short and stout? She imagined them both, like a couple of trolls, fussing around in the café serving the folks of Montsoreau before closing up for the night and climbing the steep stairs together, she with one eye on her legionnaire.

Before the mattress could be installed on the floor of the box room it had to be emptied of its contents: old suitcases, a broken chair, a number of books, and, surprisingly, an almost-new bassinet. All of which would have to sit on the small landing until a better place could be found for them. Having squeezed the mattress into the box room. Claude went in search of some bedding, returning minutes later with two cotton sheets, two blankets, and a straw pillow. Back down in the kitchen he informed Grace that she was free to go to bed whenever she wished, but that she should not leave the café without first telling him, and on no account answer the door to callers.

"On second thought, perhaps it would be wise, mademoiselle, for you not to venture out at all for a few days, until things have calmed down. You can help me in the café."

"Very well. I had to leave Azay without my case, monsieur. I have only the clothes I am wearing. I will either have to wash them or buy new things." For that she must leave the café, which, as Monsieur had made clear, was not an option at this time. However, when free to do so, purchasing clothes would not be a problem. She had not removed her money belt since leaving England. In it were funds enough to last her months, since she was carrying cash for the network to which she had been assigned. Also, she had coupons.

"We will have to think about your clothes in the morning and how you can help in the café, mademoiselle. Can you cook?"

"Yes," she hesitantly replied.

"Good. Very soon the power may go off and we will be left only with candles, which, like everything else, are in short supply. So, the sooner we go to bed the better.

Chapter Eight

<u>Milton Ernest, Bedfordshire</u>

Sergeant Hodges had arranged to meet his inspector for lunch in the lounge bar of the Queen's Head. Since yesterday morning, each had been slowly working through a divided list of those who had been present at the house where poor Henri had been so callously dispatched.

"There you are, Sergeant. I was beginning to think they might have spirited you off to parts foreign."

"No such luck, sir," he replied, taking his place at the small round table at which the inspector sat, a plate of unappetizing Spam sandwiches awaiting his attention.

"There was a phone call for you. They didn't leave a name but said they would phone back."

"Thank you, but who knows I'm 'ere?"

"Obviously, somebody. Also in your absence I've had a visitor, a military gentleman from the SOE. Odd fellow. He 'felt it best to have an unofficial off-the-cuff chat, away from Tempsford,' where it seems we were scheduled to meet him. Now that we've had our briefing, Sergeant, for what it's worth, we can get on with the investigation, though I can't say that it will help us find our killer any the quicker. How did you get on?"

"Nobody saw or 'eard anythin'. If you ask me, they were all too plastered and gettin' up to who knows what. Some party!"

"A few friends around for dinner was the way Mrs. Huntington-Brown described it. You make it sound like some bacchanalian orgy, Sergeant."

"And what would that be like, sir?"

"Something I would rather not go into at the moment. It might put me off my Spam sandwiches."

"If you say so, sir. But I'll say this, one of the two single pilots, Flyin' Officer Roy Pavitt, I reckon 'e and the missis ..."

"Mrs. Huntington-Brown?"

"Yes, that's the one. I reckon they've got somethin' goin' on, if you get my drift?"

"He's the one that was helping her in the kitchen when Henri stepped outside for his smoke."

"The very one."

"And what gives you that idea?"

"Well ..."

"Never mind. A romantic interlude over the preparation of some cucumber sandwiches doesn't advance our case very much, even if it did take place while poor old Henri was getting his throat cut."

"You're right, sir. Even so, I wonder if the squadron leader knows what's 'appenin'? 'Ow did you get on with your lot?"

"My lot were no more informative than yours, I'm afraid. Nobody saw or heard anything." The inspector eyed his sandwiches reproachfully, wondering if it would ever be possible to develop a liking for Spam. Some liquid refreshment would be needed to wash it down. "It's a bit early for a beer, don't you think? I tell you what, why don't you get us some tea when you place your order for lunch. Only sandwiches on the menu today."

"Right you are, sir. By the way, they've found me a bed 'ere at the Queen's 'ead."

"How on earth did you manage that, Sergeant?"

"I 'ad a chat with the landlord. It seems we 'ave a mutual acquaintance in the Met. It's a long story, but to cut it short, there's a sergeant at the Southwark nick who just 'appened to 'ave done us both a favour, over the years. 'E's that sort of copper, if you know what I mean?"

"I'm not sure that I do, Sergeant. But never mind."

"Funny old world, isn't it? I mean, us both knowing the same bloke. Anyway, 'ere at the Queen's 'ead, be'ind the pub, there's what used to be a stable. Above that they've converted a loft into, what 'e calls, 'overflow accommodation.' It's not exactly the Ritz, but it'll do."

"Do I take it that Mrs. Hall's establishment didn't pass muster?"

"You might say that, sir. The lady leaves much to be desired when it comes to runnin' a boardin' 'ouse. She's another one that could be workin' for the Germans."

"Sorry to hear that, Sergeant. However, having us both under the same roof will be a lot more convenient."

Such was the nature of their frugal repast that they were not late for ACW Little and her black Humber when she pulled up in front of the hotel. Throughout lunch the inspector had felt disinclined to divulge his plans for the afternoon, neither had the sergeant felt sufficiently motivated to ask. Lunch, even one as sparing as that which was on offer, had today left him feeling torpid.

"Well, Sergeant, what do you think about it all?"

"You mean this business with Henri? Well it's got to be an inside job, 'asn't it?"

"An inside job. Do you know what, I think you may be right, however, in this particular case there appear to be several insides. Who knew that Henri was in the country? Who knew where he was billeted? And who knew that he would be attending Mrs.

Barrington-Brown's little soirée? I think, though, that whoever murdered him just got lucky when Henri went out for a smoke. Come on, Sergeant, let's get back into it."

"Anythin' I should know from your chat with SOE, sir?"

"All in good time, Sergeant, all in good time."

"Good afternoon, Miss Little," the inspector cheerily said, sliding into the rear of the vehicle, closely followed by his sergeant.

"Good afternoon, sir. And where are we going?"

"Back to Tempsford to see a man about a dog."

"A dog, sir?"

"Just an expression. Sergeant, I want to talk to a certain pilot."

"I thought we 'ad covered all those that were at—"

"This one has nothing to do with Mrs. Huntington-Browns little party, Sergeant, at least not directly."

"I didn't expect to see you so soon, Inspector. I'll see if Sergeant Gifford is operational today."

Flight Lieutenant Mortlock, the stations adjutant, had secured entry for them to the camp and provided a room in which they now sat. Outside it had started to rain from a cloud base that had lowered almost to ground level. To Hodges it seemed that Bedfordshire and November equalled rain.

"That would be most helpful. Tell me, can you fly in this?" Inspector Sim asked, pointing to the heavy rain that now pelted the window.

"Not today. It's forecast to get worse. Apparently it's like this along the entire south coast and across the Channel. All ops have been cancelled for tonight."

"Then it betters our chances of meeting this Sergeant Gifford."

"Always assuming he was operational today. He wouldn't normally be here until this evening. And even then, when they aren't needed, the chaps don't tend to hang around when ops have been cancelled. Excuse me, I'll go and see if he's available."

As the door closed behind the adjutant, Sergeant Hodges asked what was, for him, the obvious question.

"Who's this Sergeant Gifford, sir?"

"He's the pilot who brought the late Henri over from France. Very helpful, our Flight Lieutenant Mortlock. I'm hoping Gifford might be able to help us with our enquiries, though somehow I doubt it."

"This SOE, sir? What kind of setup are they?"

"Special Operations Executive, some hush-hush military organisation. They're responsible for Henri being in the country, I understand. They come and go at the base. I understand from the flight lieutenant that generally SOE are only in residence when the station's operational, so it rather looks as though you are going to have to forgo the pleasure of meeting the mysterious men from the SOE today."

A few minutes later, Flight Lieutenant Mortlock returned with a sergeant pilot.

"You are in luck, Inspector. I just caught the sergeant before he returned to his mess. I'll leave you to it."

"Good afternoon, Sergeant. Please, take a seat. I'm Inspector Sim, and this is Sergeant Hodges. We're from the Met. We're looking into the death of a French gentleman who I believe you brought over from France recently."

"Yes, that's correct."

"That was on the thirteen December?"

"Correct."

"I assume you have already been questioned by your superiors concerning that particular flight."

"Yes, sir."

"I appreciate your giving up the time to talk to us today. I'm sure there are a number of other things you would rather be doing, but if you can help us that would be good."

"There really isn't much I can tell you about the man, Inspector. He was just another Joe."

"Joe?"

"That's what we call our passengers."

"I see. Was there anything about that particular flight or operation that made it different from the others you have flown?"

"I'm not sure how much I'm permitted to talk about, Inspector. The flight lieutenant said you were from Special Branch, which meant something to him but not much to me."

"I understand. Rest assured we have the highest of clearances, Sergeant, otherwise we wouldn't be sitting here. Someone wanted Henri dead. I don't believe for one minute that it was a random killing. I do believe that his death has something to do with his part in this war. Of that I'm convinced."

After a pause, the sergeant said, "There was one thing that surprised me about the flight, well, both ways, really."

"And what was that?"

"We're always short of space on these flights, at least the ones I've flown. It's normally two out and sometimes three for the return trip, in the Lizzie. That makes it a bit crammed down the back. That night I took one in and brought only one out, and I remember that the Air Transport Form for the return flight was mauve."

"Is that significant?"

"The code denotes the authority, Inspector. Black if it's for SOE, and mauve if it's for SIS."

"I see. So that flight, at least the return portion of it, was not on behalf of the SOE but for the SIS?"

"Yes."

"The Joe, as you call him, did he speak to you during the flight?"

"Although we've got the intercom, it's hard to communicate with whoever's in the rear, with the sound of the engine and the air rushing through the plane. He seemed keen for me to know he was a friend of my commanding officer."

"Squadron Leader Huntington-Brown?"

"Yes, I suppose he was trying to impress me. I must say, for a Frenchman his English was pretty good."

"Nothing else?"

"Not that I can remember."

"When you arrived at Tempsford—"

"Tangmere. Although we're based here at Tempsford, we generally land back first at Tangmere."

"Tangmere, right. Who met him?"

"I think it was the squadron leader and a civilian. They drove up to the aircraft in a big American car and drove off."

"Is that unusual?"

"No, not at all. When we're operational there, all sorts of London types are milling around. You don't really know who's who."

"Sergeant, do you have any questions for Sergeant Gifford?"

"Have you been at Tempsford long?"

"No, I'm the rookie on the squadron. I came from Coastal Command."

"This will be a bit different then?"

"You could say that, although, apart from the night ops, it's more like the sort of flying I was doing before the war, in British Columbia."

"I see. Were you in Canada long? You don't sound Canadian."

"Six years. I learnt to fly there. I would be there now if it weren't for Hitler."

"My daughter's in Toronto with 'er uncle. For the duration."

"She's a lucky girl. You must be relieved, having her safely out of the country."

"Yes, I am. The inspector and I 'ave met a number of your fellow pilots over the last twenty-four hours. They all seem to be commissioned. Are there other sergeant pilots on the squadron?"

"No. I'm the only one. Why do you ask?"

"Interest, really."

"It's something that seems to bother the CO. He says he's going to do something about it. Frankly, I couldn't give a damn. In my last squadron, at least twenty-five percent of the pilots weren't commissioned. Anyway, the beer's cheaper in the sergeants' mess."

"A definite plus, I'll bet. And you don't remember anythin' else about that flight, somethin' that was out of the ordinary?"

"Each operation's different. I can't think of anything outstanding about that particular night other than what I've already mentioned. These Joes are a mixed bunch, as I'm sure you've been told. Male, female, old, young, French, British, you never know what you're going to get. Outbound we have very little to do with them once we've given them the preflight briefing and escorted them to the aircraft. Sometimes we have breakfast with the SOE Joes when we get back to Tempsford or Tangmere, but the SIS Joes don't hang around once we're on the ground."

"Just one last question, it's probably not important, but are most of your flights for SOE, Sergeant?"

"As I said, I've not been with the squadron long, but, yes, most of my flights have been for SOE."

"Thank you, Sergeant. I don't think we'll need to bother you again."

It wasn't until the sound of the departing pilot's footsteps along the linoleum corridor had receded that Inspector Sim spoke.

"Now that was interesting."

"You mean the bit about SIS?"

"Exactly, Sergeant."

When Flight Lieutenant Mortlock returned to escort them off the station, Inspector Sim had one question for him.

"Flight Lieutenant, SIS, do they have a representative here at Tempsford? It seems we've been chasing the wrong fox. We need to speak with SIS."

"Ah, I can't help you there, Inspector. If anything, they're even more hush-hush. Can't say I've met many of them. They're a bit like SOE, they come and go from the station when we're operational, but I've had little to do with them. You're more likely to catch them at Tangmere than here. They have their own man at Tempsford, but I've never met him. You could speak with the CO, but he's not on the station at present. But no doubt Special Branch has their own contacts with SIS."

"We do indeed. Well, I don't think there is much more to be gained by our being here. Thanks again for your help, Flight Lieutenant."

When both men returned, in pouring rain, to the black Humber, wet from their short walk, ACW Little was nowhere to be seen. It was ten minutes before she made her appearance, and then in the company of a tall military policeman chivalrously sheltering the airwoman from the rain with a battered umbrella.

"Have you noticed, Sergeant, how popular ACW Little is with the men?"

"I 'ad noticed, sir. We leave 'er for just a minute, and in no time at all there's a bloke on the scene. A big favourite with the men, our ACW Little. Do you think she gives off some kind of alluring aroma?"

"Well, if she does, clearly you and I can't smell it."

Returning to the Queen's Head and having dismissed ACW Little for what remained of the day, they were informed by the landlord on entering the pub that a foreign gentleman was waiting for them in the lounge bar.

Colonel Jean-Guy Bernard of the Free French was standing alone at the small bar with a glass of red wine in his left hand. In his right was a gold cigarette holder on the end of which was a Gilanes Brunes emitting its distinctive aroma. Of medium height with jet-black hair, the parting of which ran down the middle of his skull, he wore a uniform that had not suffered at the hands of a military tailor; the well-fitted tunic, jodhpurs, and polished brown cavalry boots giving him an air of military competence he may or may not have possessed. A blue kepi sat rather conspicuously on the bar beside a large glass ashtray. All that was missing was the pencil thin moustache. Attire aside, there was no mistaking his lineage, even were he to be wearing hospital pyjamas, this middle-aged soldier could only be French. Military bearing aside, he reminded Sergeant Hodges of a waiter he had known before the war.

His name was Marcel Gillier, who liked to refer to himself as the *maitre d'hôtel*, (it was only a small hotel and rather run-down). Gillier had involved himself in matters that were the business of some unsavoury persons of Greek Cypriot origin who were smuggling goods through the King George V docks. The waiter had come to see him in the hope that he would extract him from the difficult position in which he had found himself. On balance, as one of Sergeant Hodges's snouts, an informer, it didn't seem to be an unreasonable request. Unfortunately, poor Marcel had taken their money, thus locking him into something he could no longer control, if he ever could. The only advice Sergeant Hodges could give him was to flee home to France, and that he did, leaving wife and child behind. Since then, Sergeant

Hodges had often speculated on the fate of Marcel following the invasion of his country.

"Good evening, I am Colonel Bernard of the Free French. You are Inspector Sim of the Metropolitan Police?"

"That is correct, Colonel. This is Sergeant Alan Hodges. We have been expecting you."

"*Bon*. May I offer you a drink, Inspector?"

"Thank you, Colonel. I'll have an ale. And you, Sergeant?"

"I'll 'ave the same, sir, if that's all right?"

Each with a drink, they retired to one of the tables away from the bar. Although they had the room to themselves there existed a tacit understanding between them that they would converse softly.

"I wish to talk to you, Inspector, about the death of a French national."

"Henri Bonoteaux?" the inspector queried.

"Henri Bonoteaux," the colonel replied.

"How may we help you?"

"Monsieur Bonoteaux. I wish to know how far you have progressed with your enquiries, Inspector."

"May I ask the nature of your interest in the case?"

"The same as yours, Inspector. We wish to know who killed him."

"I see." Inspector Sim slowly lifted his glass, his eyes fixating on the colonel. "Why?"

"Why? Do you mean why was he killed or . . . ?"

"We are of course interested in why he was killed, but I would first like to know why the interest in Henri, Colonel? There must be thousands of Frenchmen in England, particularly after Dunkirk. Admittedly, they haven't all had their throats cut, thank goodness. So I ask myself, why Monsieur Bonoteaux?"

"I hope you do not wish to play games, Inspector. We both know that he was, shall we say, on active service."

"We do?"

"As to the purpose of his visit to England, it may or it may not be connected with his death, time will tell. Whoever killed him was remarkably well informed as to his whereabouts, don't you think?"

"I agree. And who would that be? For that matter, who would want to kill him, Colonel?"

"Is that not for you to find out?"

"Thank you for confirming the status of Henri. We understand that the authorising authority for his visit to England was our Secret Intelligence Service, the SIS, not, as we first thought, the SOE. But I'm sure you already know that. We have yet to delve into that particular swamp, but from past experience I am not optimistic. Would I be right to assume you know the purpose of his visit? After all, if his death has nothing to do with his active service, what other reason could there possibly be? Who, other than those involved with bringing him to England, knew he was in Milton Ernest?"

"Inspector, I had not heard of the man until I was told of his death. These people are not normally my concern. There are obviously those in France who knew he was coming here as well as those in England who authorised his visit."

After a lengthy pause, the inspector asked, "Who do you think would want him dead?"

"It is not a simple question to answer, Inspector."

"Would you like to try?"

"Since my country has been occupied, we French have been at each other's throats. There are many who claim the right to represent France. But only the Free French can speak for all of France. However, not all agree with the way we carry out the fight to liberate our country."

"Are you saying it's possible that a rival resistance group may have ordered his killing?"

"It is not impossible."

"And the Germans?"

"It's possible. Surely you are not so naïve as to believe that the Boche are not active here in England?"

"I'm sure they are. Germans. An interesting thought, Colonel," Inspector Sim replied.

"If it was a rival resistance group, why wait 'til 'e's in England? Surely it would 'ave been easier to 'ave 'im bumped off in France?" Sergeant Hodges's interruption was received with acceptance by his superior but with surprise by the colonel, who had yet to acknowledge his presence.

"A good point, Sergeant," Inspector Sim said.

"Perhaps those who killed him wanted to also embarrass your government," the colonel parried.

"And who would want to do that?"

"England, Inspector, is not universally popular in France. There are those who feel deserted, betrayed by your country."

"That's unfortunate, Colonel. I think the BEF did the best they could, under the circumstances. I think your country needs to look closer to home when searching for those who betrayed the French people. It is perhaps a subject upon which we must agree to disagree, wouldn't you say?"

"You are of course correct, Inspector. I should add that I am not one of those who feel betrayed, at least not by England. The people of France were, as you suggest, betrayed by their politicians and the army high command. Then there are the communists. Perhaps it is they who killed him."

"Yes, there are always the communists. Are you staying here at Milton Ernest, Colonel?"

"I have a room in Bedford at the Swan Hotel. My time is limited, Inspector. I am wanted in London. The sooner we can, as you British say, get to the bottom of this murder, the better."

Inspector Sim was not completely sure that he welcomed the introduction of the pronoun 'we' into the conversation. Had the colonel ambitions of a constabulary nature? If so, they needed to be squashed.

Chapter Nine

Auxerre, France

Two days after his meeting with the men from the Met, Sergeant Gifford was again operational, taking a routine sortie into a field near Auxerre to a landing strip he knew to be barely suitable, given its very rough surface. The approach, however, at least from the east, was perfectly acceptable, but less so from the west. But getting there had not been straightforward.

With a full fuselage tank situated right behind him holding 106 gallons and a further 150 gallons of fuel in a tank between the undercarriage struts, he had left Tangmere with two Joes in the back – one male, one female, both French – seated side by side and facing aft. Again he had been impressed with their high level of training and dedication. Neither seemed at all nervous about flying into occupied France, quite the contrary. They couldn't wait to set their feet back firmly on the soil of their mother country. The broken cloud ceiling at around 8,000 feet had made life easier most of the way until just southeast of Orleans. It had also offered a certain amount of cover from German night fighters, but then low cloud began to form. At the confluence of the Yonne and Armançon rivers, north of Auxerre, he lost all sight of the ground but picked it up again north of Chablis. The weather change was against him, with the low cloud forming fast. It was important to get on the ground as soon as possible, drop off the Joes, pick up his outward-bound load and be airborne before the meteorological conditions made it impossible to operate into the field. He started to descend.

Five minutes after his turning point, over Yrouerre, it started to rain, but he could just make out the Serein River, at which point he started looking for the ground signal, the letter J. At two thousand feet he caught sight of a flashing light to port – dot followed by three dashes. He signalled back, and a few minutes later he was bouncing almost uncontrollably along the rough strip, wondering how it was the Air Ministry had approved its use. It was certainly equal to the roughest strip he had ever had the misfortune to fly into on the West Coast. It was only as he tried to turn at the end of his short landing roll that he realised that the tail oleo was damaged. No matter how much differential brake he applied he couldn't turn the aircraft. After a few minutes the reception committee, having realised that something was wrong, sprinted across the field.

Shutting down the engine he ordered the Joes out, along with the removal of the freight. After which he slid back his canopy and climbed out. It was the first time he had actually set foot on French soil, a moment on which he had little time to reflect. With the help of one of the inbound Joes he quickly explained to the reception committee what he required of them. They were to lift the heavy tail of the aircraft and turn the machine around. There was now so little wind that he would be able to take-off in the opposite direction to that which he had landed. The three-point take-off would serve him well in this instance. His outbound Joes, two elderly, suited gentlemen, had trouble climbing the short ladder. They were preceded by four containers and a gift of a bottle of Chablis from the head of the reception committee. Sergeant Gifford climbed into his cockpit and slid his canopy shut. Lateral control on take-off notwithstanding, there was another problem that now confronted him.

When over-rich, a hot Mercury engine could be very difficult to restart. The last thing he needed was to run the battery flat attempting a restart. Were that to happen, there would be nothing for it but to destroy the aircraft and go into hiding. It was on the third attempt that the engine reassuringly burst into life. With thumbs-up from the field controller, they were ready for take-off. Just then he was distracted by a set of car lights speedily approaching along the adjacent road. With no time to lose, he stood on the brakes and slowly advanced the throttle. Releasing the brakes, the Lysander shot forward and upward. Behind them the reception committee, along with the inbound Joes, scattered, tossing two of the inbound containers into long grass to be retrieved later.

He increased speed to 110 mph so that the flaps and slats would retract and then checked that the gill opened. Cloud ceiling had lowered to five hundred feet. He was entering cloud. Quickly but cautiously he pushed forward, lowering the nose to reduce height, popping out of cloud into relatively clear air above a river. There was no other choice than to fly northwest and hope that the cloud ceiling would rise along his track. He adjusted the mixture to weak and reduced power to 2,200 rpm. That night was particularly dark, and little of the moon's light penetrated his part of the world. The chances of flying into rising ground or hitting a power pylon were considerable were he to attempt a low-level flight all the way to the coast, always assuming he could find his way. There was small comfort in the fact that there was little chance of them running into night fighters all the time they remained at that altitude, but such a haven was a fool's paradise. He would, at some stage, have to climb but preferably in clear air. He had to gain height before attempting to cross the French coast.

It was not until they were level with what he hoped was Montargis, off to starboard, that the cloud began to lift a little.

Seizing the opportunity, they climbed up between layers of cloud, levelling off at 9,000 feet and catching occasional glimpses of the night sky above. Better, he reasoned, to stay partly hidden in the tops rather than risk running into the Luftwaffe on top, clear of cloud. If his dead reckoning navigation was correct they would pass between Chartres and Paris to cross the coast just west of Le Havre. From the drift he was experiencing, the wind at 9,000 feet was from the northeast and possibly up to twenty miles per hour. By laying off ten degrees to starboard, he hoped that it would be sufficient to prevent them from being blown further west, risking a greater chance of running into the Luftwaffe if they crossed the coast west of Caen. It was navigation at its most basic. They flew on.

Since leaving Auxerre he had been too busy to converse with his passengers, neither of whom had uttered a word over the intercom, or, if they had, he had been too preoccupied to hear them.

"*Bonsoir, messieurs,*" he shouted, a greeting he felt rather proud of, given the need for his attention elsewhere. "Sorry about the rough take-off. Not the best strip, I'm afraid. If all goes well we'll be landing in about an hour and a half." *Preferably in England*, he thought.

"*Nous ne comprenons pas.*" At least that is what the reply sounded like above the roar of the engine. Clearly, he was wasting his time attempting to converse further.

With every hour flown, a pilot builds up confidence in his ability to handle most situations in the air. It's called experience. But in the absence of any discernible landmarks from which he could fix his position, Sergeant Gifford was beginning to have his doubts as to his position. If only he could observe a crossing of the coast, that would be something. Suddenly the air lit up beside them, then shells started exploding all about the aircraft.

They had flown into a flack barrage. Had he flown further east into the area of Le Havre? In that case they were not only further east but also more to the north than he thought, or was he west of Cotentin, where it was known there was flack? With the northeast wind they had encountered since leaving Auxerre, he estimated their speed across the ground to be around two miles a minute. If this remained true they still had some distance to run to the coast. Perhaps a new flack site had been set up on his route, one Tempsford knew nothing about. These thoughts flashed through his mind as he threw the aircraft into a steep dive to port into thicker cloud, but not before the Lizzie sustained a number of hits and the gyro horizon had toppled.

"*Qu'est-ce qui s'est passé?*" yelled a voice over the intercom.

The pilot switched off the intercom; screaming Frenchmen he did not need at this time. Levelling out at 5,000 feet he gingerly tested the controls, first the ailerons, then the elevator, and finally the rudder. Neither the fuel nor the oil tank directly behind him seemed punctured. Shining his torch, he inspected first the starboard and then the port wing; both seemed undamaged. Unable to identify what part of the aircraft had been hit by the shell or shells, he flew on, gradually climbing back up to 9,000 feet, from which he hoped to gain sight of the ground and establish his position.

Twenty minutes later he caught sight of the sea beneath them. They had crossed the coast, but where? The homing beacon at Tangmere, if he could receive it, would not only help establish his position but also tell him what course to steer. It was not to be. Silence pervaded the ether. *Had the aerials been damaged by the flack*, he wondered?

Eventually they crossed a coast, which, from his heading, could only be England, unless he was flying around in circles. Here the cloud was more broken and, having established his position, he was further west than he had calculated and made course for Tangmere. With an unannounced arrival in the area it was always possible that their own anti-aircraft defences might mistake his Lizzie for a German raider. His luck held. He was aware as he lined up on the emergency flare path that he was bringing back a crippled aircraft, just how crippled he was about to find out. One thing he did know was that once on the ground he would have little lateral control, a result of the damaged rear oleo. Cutting the engine, he flared out. Both land flap and forward slats had deployed, neither having sustained damage. The Lizzie was one of the first STOL military aircraft, made for short take-off and landing, and as such could be flown onto the deck at comparatively low speeds. Sergeant Gifford tried to keep the aircraft airborne as long as possible, keeping the wings level, allowing the speed to drop away as the engine quickly wound down to idle. Holding off until he could no longer expect the aircraft to continue flying, he eased forward on the stick and the Lysander settled smoothly onto the runway.

Almost immediately it went into a violent ground loop to the left before coming to rest, and then slowly the port undercarriage collapsed, the wing striking the tarmac with a thud. Shutting down the engine, Gifford ordered his passengers to evacuate the aircraft, there being enough fuel left on board to destroy the aircraft and all aboard were it to catch fire.

Sliding back his canopy, he quickly undid his safety harness and parachute straps and exited the aircraft, moving aft to assist his passengers. Maybe the rear cabin canopy was jammed, because neither passenger seemed to be attempting an evacuation. It was then that he remembered he had switched off the intercom shortly after coming under fire and so they would not have heard his order to evacuate. Even so, there appeared to be no movement within the rear cabin. Aft of the front cockpit, on the port side of the Lizzie, there were a number of large holes. Vehicles were making their way across the grass towards the stricken craft as he pulled hard on what was obviously a jammed canopy. Eventually it slid back. Both passengers were still in their seats, both covered in blood. One moved his right arm and muttered something. At least he was alive, but the other looked decidedly dead. *There will be all hell to pay for this*, was Gifford's immediate thought. To his knowledge, nobody had lost a Joe en route except during the medical evacuation for MI9 of a downed aircrew member, from a field near Pocé-sur-Cisse, and he had been near death when loaded aboard the Lizzie.

A medic pushed him aside and shone his torch into the rear cabin.

"Gawd, luv-a-duck, what a mess. Bad luck, Serg. Just not your night, was it?"

The next morning, without having slept, he was on the mat in front of his flight commander and the station's commanding officer.

"This is a bad business, Gifford," his CO intoned, followed by some words that got lost in his Kitchener moustache. "I want your report on my desk before you leave the unit today, do you understand?" Rubbing the top of his cropped head, he continued. "We're not in the business of killing our passengers. They expect us to deliver them safely to England. Needless to say, SOE is not happy. As if that's not enough, you've buggered a perfectly serviceable aeroplane. What have you got to say for yourself?"

As official bollockings went, it was much as could be expected, although it was a bit rich to suggest that he alone had been responsible for the death of one passenger and the injury of another. Had not the Germans or the Vichy French had a hand in the affair? After returning to Tempsford from Tangmere that morning, he had learnt that weather conditions the previous evening had deteriorated over northern France to such an extent that no other aircraft had successfully completed its mission, including two Hudson pickups. Not that it in any way exonerated him from blame. He had inadvertently blundered into that flack barrage due to his poor navigation. But what else could he have done other than rely on dead reckoning, taking into consideration the wind and work on his heading, time, and speed as best he knew them? He would relive the flight in his mind into the foreseeable future; nothing would change that.

"Well?"

"I miscalculated the strength of the easterly, sir."

"You miscalculated the strength of the easterly. Is that it?"

"Also the flack battery was not included in the preflight briefing I received."

"Yes, well, for what it's worth, that particular battery was installed just a few days ago to protect some kind of new ground installation the Germans want protected. We've asked the chaps in reconnaissance to have a look at it." There followed a short pause. "Well, it's just not good enough, Gifford. Then there's this business of the late Mr. Bonoteaux. It seems your passengers aren't even safe once they're on the ground. Squadron Leader, do you have anything to add?"

Here it comes, Gifford thought. In the short time he had been with the squadron, his flight commander, Squadron Leader Huntington-Brown, had not tried to hide his dislike of the only sergeant pilot under his command, someone who had learnt to fly outside of the air force and, to heap Pelion upon Ossa, in the colonies. He could expect little support from that particular corner. As for the murdered Frenchman, what the hell had that to do with anything?

"I don't think so, sir," his flight commander replied. Gifford could almost feel the satisfaction the man was exacting from the situation. "Perhaps Sergeant Gifford would benefit from some time spent on the Hudson, since we're now short of one Lizzie, for a while."

"A splendid idea. Do we know how long before we'll have the damaged aircraft back in the air?"

"At least a week, sir," the squadron leader answered.

"That long, well, I don't suppose there's much we can do about that. If necessary, we'll borrow one of the chaps in 321 Squadron. Meanwhile, Gifford, consider yourself severely reprimanded. Your record will duly reflect what has happened."

"Yes, sir."

"Have you seen the MO since you landed?"

"No, sir."

"Right. Get yourself along to the sickbay and get the MO to have a look at you. But only after you've written that damn report, understood?"

"Yes, sir."

"See that Sergeant Gifford becomes reacquainted with the Hudson, will you, Squadron Leader."

"Yes, sir."

"You can go, Gifford."

"Yes, sir."

Chapter Ten

<u>Café Brion, Montsoreau, France</u>

For two weeks, Grace Harris had not set foot outside the Café Brion. Her world had shrunk. It was reduced to the confines of the gloomy kitchen at the back, the even more depressingly cloistral-like box room in which she slept, and she was exhausted after labouring from dawn to dusk for Monsieur Claude. Her routine was unrelenting in its indifference to her circumstance. It was not something she had planned. The rhythm of the day and the very presence of each other in such a small space dictated some kind of order. What she had not realised was that it was one into which she had unwittingly been manoeuvred by Monsieur Claude. Their relationship had developed into that of employer and employee, with her remuneration being a safe place in which to hide from the Germans.

Sometimes, when the last customer had left and more often than not by candlelight, she would venture into the café proper, inhale the cigarette smoke and experience something of the outside world from which she had been excluded for her own safety. He had assured her that the Germans had carried out fearful reprisals for the incident two weeks earlier in Saumur and were still scouring the countryside for the perpetrators. It was not safe for her to leave the café, he insisted, and when they were open her movements were restricted to the kitchen. Sometimes, but not often, she would hear German voices in the café, which solicited from Monsieur Claude nervous and erratic behaviour, at which point she would attempt, in whispered tones, to calm his fears.

Occasionally a customer would leave a newspaper in the café, and, if she were quick enough before Monsieur Claude could grab it, she would eagerly snap it up and hide it under her apron to read when he left the café on one of his many errands, some of which, she assumed, were on resistance business. It was curious that he seemed to want to restrict her knowledge of what was going on beyond the walls of the café. If someone came to the kitchen door, he would send her into the café if they were closed, and if they were open he would ask her to go up to her room until the visitor had gone. All in the interest of security, he would say. On no account was she to answer the door. The few copies of the newspaper that she had been able to obtain carried nothing of the shooting in Saumur, which, in itself, given German censorship, was not surprising. But neither was there any mention of the terrible retribution exacted by the Germans, which, she thought, they would have been only too keen to see in print to put fear into the local populace. His desire to deny her a window on the world was only one of the things that were odd about the situation in which she found herself. How had Monsieur managed before her arrival? Since commencing her work for Monsieur Claude, the most casual of observers would have noticed that business in the café had gradually increased. By doing all the cleaning, most of the cooking, as well as meal preparation, keeping an eye on the pantry, and ordering supplies (those that were available), she was, in effect, running the café. The experience she had gained at her aunt's hotel in Bristol had equipped her for the task.

Above all, in the back of her mind, each and every day was one question: Why had Monsieur Gilbert not contacted her?

Was he staying away until the Germans moved their attention elsewhere, always assuming there had been an incident in Saumar? It was something she was beginning to doubt. Or had his luck eventually run out and he had been arrested? If she ever mentioned Gilbert to Monsieur Claude, a silence would follow, to be broken by some talk of the travails that confronted France.

On the fifteenth day of her residency at the Café Brion, at 09.00 am, there was a knock on the kitchen door. She was alone. Monsieur Claude was away on one of his commissions. It was not a loud knock, and yet it carried with it the sound of persistence, one that would not be ignored. Grace did as she had on previous occasions, nothing. She stood in the middle of the small windowless kitchen waiting for the knocking to end and for whoever it was on the other side of the wooden door to walk away. The knocking continued but then suddenly stopped to be replaced by a voice.

"Simone, are you there?"

"Monsieur Gilbert, is it you?"

"It is. Mademoiselle, let me in."

"I can't. Monsieur Claude has the key and he's away."

"So that is how it is. You are well? You haven't been harmed?"

"No, I'm well."

"Do you know when he'll be back?"

"No, but he's seldom away more than a couple of hours. We must open the café for *d*éjeuner."

"Right. I'll come back at midday. It would be best if you didn't tell him I've called. Do you understand?"

"Yes, of course."

"Till then, mademoiselle."

She heard his footsteps recede on the cobble stones.

The rest of the morning she spent trying to control her thoughts while preparing the café for opening. She was filled with anticipation. Gilbert had at last made contact. Now her reason for being in France could be realised. If her behaviour seemed out of the ordinary, Monsieur Claude didn't seem to notice upon his return, having secured from the *p*âtisserie a number of loaves of bread, which was nothing short of a miracle given the shortage of flour. She had observed, since her arrival in Montsoreau, how Monsieur Claude worked the black market for all it was worth. There seemed to be nothing he couldn't find. Recently they had received the whole hindquarter of a pig. What currency had the owner of the Café Brion to trade with, that he should have been so fortunate? Monsieur Claude was in a buoyant mood, but it was not to last.

At midday, just as they were opening the café, Gilbert returned. Again the kitchen door, which remained locked at all times, received the attention of Monsieur Gilbert's knuckles, at which point Monsieur Claude told her to go up to the box room and to remain there until the visitor had left the café. From the small landing she heard the kitchen door being unlocked, followed by the hasty entrance of not one but several men. Monsieur Gilbert had not come alone. She could hear Monsieur Claude protesting at the intrusion and the raised voice of someone she didn't recognise. Seconds later, the sound of furniture being thrown around in the kitchen reached her along with a yell of pain from Monsieur Claude.

"Simone?" Gilbert called out.

Grace descended the narrow stair to see the table and two chairs turned over in the centre of the kitchen and the small cowed frame of Monsieur Claude in the dark corner, by the stairs. A large red mark had appeared on his left cheek. Over him stood a tall broad-shouldered man holding a large hammer, the handle of which was painted an incongruous yellow.

"Mademoiselle, you're leaving. Gather your things and be quick. Is this your bicycle?" Gilbert asked, pointing to a dust-covered machine, unused since her arrival two weeks earlier.

"Yes, but, what has happened?" she asked.

"I'll explain later. This man will have to find someone else to help him run the Café Brion." At this, the man with the hammer kicked Monsieur Claude in the ribs, causing him to scream and curl into an even tighter ball.

On leaving the café, Gilbert's companions cycled away, waving as they went. Grace and Gilbert rode together to the southern end of the village through deserted streets.

"Ride to Thouars. Go to the Church of Saint-Leone. There's a crypt, wait there. If I haven't joined you by five this afternoon, go on to Pas-de-Jeu. It's on the Loudun Road. You'll find a small red garage in the centre of the village. The owner is a Jean Badia. You are to talk only to him. Tell him I sent you. Do you understand?"

"Thank you, monsieur."

"And remember, trust no one. By the way, our friends have been asking after you. With no news they had assumed the worst. We'll surprise them."

After two weeks of confinement in the café, Grace felt she had been given a fresh start. She felt a *frisson* of pleasure on her ride to Thouars in the warm sun, with the wind blowing through her hair and her body responding to the need for exercise. For a few short hours all thought of war and the German occupation were left behind in the Café Brion with the Lilliputian Monsieur Claude. Such feelings were a luxury she could not afford if she wished to remain free, so, by the time she had reached the outskirts of Thouars, reality and the need for vigilance had taken their rightful place in her mind. Since leaving Montsoreau she had not seen one German. However, on approaching the River Thouars and the bridge that takes the traveller into the centre of the town, two policemen blocked her path. One held up his hand, indicating that she should stop. Dismounting, she walked the few paces that separated her from the policemen.

"Bonjour, madam. Your papers, please," said the older of the two. Both men seemed friendly enough, although the younger of the two, a fair-haired youth with a short neck, eyed her licentiously, undressing her with his eyes. Her mind was in overdrive; she needed a plausible explanation for her visit to Thouars, all previous backup stories having been made redundant by her lengthy stay in Montsoreau.

While one examined her papers, the other asked, "Do you live in Thouars, madam?"

"It is mademoiselle, and no, I don't live in Thouars."

"Then what's the reason for your visit?"

"To visit the grave of my father. I've cycled from Montsoreau."

"I see. In which church is he interned, the Church of St. Medard or in the Chapel of Joan of Arc?"

Was it a trap? He hadn't mentioned Saint-Leone. Was there a Church of St. Medard in Thouars, or for that matter a chapel celebrating Joan of Arc? Had Monsieur Gilbert made a mistake? Trust no one, he had said, yet now she must do just that and trust that he had not made a mistake, one that could see her arrested and handed over to the Germans.

"Neither, he's interned in the Church of Saint-Leone."

"Saint-Leone," the older man repeated, "my mother is also interned there. It's a lovely church. I see from your papers you don't live in Montsoreau. Where do you live, mademoiselle, when you aren't travelling around on your bicycle? Here it says Paris, is that correct?"

"That is correct, officer."

"You're a long way from home. It's not safe to be riding around the countryside on your own, mademoiselle. The Germans are also a long way from home, and they like pretty young French women, such as yourself," sneered the younger one. "Perhaps you should have someone to look after you during your visit."

"Thank you, but that will not be necessary. May I go?"

The older policeman handed Grace her documents. "Yes, but he's right, mademoiselle, there is a war on. Take care."

Eventually she found the Church of Saint-Leone, but not before visiting first the Romanesque St. Medard and the Chapel of Joan of Arc. Just as well there were only the three churches in Thouars, she thought, or she might have spent the rest of the day going from church to church searching for Saint-Leone.

It was past midday when she pushed on the heavy wooden door with its metal bracing and studs. At first she thought that it might be locked, but after putting her shoulder to it she managed to pry it open. The church was from the twelfth century, not too dissimilar from the sort that she had attended with her mother most Sundays, although, from time to time, she liked to hop about, visiting first one church and then another, much to their local priest's chagrin. When she was seven, her mother had decided that they should both carry out a pilgrimage to Chartres to pray before the chemise said to have been worn by the Virgin Mary at the birth of Jesus. But the untimely passing away of an aunt had put the kibosh on that particular adventure. Her father, who claimed to be Anglican, that vague and ambiguous of creeds, never went near a church and found his wife's ecclesial touring amusing. He did, however, voice no objection to his only daughter being brought up under the teachings of Rome.

Leaving her bicycle in the porch, she went in search of the crypt. There were within the nave a few worshipers, their heads bowed, and a young woman who Grace saw sitting alone to one side, gently weeping. At the end of the nave, in the chancel, an old priest was arranging a few chairs by the altar. Behind him, covering almost the entire eastern wall of the chancel was a faded reredos, a carved ornamental panel that incorporated a number of small statues. To Grace it was all very familiar – the alchemical light streaming through the stained-glass windows transforming the gloom, even the smell, the most underrated of our senses, evoking within her something from another time when her life seemed secure and predictable and so different from the precarious situation in which she had placed herself. It was the closest she had come since landing back in France to feeling emotionally ill-equipped for her mission, in spite of all her training.

As she walked along the northern side of the nave, set into the wall was an Easter sepulchre on the floor on which someone had chalked the Cross of Lorraine, the Gaullist symbol. Had the old priest seen it and turned a blind eye? Halfway along there were two ornately carved confessional stalls, which she had noticed when first entering the church. Tortured memories of her first confessional came flooding back. The trouble had been that she had nothing to confess, at least nothing she thought her priest would want to hear. Later it would be different, but by then she had given up seeing her priest as the interlocutor between herself and God. The doors to both confessionals were open, but in one sat a toddler swinging her feet and humming. In the past, such behaviour would have brought a swift response from her mother, had she been present. Further on there was a small chapel to the left, dedicated, she assumed, to the Sicilian, Saint Leone of Catania, remembered for his love and care for the poor. Beyond that there stood a large statue of Mary, the bottom of which had suffered some damage. Two toes of Mary's left foot were missing. It was also in need of a fresh coat of the mandatory pale blue. Minutes later she had covered the interior of the church but was unable to find the entrance to the crypt. There was no hurry. Gilbert could not possibly have arrived before her, unless he had driven to Thouars. A thought occurred to her; he could be waiting for her in the crypt. No longer content to continue her search, she approached the priest. The man, an asthmatic, breathlessly directed her outside to a small wooden door set in the western wall, secluded from prying eyes by an ivy-covered wooden trellis that lent at an alarming angle. Again, because of its weight, she had trouble opening the door, but it was evident that the entrance to the crypt, as well as being unlocked, had recently been used, for once in motion it swung easily on its rusting hinges. Closing the door behind her, she descended into the dark, down a flight of stone stairs, feeling her way and maintaining her balance, with her left hand sliding along the smooth stone wall. It was cold and damp and not a good place to meet a contact, there being no other way out. As she reached the last step, just as her eyes were becoming adjusted to the gloom, someone struck a match.

"Bonjour, mademoiselle."

Before the light from the match was extinguished, Grace caught site of a woman sitting on a tomb.

"Relax, mademoiselle, I am here for Gilbert. It was arranged that I should meet you."

"He said nothing about this. Who are you?" Grace asked.

"It doesn't matter who I am." There was a pause. "Did you know that beneath me lies Margaret Stuart, the first wife of Louis XI? It says here that 'Marguerite d'Écosse, first born of King James I of Scotland, married at eleven and died childless, aged twenty on twenty-fifth of June fourteen thirty-six.' A short life for a Dauphine of France, wouldn't you agree?"

"Twenty is young. But ..."

"Let us both hope that we can live a little longer." The voice permeating the darkness was soft and, although little more than a whisper, resonated around the crypt. The faint accent was that of the Alsace. "You must trust me, mademoiselle. Although there aren't many Germans in Thouars yet, there are many collaborators, including the police. And now with the end of demarcation many *attentistes* will find the fence a difficult place on which to sit and may come down on the side of Vichy. We must move from here. I'm to take you to a safe house."

In the darkness Grace felt the woman brush past her and mount the steps, carrying with her a whiff of cheap scent. "Come on, we're in the company of death down here, and that's not something I want to cultivate."

"My bicycle, it's in the church."

"We'll get it on the way out."

Outside, in the blinding light, Grace got her first good look at the woman from the crypt. She was about the same age and height as herself, slim with a mop of dark hair swept back to reveal a broad forehead above a pair of alert eyes. There emanated a distinctive aura of challenge about her that was only intensified by the resolute set of her chin on a tanned face.

"This way. If we're challenged leave the talking to me. You have papers?"

"Yes."

"Good, it wouldn't be a good idea to be caught out and about without papers," she said, giving Grace an insightful smile.

Her new companion didn't walk but strode, and Grace found herself having to step out with her bicycle to keep up.

"Come on, we haven't far to go."

The medieval town of Thouars sits on a hill behind a dominant seventeenth century chateau, the castle of the Dukes of Trémoille. As with the other towns she had visited since arriving in France, she had to continually remind herself, in the absence of any Germans, that she was in an occupied country and that France was at war with itself and, for a few, with the invader. Everything seemed so normal, if you ignored the long queue of women standing patiently outside every food shop.

After crossing the Place Saint-Medard, something Grace had done just an hour earlier, they navigated their way through hilly, narrow streets, seeing few people, before arriving outside a large, wooden double gate set in a high stone wall. On entering the cobblestone courtyard they were confronted by a row of empty stables to their right and to the left a cavernous but equally empty hay barn. Completing the square was a single-storied wooden house, the door and windows of which appeared to be boarded up.

"Put your bicycle in the far stable. It'll be safe there."

Grace did as she was told, after which her companion led the way, as she had done since leaving the church, striding out purposefully across the courtyard. The door of the house that gave all the signs of being nailed closed opened with the use of a metal key from around the neck of the woman from the crypt. Inside both the low ceiling and the darkness, as dark as the crypt, contributed to a feeling of confinement.

"Leave the shutters opening onto the courtyard closed. These we can open." When the shutters of the windows set into the back wall were opened, the view was into an ivy-covered hillside less than a metre from the house.

Grace had observed on entering the courtyard that directly opposite the large gate across the street stood a row of very old, narrow, three-storied houses, their large, faded shutters a testimony to their age. The middle house was a distinctive yellow. The top floors of all three dwellings overlooked the stables. It was an ideal place from which, if one were so inclined, to observe the comings and goings of this 'safe house,' and harmless if they were in friendly hands. Hands that could be trusted, but, then, who could you trust in these times?

The place in which both women now stood had been the residence of whoever it was who looked after the horses, the equestrian odour of which lingered on. It was essentially not much more than one large room with a small scullery to the left and at the far end a partition, behind which was a small area that served as sleeping quarters and was home to an iron bedstead, on which lay a badly stained horsehair mattress and a *garderobe* that had once had a door. In the largest room there was a *chaise longue,* the *cloqué* fabric of which was torn and, like the horsehair mattress, badly stained. Also it was missing a leg, but four strategically placed bricks helped maintain its equilibrium. There was a bookshelf, minus books, and an armchair, the springs of which had long since given up the ghost. The floorboards creaked under their weight as they walked about the room. A thick coating of dust throughout the safe house lay testimony to its disuse.

"You see, there is water," she proudly proclaimed to Grace, turning on the tap of the large wooden sink in the scullery. "But no lighting, I'm afraid, but anyway, it would be wise not to show a light in here after dark. If all goes well you will not be here long."

"Thank you. Unfortunately, I had to leave my last place with almost nothing. I need to buy—"

"Ah, we have a surprise. There is something for you. I'll go and get it. It's hidden in one of the stables, along with some bedding I delivered yesterday."

Upon her return she asked Grace to close her eyes and not to open them until told to do so. It seemed so incongruous to be playing such a game under such circumstances and in such an environment, but there was obviously a fun side to her companion that she felt bound to humour.

"You can open your eyes now."

There on the scarred wooden floor stood Grace's suitcase, the one that had accompanied her to France, so long ago.

"It's my case! But how ...?"

"It arrived a few days ago and I was asked to care for it."

"But how ...?"

"Don't ask. It's so much better if we don't know something that involves others."

"I thought I had seen the last of my case. This is amazing."

"Isn't it? Strange things happen during a war, or so I'm told."

"It's amazing," she repeated. "I don't even know your name," Grace exclaimed.

"Danielle. They know me as Danielle. I'll be your contact until Gilbert arrives."

"When will that be? He said—"

"What Gilbert says and does are not always the same. That is just one way he's been able to stay free for so long. He'll come. We'll fetch the bedding later, but first some food. When did you last eat, mademoiselle?"

"I can't remember."

"Then it's time you did. There's a place I know that has food. I'll go and see if I can get dinner for us both. When this war ends I promise you I will spend every hour of the rest of my life eating! I won't be long. Do you have money?"

"Yes. Let me give you some." Grace undid her dress and removed some notes from her money belt. Handing them over, she said, "Before you go, Danielle, is there another way out of here other than through the gate? I couldn't help noticing the courtyard. It's overlooked by the houses across the street."

"I was going to mention that. Those houses are occupied by families who have good reason to hate the Boche. We would be informed immediately if there was any change. However, if you should see the blinds down in the top windows of the yellow house, you know that the stables aren't safe. But to put your mind at rest, come with me."

Danielle led her into the scullery. "As you've probably noticed, this place hasn't been used for ages, and when it is nobody stays very long. See here?" she said, pointing to a trap door to the left of the sink. "Lift it up."

Grace did as she was told, inserting her right middle figure, as it had always been her strongest, into a small brass ring. She pulled with little effect, at first. "You are not very strong, mademoiselle, if I may say. Try again."

Determined this time to lift the trap door and put her strength beyond question, she heaved until it suddenly gave way, sending her falling back onto her bottom and the door falling back in place. Danielle laughed out loud and, reaching down, effortlessly opened the trap door. A foul smell immediately engulfed the room.

"That's disgusting!" Grace exclaimed, holding her hand to her mouth and nose.

"Isn't it? I understand it isn't so bad once you're past the first fifty metres. It's tiled all the way, but you have to crawl for most of it. The tunnel was ... Well, perhaps it's better if you don't know. If you have to use it, perhaps the perfume will spur you on. It comes out in a garden the other side of the road. The smell is a good deterrent if anybody wanted to follow you, don't you think?"

"I believe you. Can we close it up now? I don't particularly want to live with such a stink."

"I'll give you a key for the gate and for this place. Should they come for you they'll have to break both down, which should give you enough time to get into the tunnel."

It was almost dark when Danielle slipped out of the stables, having first arranged to meet Grace in a park the following day. She locked both the gate and the door to the house, neither of which, she observed, would put up much resistance to a determined aggressor, but it was something. The bedding Danielle had retrieved from one of the stable stalls smelt of horse and straw, not that it mattered, she was asleep the moment her head touched the horsehair pillow.

Chapter Eleven

Tempsford, Bedfordshire

Twelve days had passed since that disastrous flight in the Lizzie that had claimed the life of one of his Joes. Since then he had, as ordered, taken a brief refresher course on the Hudson back at RAF Silloth. Leaving the Lizzie to become reacquainted with the twin-engine Hudson would, under other circumstances, have been a welcome change, but not now. He was in the dog house, and if he was to consolidate his position within the squadron there must be no repeat performance.

Prior to that flight there had been little time during that moon period for anything other than flying and resting. As always, the weather had dictated play, and on that fateful flight it hadn't been particularly cooperative. Either fog or low cloud over the target areas or at Tangmere and Tempsford had managed to disrupt many operations. Since arriving on the squadron, flying only the Lizzie had given him the opportunity to come to grips with its peculiarities. As aircraft went, it was relatively free of any real vices if you remembered not to stall or spin the thing, but you had to remember that damn tail actuator, making sure it was properly set. There was, of course, the matter of the mixture control, something that had proved fatal for one pilot. Before landing it had to be moved from WEAK to NORMAL or it was impossible to throttle back completely. Another possible problem associated with the mixture control was when over-rich a Mercury engine could be a bitch to restart, and there was the risk of running the battery flat. It was something he had been acutely aware of twelve days earlier on the ground at Auxerre. Others had not been so lucky and had ended up burning their aircraft and going into hiding. Also, the engine could 'Rich-Cut' if the pilot were to rapidly move to a high-power setting. For a single-engine aircraft, the Lysander was large, certainly when compared with the ones he had flown in Canada, and yet it was reasonably manoeuvrable with good handling characteristics. The automatic leading-edge slats and trailing-edge flaps he thought a clever idea, giving the pilot freedom to concentrate on his landing. You just had to be aware of your angle of attack and speed. For the job in hand, cockpit visibility was good except forward, where the Mercury radial engine got in the way. For a British aircraft the cockpit layout wasn't too chaotic, although the folks at Yeovil, home to Westland, could learn a few things off American aircraft manufacturers. The robust undercarriage seemed capable of withstanding the worst of landings, whether on surfaces that would have written off other aircraft or even when dropped from a great height onto a runway. This had been amply illustrated to him on his second operative flight when landing back at Tangmere. Fog and low cloud had covered most of southern England. He had elected to first try Tangmere, where they had funnel lights on poles that were just above the fog level. The lights were barely visible, giving off a ghostly glow as he rounded out. With minimum power he crossed the fence and held the aircraft level, allowing the speed to wash off, slats and flaps having deployed. Finally, the Lizzie decided that it had run out of lift and plummeted through the fog onto the runway, a landing that in any other aircraft would have sent the undercarriage up through the main plane.

Now he had been detailed for his first Hudson flight with the squadron, weather permitting. The black Air Transport Form showed four in and eight out, with details of the agents and a description of the target. He had armed himself with map references and the local sheet of the Michelin road map and, as usual, he had prepared his own 'gen' sheet that included course notes, headings, and landing codes. Having a navigator helped, but he wanted to be prepared. Getting back into the Hudson had been easy. After only a few night circuits he felt at home in the aircraft. Additional power came with the extra engine. Two Wright R-1820 Cyclones, each generating 1,100 hp. would make the job easier, although it needed longer landing fields than the Lizzie and longer turn-around time. He had been assigned a Norwegian sergeant navigator, Anders Tosen, who spoke perfect English, and a Yorkshire wireless operator, Sergeant Bert Copperwood, whom he found hard to understand. They accompanied him on all his Hudson flights out of Tempsford, by the end of which they had become a formidable team. Tempsford was not like other stations. Most of the pilots were not careerists but in the RAF only for the duration. Due to the nature of the operation, there existed a spirit of individualism at Tempsford that suited Gifford. Military discipline, of the sort he had experienced on his previous station in Cornwall, was not to his liking. As a crew they operated in more of a civilian atmosphere of equality when aboard the Hudson, something Sergeant Gifford had subconsciously fostered.

Having briefed both Tosen and Copperwood on the flight, he was taken by the escort officer to meet the four Joes who were already at Gibraltar Farm, Tempsford's nerve centre. Of all the agents he had carried to date they were the oddest: three males, one female. That they were neither French nor British was the first thing that struck him about the quartet. He hadn't much of an ear for accents, but if he wasn't mistaken their spokesman, a rather serious chap, Milch, sounded decidedly Germanic. All four seemed to exude a demeanour of foreboding, almost despair, as if they already knew what fate had in store for them across the Channel. Also, milling around that evening were more than the usual number of London types, including a couple in ill-fitting suits who looked decidedly Slavic, one of whom was never far away when he talked to the Joes. Everybody appeared to be on edge, more so than normal. Would the weather suddenly put a stop to everything? Would they all end up right back here at Tempsford or Tangmere after eight or nine hours in the air, unable to complete the mission due to weather over the target? These were the usual concerns prior to every operation, but that evening had about it something else, a level of urgency that was out of the ordinary. Whether the name of the operation had anything to do with it he didn't know, but it was being called Pickaxe. The weather over the target, just east of Angers and close to Beaufort, had the potential to cause trouble. It was not something he would pass on to his passengers.

After they had been kitted out, the Joes walked with him to the aircraft. Access to the Hudson was through a small oval door on the port side, aft of the wing. He noted that the female Joe found her jumpsuit cumbersome and had trouble getting into the aircraft. Compared to others that he had flown into France, the four appeared unfit and not at all agile. This did not bode well for a speedy turn-around time on the ground. If necessary, Bert Copperwood would have to assist their exit from the aircraft. Sergeant Gifford was determined to make his first Hudson flight trouble free where possible. He needed to win back his spurs. The interior of the Hudson was spartan. The bulkhead and walls were bare of internal cladding. His passengers had to sit on their baggage with their backs to the bare metal wall and hang on as best they could. As they were settling down onto the floor of the aircraft, their spokesman shared what might have been the reason for all four appearing downcast.

"We are going to France. Is this true?"

"That's the plan. Is there a problem with that?" Gifford replied.

"It is a change for us. That is all. We had not expected this. We are Austrian and trained for . . . It is not important." One of the other Joes had said something that abruptly terminated their discussion.

Gifford moved forward into the cockpit through the small door that separated the crew from the main cabin.

With the take-off checks complete and fifteen degrees of flap selected, they lined up on the runway. Rain began to cover the windscreen just as they received the green light from the tower. They would first have to climb up through cloud. The ceiling at Tempsford was only 1,500 feet and clear sky was at around 5,000 feet as far as the French coast, if the weathermen had got it right, which they seldom did. As he pushed the throttles forward, Tosen's left hand followed him through, leaving the captain free to use both hands on the controls. The boost went to forty-five inches and the rpm to 2,500 on both radial Cyclone engines. A fifteen-knot left crosswind, along with the aircraft's tendency to swing to port, meant applying some left rudder as they sped down the runway. Many were the RAF pilots who, when switching from the docile Avro Anson, the basic twin trainer, to the Hudson, had been caught out by the swing on take-off or landing. The Hudson possessed twin rudders which, although not as effective as some aircraft he had flown, still provided effective lateral control. At 50 mph he pushed the nose forward, lifting the tail off the runway. At just over 100 mph he eased back on the stick and the Hudson parted company with the ground. Climbing away at 115 mph he asked Tosen to apply brakes to the spinning wheels before retracting the undercarriage and then raise 15 degrees of flap. When he had first converted onto the Hudson at Silloth he had been impressed by the size and effectiveness of the aircraft's Fowler flaps. Lockheed-Vega, he concluded, had built a good aircraft. With the airborne checks complete, the crew settled down to their respective duties. Tonight they would cross the French coast at Cabourg before heading farther south, skirting around the Luftwaffe airfield at Argentan and then on to Alençon, passing to the west of Le Mans before descending towards Angers. With a dedicated navigator and additional navigational aids aboard the Hudson they would not have trouble locating the landing field.

The noise from the two Cyclone engines, accompanied by the air rushing through the unpressurised fuselage, made it impossible for the four agents to converse, had they a mind to do so, which was not the case. Each was left with his or her own thoughts. Milch speculated on the reason for Moscow changing Operation Pickaxe at the last minute, and instead of dropping them into Nazi Austria, for which they had been trained, they were now to operate in occupied France, for which they were totally unprepared. Their original destination held enough risks, and any chance of success in Nazi Austria had been highly unlikely, but now, even with the set of new documents they had been hastily issued with, their future looked perilous. They were ignorant of conditions on the ground in France, making their new assignment nothing short of a suicide mission. Only Freda spoke passable French, although Milch and Hans had picked up a little while interned by the French in 1938/39, but Karl could remember little from his pre-war time in Paris. Dekanozov, if he was to be believed, had said that the agents earmarked for this particular operation had been delayed in Russia because the British had failed to provide room aboard a ship out of Murmansk. He had stipulated that there was an urgent need for Moscow to re-establish contact with Paris. What he did not tell them was that the Abwehr and the Gestapo had broken up Moscow's network the previous year, rounding up many agents, and all attempts to set up a new network had failed. Karl, as with the Austrian operation, was to act as the wireless operator, using a set provided by the British. They had landed in Scotland with a Russian model, which had proved to be useless when tested by the British in London. It was meant to be of such strength as to provide direct contact with Moscow. That it did not was of no surprise to Milch. Little that was made in Russia, in his opinion, was of a decent quality.

In an attempt to encourage them, Dekanozov had suggested, half-heartedly, that were they to be arrested, as was more than likely, they might try, as Austrians, to pass themselves off as part of the occupation, but without proper documentation to support such a claim, who would believe them? Likely as not, they would be charged as deserters and shot.

They were to be met at Angers by communist members of the *Francs-Tireurs et Partisans* (FTP), who would see them safely to Paris, but what then? Once wireless contact had been re-established between Paris and Moscow, what was their mission? Knowing the Soviets as he did, they, like all who serviced the state, were disposable. Nothing was as cheap as the life of others to those running the Soviet Union.

Only Milch knew how much the change had thrown his plans into disarray. At the first opportunity he had intended to separate himself from Hans, with whom he had been paired for the Austrian mission, and merge back into Austrian life to await the end of the war, which, in his estimation, with America now on the side of the Allies and Russia having halted the advancing

German army, was not too far off. He had an uncle living high up in the Niedere Tauern, on a farm, where he would be able to hide, assuming he was not arrested en route. At least, that had been the plan. He wanted to sever all contact with Russia. Shortly after returning from Spain in 1939 he had decided that his future lay elsewhere, preferably in a free and independent Austria. He had never looked upon communism as the answer, and he had discovered when it had infested his native country and Russia that it was not the worker's paradise it purported to be. But all that was now history. He couldn't see himself hiding out in France until the end of the war or making it safely all the way to his uncle in Niedere Tauern. It was obvious to him, as it must be to his compatriots, that, ill-equipped and untrained as they were for their new mission, they were doomed. To save time, Moscow might just as well have delivered them direct to Berlin.

With little or no cloud over the Channel, a full moon reflecting off the sea below, and a light southerly wind, it was easy flying all the way to the French coast, although the threat of interception by the Luftwaffe was, on such a night, more than probable. It was with some relief that he saw that to the south of Cabourg land was partially obscured by layers of stratus, just as long as it didn't extend to Angers. Further south there was still more cloud, with broken cumulus up to what appeared to be 15,000 feet. With several night fighter squadrons based in the area, any one of which could be on patrol, the cumulus cloud, albeit only five-tenths, offered some cover.

Between Sabie and La Flèche they started their descent. The low stratus to the north had lifted south of Le Mans, providing them with ideal conditions for spotting the landing field through what had become broken cumulus. The Hudson required 1,000 metres to land. The field near Angers was a little longer. Having become used to flying the Lizzie, Gifford was surprised how quickly he felt at home in the Hudson, but he would consciously have to make allowance for the larger aircraft's reduced manoeuvrability, particularly at slow speed. It required a larger circuit and was not so easy to line up for the final approach at night, no matter how accurately a circuit was flown.

Because of the increase in the required landing distance, the torch layout on the ground for the Hudson differed from that for the Lysander. For the larger aircraft it was 400 metres long, with 150 metres between torches, with one torch to the right at the end. It was Tosen who first spotted the lights below to starboard. They were down to 1,500 feet above ground level, and from the direction of the torches they could expect a northerly wind for the landing. Crossing over the field, Gifford carried out his pre-landing checks – carburettor intake switched to COLD, check brake pressure, making sure the brakes were off, and, with the speed below 145 mph, calling for the landing gear to be lowered, check that the mixture controls were in AUTO RICH, propeller controls fully forward, superchargers were in M ratio, and 15 degrees of flap selected. He reduced power to just above idle and, keeping the field in sight below to his left, they joined downwind. Copperwood sent a coded message that they were about to land. Tosen flashed the code F and back came the correct response from the ground. They had now passed the field and started their base turn to port, with Gifford straining to pick up the lights on the ground. He kept the rate one turn going, all the time checking his compass heading. Assuming he hadn't messed up when swinging into the direction to which the landing strip was aligned, it should be directly in front of them. And there it was, only to port. They were too high and too fast! An old saying given to him by his first flying instructor came to mind, 'Good landings come from good approaches.' The reverse he knew also to be true. There was nothing for it but to put the power on, wheels up, and go around. With flaps retracted to 15 degrees they climbed away. The entire neighbourhood must have heard the Hudson overshooting, including any Germans who just happened to be hanging around. What was now evident was that there was a westerly component to the wind that he hadn't allowed for. This time he would get it right. After extending his crosswind leg, he again turned downwind, undercarriage down, flaps still at 15 degrees. He also extended his downwind leg before turning to port onto his base leg. With a tailwind, he shortened his base leg and turned onto the grass runway heading, laying off some drift. They were perfectly aligned with the lights and at the correct height, the speed was also right. He called for land flap. The pilot's notes for the Hudson stipulated a final approach speed of 75 mph (power assisted) which, given the length of some of the fields the squadron operated from, was a luxury. As a squadron, they had reduced the speed across the fence to 55 mph (engine assisted) without stalling or dropping onto the field, though at such a speed the aircraft was even less manoeuvrable.

Touching down on the main wheels, Gifford quickly closed the throttles and lowered the tail, reducing both speed and landing distance while maintaining a little left rudder. The surface, though undulating, was firm, perfectly acceptable for the operation. At the end of his landing roll he turned the aircraft left through 180 degrees and taxied back to where the first torch had been placed and where the reception committee waited. In addition to the reception committee, with most Hudson operations the French included in their équipe de terrain armed pickets on every approach road and lane. Lightly armed, they would do little more than warn of approaching Germans but possibly give enough time for the reception committee, along with the Joes, a few moments to scatter. The field was under the control of the *Bureau Central de Renseignements et d'Action* (BCRA), a Gaullist resistance group that covered both intelligence and operations. Perhaps it was their presence that prompted the communists not to show, the relationship between the communists and all other resistance groups being at best fractious.

With both engines set to idle, Gifford remained at the controls while Tosen and Copperwood bundled the reluctant quartet of Joes out of the aircraft, along with fifteen packages that included various supplies for the resistance. From the cockpit he could see the shadowy figures of individuals running towards the aircraft, which he assumed to be his return load, but then Tosen suddenly appeared beside him.

"We have a problem. The reception committee for the four has not appeared. The agent in charge of the field wants to talk to you," Tosen informed him

"Damn. I should have known it was all going too well! Where is the man?" He could see his position in the squadron evaporating before his eyes.

"Captain, *qu'est-ce qui se passe?*" A small bald-headed excited Frenchman had squeezed his way into the cockpit. "I am Lucien Galtier. You have brought to us these communists. *Nous sommes pour le général de Gaulle.* We cannot be responsible for them. They are Boche! You understand?"

"They were to be met by—"

"We know who was to meet them, Captain, the PCF. They are not here. They are communists, the *Parti communiste française.* We don't trust them. *Comprenez?*"

"Anders, can you go back and give Bert a hand. We need to be out of here!" Addressing the Frenchman, Gifford said, "Can't you look after them? They are not coming back with us, and I want your people on board, now!"

To further fill an already full cockpit, Copperwood's rotund frame tried to put in an appearance but was restricted to no more than a voice from the cockpit door.

"Skipper, the Joes we brought in, two of 'em are tryin' to get back on board like. What do you want me to do?"

"What next? Right! Bert, go back and stop them from getting on board. Threaten to shoot them if they don't comply. We've got eight out and that's a full house. Get our outbound passengers on. All inbound freight off?"

"Yes, Skipper, and Anders is supervisin' loadin' of the outbound."

"Thanks. Okay, Bert, go back and make sure none of our inbound passengers get back on board, understood?"

The two remaining occupants of the cockpit felt the aircraft bounce as Copperwood ran aft.

"You. What did you say your name was?"

"Galtier, Lucien Galtier."

"Monsieur Galtier, I want your people on board the aircraft now! What you do with the four we brought in is your problem. *Comprenez?*"

"I cannot be responsible for them, Captain. Impossible!"

"I'm afraid you have no choice. I'm sorry to land them on you, but I can't return with any of the four passengers we brought in."

"Captain, this will . . . *réverbérer* to London, *comprenez?*"

"I'm sure it will, monsieur. But if I take them back on board we will have to leave four of your group behind, *comprenez?* Now, can we go?"

"Very well. I will see that they are removed from the field then—"

At that point Anders Tosen reappeared.

"All clear, Skipper. We are loaded and ready."

"Thanks, Anders. See that Monsieur Galtier safely leaves the aircraft. Let's get the hell out of here!"

What Sergeant Gifford could not see from his position in the cockpit was the four inbound being encouraged by two of the armed Gaullist reception committee, albeit reluctantly, to position themselves away from the aircraft on the edge of the field.

"We're all clear, Skipper," Tosen reported, taking up his position in the cockpit. Both checked to see that the rear door warning light was out.

Outside Gifford could see a man wielding a torch and giving the thumbs-up.

Check flight control trims in neutral, flaps 15 degrees selected for take-off, check engine and oil temperatures. Holding the aircraft on the brakes, Gifford slowly advanced the throttle. Upon reaching full travel he released the brakes and the Hudson began its take-off run. Almost immediately the tail began to rise as they sped down the grass strip. If anything, the westerly was stronger than when they landed, necessitating some left rudder and left wing down. At 100 mph he pulled back on the controls and the aircraft took off into the night, immediately adopting ten degrees of drift as they climbed away.

Three kilometres to the east, on a small rise, Standartenführer Heinrich Hoffmann of the Sicherheitsdienst (SD) stood beside Major Hermann Danner of the Abwehr, observing the goings on of the French Resistance and the British flyers. In occupied France, as in the Third Reich, there existed little cooperation between the SD and the Abwehr, but Hoffmann and Danner were friends from schooldays and, unbeknown to their superiors, shared information meant only for their respective organisations. It had long been the policy of the SD to let the communist fox run and pick up all those who would meet with the vulpine. Not only was this procedure more inclusive, it was also cost-effective. German intercepts of Moscow's intention left little to chance. For Hoffmann this meant that the game had become less of a challenge. The four new arrivals would be scooped up in Paris by the Gestapo after making contact with what was left of the communist network, one that would be totally eliminated this year, if he had anything to do with it. The various informers among the French meant that, although the identities of those leaving for England on the flight that was under observation was not immediately known, those running the Gaullist group were and could be rounded up at a time and place that suited the SD.

Hoffmann wondered yet again why so many of the French were willing to accept not only the occupation but also actively cooperate with those who had seized their country. France was the only occupied country that had put its armed service at the disposal of Germany and to which Germany had accredited an ambassador, making it more of an ally than an enemy. Locally, the Milice he found particularly useful, a more-than-willing tool when it came to rounding up Jews and running the resisters to earth. He had less time for the political dreamers who inhabited their own little Vichy world, accepting at the same time that they, like the Milice, served a useful purpose, maintaining a pretence of independence to which so many French men and women foolishly clung. That the demarcation line no longer existed and that the whole of France was now occupied didn't seem to dent the enthusiasm of those who supported that ridiculous old marshal. Without active collaboration from the French it would have been impossible to occupy their country and at the same time prosecute the war. Hoffmann could not envisage such compliance, such cooperation, if the roles were reversed and Germany had been taken over by the French.

With the departure of the aircraft he realised how cold he had become, the night's winter chill penetrating his heavy military coat. Even his feet were frozen, although protected from the winter's cold by fur-lined leather boots that had been made for some poor sod on the Eastern Front. It was time for him and Major Danner to retire for some schnapps and then to their beds and leave the rest to the Gestapo in Paris.

Chapter Twelve

Milton Ernest, Bedfordshire

Inspector Sim had last seen him ten years ago? No, it was more like twelve, during the second disobedience campaign, when Gandhi had marched to the sea at Cambay and begun to make salt illegally as a protest. They had both been conscripted into the government's widespread crackdown, imprisoning the leaders and attempting to hold back the inexorable tide of Indian nationalism. Adrian J. Padmore was a man for whom India had been nothing more than a step on the ladder to higher things. Had he reached those heights for which he had so diligently striven, or had the war stripped the rungs off his ladder? What was of more immediate interest, what was he doing in Milton Ernest, interrupting his breakfast at the Queen's Head? Sergeant Hodges had briefly taken off to his quarters, leaving the inspector to finish his meal in peace, but the easily recognisable voice from reception had put paid to that idea.

"Sim, fancy running into you here," the man had said when entering the dining room. The *bonhomie* was still there, if a little forced. "Simply spiffing to see you again." He had put on a bit of weight and lost some hair since they had last met, but probably Padmore had similar thoughts. He wore a three-piece tweed suit, a silk handkerchief that gushed from the breast pocket, and shiny brown brogues, and he was shorter than Sim remembered.

"Adrian J. Padmore, if I'm not much mistaken." The man had retained that strong handshake that was meant to mark his sincerity.

"Flattered that you remembered, old boy. How long has it been? Ten years?"

"Twelve."

"Damn me if you're not right, Sim. Cambay, wasn't it?"

"You tried to put the cuffs on Gandhi but they didn't fit. He was too thin."

"That's right. Fancy you remembering that. Well, what do you know? Milton Ernest of all places, who would have believed it?"

"Who indeed? Will you have some tea?"

"Damn good idea. Had breakfast hours ago. Left the City at sparrow's fart."

Sim got up from the table and left the otherwise empty dining room to order tea for the man who had been attached to India's Special Branch. Padmore had been in India on temporary assignment from London.

While Sim ate his last slice of toast he eyed his visitor. He didn't believe in coincidences. The appearance of Adrian J. Padmore at the Queen's Head was no accident. Of that he was sure.

"So, what brings you to this neck of the woods, Sim?"

"Police business. And you?"

"So, you're back in harness then. I heard that after India you had retired. It's this damn war, I suppose. All hands to the pump. That sort of thing."

"Something like that. And—"

"Do you know, I don't believe I've ever been to Bedfordshire before? A bit damp for my liking – ah, the tea."

The young woman who had served the inspector's breakfast delivered to the table not only a fresh pot of tea and an extra cup, but also more toast.

"I say, Sim, they certainly look after you here. Toast and tea. Just what the doctor ordered."

"You didn't say what brought you to Milton Ernest."

"Didn't I? I thought I did. FO business. It's Padmore of the FO these days, I'm afraid. Can't say it's much fun."

"The Foreign Office? The last time I checked Bedfordshire was still part of England. Have things changed?"

"Oh, very droll, Sim. Pity there's no marmalade. Before the war I used to get a damn fine ginger marmalade from Fortnum and Mason. Gone for the duration, I'm afraid, like everything else. I've always thought that you could judge just how civilized a nation was by the quality of its marmalade. Do you know what I miss most of all? Being able to tootle down to the coast on a Sunday. I've had to put the Lagonda up on blocks. At four and a half litres it's a bit of a guzzler, you know. Damn fine car, though, the M45 Sports Tourer."

No, he didn't know, nor did he care. Padmore may be on business for the Foreign Office, but who was his employer? Inspector Sim had a shrewd idea. It was, however, not something he could expect Padmore to either confirm or deny. Out of the corner of his eye Inspector Sim saw the Humber pass the pub window before parking outside the hotel entrance.

"My transport has arrived. I must go. Are you staying in these parts or just passing through?"

"I'll be around for a few days, I expect. I'm staying at the Abbey. I'm sure our paths will cross."

"Quite possibly."

Sergeant Hodges was waiting for him by reception.

"Are we all set to go, sir?" Sergeant Hodges asked.

"We are, Sergeant. How is the accommodation working out, everything okay?"

"Can't complain, sir." Getting into the car, Sergeant Hodges asked, "That man you were talkin' to, was 'e a guest or part of our enquiries?"

"Someone from the past, Sergeant. But I wouldn't discount that idea. Good morning, ACW Little."

"Morning, sir, where are we going this morning?"

"RAF Tempsford."

"Right you are, sir."

"We have an appointment, Sergeant."

"We do? That should be interestin', sir."

"I hope so. This investigation is about due for some clarification, wouldn't you say?"

"I would, sir."

Flight Lieutenant Mortlock escorted them past a duck pond to a cowshed that turned out to be one of the camouflaged Nissen huts scattered about the airfield. So detailed was the deception at Tempsford that sacks were draped across the inside of the window frames in front of the blackout curtains. Doors were left hanging from only one hinge. All of it designed to make the Germans believe that Tempsford was an old, disused airfield given over to agriculture. The subterfuge did not end at Tempsford. At nearby Cardington the roofs of the massive balloon hangers were disguised to look like the rooftops of Victorian terraced houses.

"I thought you might first like to meet the station's air liaison officer, a Captain Brockelhurst, army. The Security Intelligence Service is rather busy at the moment. The station was on ops last night. The captain will take you to them when you're finished."

The captain introduced himself and led them down a windowless corridor that ran the length of the hut to an office outside of which sat a number of WAAF secretaries, hard at work.

"Thank you for seeing us, Captain. We're investigating the death of a French gentleman who had the misfortune to be murdered shortly after arriving in this country. We believe he was a passenger on one of the flights into Tempsford."

"I am familiar with the incident, Inspector. Most unfortunate, as you say." The officer was a Scot with a Highland lilt. "How may I help?"

"We understand the security implications associated with such an incident, but unless we can establish the reason for the man's visit to this country, who he met, et cetera, we're at something of a loss as to a motive for his murder."

"I'm not the right person to answer your questions, Inspector. You should direct them to the Security Intelligence Service when you see them. I don't know if you've been briefed as to how things work around here. I'm with SOE, which, as you know, is a military organisation, and we decide who and what is to be carried and flight priorities. We're travel agents, you might say. We then give the job to the RAF. Other organisations work in with us, but we aren't always informed about what others are doing, nor do we necessarily inform them of our requirements. If the murdered man was here on SIS business, then only they will know what that was. I take it you've spoken to the station commander, the wing commander?"

"Yes, we have."

"I don't know if it's of any help, but you have to understand how things are across the Channel; what with the Vichy, the Gaullists who, on the orders of the general, refuse to have any dealings with our people in France, and the communists, who take their orders from Moscow. Would you believe there's even a group who claim to be Royalists, but whose side there're on is anybody's guess, and, since America entered the war last year, they've established their own network over there. It's all a mess, and there's no trust between them. I'm sure there are lots of scores being settled between the various groups. That sort of thing. Perhaps one just spilled over to this side of the Channel. Who would know? But Vichy supporters must be starting to realise that they've backed the wrong horse, now that things are going our way, at long last. The communists are trying to position themselves to take over when the Germans eventually leave, and de Gaulle is out to make sure that they don't. That's something of a thumbnail sketch of what's happening on the other side."

"Thank you. Does your organisation have any direct contact with the communists?" the inspector enquired.

Whether it was the look on the captain's face or the brief pause that followed the question, neither policeman failed to miss the impact the inspector's question had made.

"Lord no! We have no direct contact with the communists, to my knowledge. Does that answer your question, Inspector?"

"Thank you, Captain." At that point a telephone rang on the desk of one of the WAAF secretaries, and shortly after a brunette poked her head around the door.

"Captain, they're ready for these gentlemen in B Four."

"Thank you, Anne. If you have no further questions, Inspector, I'll take you to B Four. This way, please."

B4 turned out to be another disguised Nissan hut set aside from all other buildings. A military policeman examined their identification before allowing them to proceed beyond the first office.

On entering, Sim should have been surprised to see Adrian J. Padmore, but he was not. His presence merely confirmed what he had suspected. Standing beside him was a younger man of medium height with unruly red hair wearing a crumpled dark grey suit, the front of which was covered in cigarette ash. He wore a regimental tie that was vaguely familiar to the inspector, but he couldn't put it into context. The room was sparsely furnished: a metal desk and four wooden chairs. Missing were the usual accoutrements one would expect to see in an office: a filing cabinet, a bookshelf, a wastepaper basket.

"Sim, fancy meeting you so soon," Padmore gushed.

"Fancy," the inspector coolly replied.

"Robert, this is Inspector Sim, who I was telling you about. We were in India together. And this is ...?"

"Sergeant 'odges. Didn't I see you at the 'otel earlier?"

"How perceptive of you, Sergeant. Shall we sit?" Padmore suggested.

"Now, Sim, I'll pass things over to Robert here, if that's all right. He's Johnny *in situ*, so to speak."

"Thank you, Adrian—"

"Before we start," the inspector interrupted, "may I ask who we are speaking to? Is it the Foreign Office, the Security Intelligence Service, or possibly the Bedfordshire Drainage Board?"

Adrian J. Padmore and Robert looked at each other. "I think we can say that you're speaking to the Security Service, Inspector," Robert loftily replied.

"Yes, I think we can, Robert." Adrian J. Padmore added, with feigned solicitude.

They were two of a kind, Sergeant Hodges observed, smarmy middle-class smarties from privileged backgrounds: public school, possibly even university, their position within society set firmly in concrete since the beginning. Perhaps this war will change all that, but hadn't they harboured similar thoughts at the end of the last one? Certainly, from where he sat, things remained the same. It was safe to assume that neither of the two men with whom they shared the room would have any idea of the world he inhabited back in the smoke. No doubt they would consider those whom he normally came into contact with on a daily basis as no more than dross. In military parlance, cannon fodder. If pressed, where would their allegiance really lie, to class or country? It was an interesting thought.

"I rang my superiors in London, at the Met, to get some answers from you people as to who was Henri Bonoteaux and what he was doing in this country. I'm still waiting."

"Yes, Henri Bonoteaux. Well, Inspector, collective wisdom has it that even were we to tell you who he was and what he was doing in our fabled land, assuming we knew, you would be no nearer to finding his killer. Wouldn't you agree, Adrian?"

"Yes, Robert, I agree."

"I'm sorry if that's not what you expected to hear, but that is the way of it." He lit another cigarette from a silver case, his second since they had entered the office.

"On the contrary, Robert, that's exactly what I expected to hear." Inspector Sim looked out of the small window at a rusting harvester. "We know from the RAF that authorisation for his flight to England came from you people, not SOE. Are you in the habit of bringing foreigners into England without any knowledge of who they are or what they do? If so, then no wonder it's taking so long to win this war!"

"Well, I don't know what to say?" Robert replied indignantly.

"Me neither," parroted Padmore.

"Try the truth, it's always the easiest," said Inspector Sim. Sergeant Hodges was beginning to enjoy the exchange, although he was doing his best to avoid showing it. The Security Intelligence Service had hit a nerve in Inspector Sim, something that his sergeant, in retrospect, should have seen coming.

"Sim, always black and white. Always the policeman. Do you know something, Gerald, you were the same in India. I'm afraid you lack the imagination necessary for the situation in which you find yourself. It's a different world now, and, if I may offer a bit of advice, you're swimming in deep waters. I wonder if you realise how deep? Are you a good swimmer, Gerald?"

Adrian J. Padmore's reference to their time together in India, suggesting some spurious level of comradeship, annoyed the inspector. In the short time Padmore was in India, their paths had seldom crossed. And to claim some intimate knowledge of his personal philosophy on life was, at best, fatuous. It was true, they had both been at Cambray, but so was half of India's Special Branch. As to how well he could swim, clearly Padmore had been seeing too many American crime films. He did so detest these American metaphors.

"As I have already said, the RAF has confirmed to us the fact that Bonoteaux was brought to this country by your people, or do you deny that?" said Inspector Sim.

"I don't believe we have, have we, Adrian?"

"No, Robert, I don't believe we have."

"I have enough imagination to associate his death with the purpose of his visit to England. And, since you know why he was here, it doesn't take too much to believe that you know why, if not by whom, he was killed."

There followed a pause, each side waiting for the other to break the impasse.

After a while, Robert said, "Do you think we should enlighten the inspector, Adrian?" His tone was condescending, and it was all Sergeant Hodges could do to contain his anger. He had a sudden desire to wipe the supercilious grin off Robert's face in a manner that would make it hard for him to smile for a long time.

"As much as we are able, Robert. Why not?" Adrian J Padmore intoned.

"Very well. Bonoteaux was one of a number of people who helped us out in France, organising various Resistance groups, landing fields, that sort of thing. His position was, however, as much political as it was operational. That's what made him our man rather than SOE's. When this war ends, HMG wants to be sure the right people are running things over there. Does that answer your question?"

"Are you suggesting that his murder could have been politically motivated?"

"No, I'm not saying that. I'm not saying that at all, am I, Adrian?"

"I don't believe so, Robert."

"Then what are you saying?" Sim asked.

"Look, we're not going to be able to help you, Sim, are we, Robert?"

"No, I don't believe we are, Adrian."

"You might say that Monsieur Bonoteaux was just another casualty of this unpleasant war," Padmore added.

"Is that why you've driven all the way up from London, Padmore, for just 'another casualty of this unpleasant war'?"

"My visit to Tempsford has nothing to do with Bonoteaux's death. As we have said, we can't help you, Sim. No doubt you will continue with your enquiries, and we wish you and your sergeant the best of luck, don't we, Robert?"

"Yes, indeed, Adrian," replied Robert.

"You can be sure that we will continue with our enquiries. Perhaps you would like to tell us, does the SIS have any direct dealings with the French Communist Party?"

As with the air liaison officer, both policemen detected a slight hesitation and an awkwardness in the reply.

"Certainly not!" cried Robert.

"Certainly not!" Padmore parroted.

"HMG likes to keep such people at arm's length. Let the Froggies deal with their own mess, isn't that right?"

"Absolutely, Robert. Wouldn't be surprised, though, if the Reds weren't behind the death of your chap Botoneaux. Happy?"

"Actually, he was *your* chap, not ours, but that will have to do for now. If you didn't come here because of Bonoteaux, why are you in Milton Ernest, Padmore?"

"Sorry, old chap, that's on a need-to-know basis."

"So why did you bother to search me out at the Queen's Head if your visit has nothing to do with the death of Botoneaux?"

"Simply heard you were in the area, old chap. Thought it would be nice to make contact after all this time, India and all that."

Flight Lieutenant Mortlock was waiting outside B4 to escort them off the base. The Humber was parked by the main gate where they had left it, but there was no sign of ACW Little.

"Your driver appears to be missing, Inspector," observed the fight lieutenant.

"That girl is a problem," Sergeant Hodges observed.

Chapter Thirteen

Thouars, France

Bereft of breakfast, Grace sat in the park listening to her complaining stomach. It had been over twelve hours since she had eaten, and only then lightly, even longer since her last cup of either coffee or tea. The little birds that had gathered around her feet where she sat were obviously equally as ravenous. It occurred to her how oblivious the animals must be to the plight of her homeland, those, that is, who weren't slaughtered and sent to feed the Third Reich. The directions she had been given by Dannielle were quite explicit as to which park was to be the location for their meeting, and yet, after waiting an hour, she was beginning to wonder if in fact she had got it wrong and Dannielle was waiting for her elsewhere.

To Grace it seemed as though the country was asleep, perhaps hoping to wake and find the occupier gone, but such a peace can be deceptive. No doubt, away from the provinces things were more active and the presence of the enemy more obvious. A few people had passed by, most with a cautious greeting. There was an old man walking a small dog, and once a policeman had walked past offering his salutation. It was as she rose to leave in search of some much-needed food that the old man with the dog, having twice circled the small park, came and sat beside her, putting her feathered entourage to flight.

"Do you think it might rain, mademoiselle?"

The voice and smell was that of Gilbert, but from a body that looked twenty or thirty years older. Grace attempted, unsuccessfully, to hide her surprise.

"Monsieur Gilbert. Excuse my surprise, I was expecting Dannielle."

"I'm sorry, I didn't mean to startle you. You are well?"

"Yes, thank you. A little hungry, that's all."

"All of France is hungry, mademoiselle. But we have work to do. Are you ready?"

"Yes."

"Good. You're to go to Pas-de-Jeu. Do you remember? It's on the road to Loudun, to the red garage. The message is for Jean Badia. Give it only to him."

Grace repeated the instruction. "And then?"

"After you have done that, return here, to Thouars, to the stable. There will be another job for you. We've lost a lot of time, mademoiselle, and there's lots more that has to be done. But you must acquire a shopping basket. Didn't they tell you that? No French woman walks out without a shopping basket. You never know when and where food might be found."

"I understand."

"I'll remain here. Walk away as if we've just met. And good luck."

"But the message?"

"It's attached to the underside of the saddle of your bicycle in the stable. Put it in a safe place. You know what to do if you're searched."

"Yes. Good day, monsieur."

Over the following weeks, her job as Gilbert's courier became evermore busy. Gilbert, she came to realise, had evaded arrest through sheer cunning and disguise, although, after their meeting in the park, she seldom met him; he preferred to use cut-outs. She would receive her instructions from a number of people, of whom Dannielle and a young lad named Pierre were but two. At no time would she have been able to divulge, even under interrogation, the location of the wireless set used by Gilbert to communicate with London. She simply didn't know. On a more fiscal note, she had surrendered most but not all of the money from her money belt to the network for whom she and Gilbert now worked. No doubt the group for whom it was initially intended would be resupplied. It had been around her waist for so long that she almost missed its discomforting weight. Her stay at the stable had, as promised, been short-lived. After a few days she left the smell of horse and the threat of a hasty exit down the putrid tunnel for a terraced house kept by an old lady whose son was a prisoner of war in Germany. On moving in, she had warned Grace that the neighbours, both sides, were Pétainists and that the daughter from one of the homes was trotting out with a German officer from Cholet. It had been explained to both sides that Grace was a refugee from the north who had lost her parents and younger brothers to the filthy British, who had bombed their home. Such news had been received with the appropriate commiseration and understanding. This hatred for the British in so many French hearts had come as no surprise. She had experienced it often while being brought up in Saintes, the child of an Englishman. The war had simply given it freedom to be expressed more vehemently. It seemed that for many French men and women, it was better that Germans remained in France than one British soldier again set foot on French soil.

Aware that it was only a matter of time before her perambulations would attract attention, Grace attempted to change her appearance often while residing with the old woman. This she accomplished in the seclusion of a disused bakery not far from the house where she boarded. She changed her identity card as often as her hair colour and style, along with her clothes – one day a woman of the land, the next a woman of the bourgeoisie. In the end, having the committed Pétainists as neighbours made it necessary for her to move house, something she continued to do every week or so thereafter, even moving out of Thouars to a town or village close by, but always using narrow, uncomfortable back roads to avoid German roadblocks. Sometimes she had to cycle miles, zigzagging back and forth long distances just to cover what in a straight line would be a few kilometres. Although it was the job for which she had been trained, Grace found it paradoxically as unappealing as it was exciting. Often sleeping in strange surroundings without taking her clothes off, going days without a good wash, eating at odd hours and in odd places and sometimes not at all. She was concerned as much for the roadworthiness of her trusted bicycle as for her possible arrest. With each passing day, Gilbert became more active and more demanding of her, as if he knew that his time was running out. He had defied the odds for so long.

Two days before a prearranged meeting with Dannielle in Thouars, while staying at a farmhouse outside Moncontour, Grace experienced the closeness of war, which she felt had, until then, evaded her. She was returning from delivering a set of heavy printing plates for the resistance newspaper *Combat* to a team in Bressoire. It was early evening as she turned into the farmyard, after having spent a tiring day cycling. A German army lorry and three soldiers, along with her two elderly hosts, filled the yard. The two old people, who had risked so much to look after her, now knelt on the stone cobbles in front of the German invaders. Aware that if she were to try and turn around she might be shot, there seemed no other course than to dismount and face the Germans. They were *Landser*, infantrymen of the Wehrmacht, probably part of a contingent that had recently shipped into the area on a rotational rest period from the Eastern Front and were no doubt out pillaging. The largest of the three, an *Unteroffizier*, a corporal, stepped forward and, before she had a chance to explain her reason for being at the farm or to protect herself, he pulled her off the bicycle and, grabbing her by the hair, dragged her towards the hay barn, the door of which was partially open. All the while, his two colleagues offered verbal support and suggestions as to what he might do with the young French girl.

Inside he threw her down onto the ground in front of some rusting farming machinery. As he crouched over her and made a grab for the top of her dress, instead of attempting to push him away, she took hold of his uniform jacket and pulled him to her at the same time, using the forward motion of his heavy body to propel him with both her legs over her head. She had acted instinctively but to good effect. Unable to prevent himself falling among the machinery, he flung his arms forward but found nothing to arrest his fall. Two metal spikes of an old harvester penetrated his head, one through his right eye, the other between his left ear and jaw. Grace lay pinned under a body that twitched for a few minutes before laying deathly still. Pushing herself free, she stood, her legs shaking but strangely unmoved by the body in front of her, the man she had just killed. Outside, the soldiers were still yelling and offering up lurid suggestions, out of sight and oblivious to what had happened. Her mind was racing as to the immediate possibilities. There was no way out other than via the barn door through which she had been dragged. Also, by killing the German on their property, she had sentenced her two hosts to death, as well as herself. She had but one choice. Bending over the body, she took his pistol from its holster as well as bullets from a pouch attached to his belt. It was a Walther designed P38, 9mm with a five-inch barrel, easier to make and cheaper than the Lugar. It was now standard equipment with all German forces. She had become familiar with the Walther while at Airsaig, where, along with other weapons, she had not only fired it on a number of occasions but been expected to be able to strip it down, clean it, and put it together in working order. Ensuring that the safety catch was off, she approached the door of the barn. Suddenly the raucous yelling stopped, followed by two rifle shots and then another. Peering out, she saw the old people lying in a fast-growing pool of blood, their killers wandering off to search for chickens and anything else that took their fancy. One of the soldiers disappeared into the farmhouse, the other began chasing a chicken around the yard. Grace waited until both chicken and soldier were approaching the open door of the barn. With his rifle slung over his shoulder, he might as well have been unarmed. Stepping out in front of him, her right arm fully extended, she aimed the revolver but waited for him to rise from the crouching position he had adopted in pursuit of the chicken. A look of astonishment crossed his face as he straightened up and faced her. Whether or not he fully comprehended the full import of his situation she would never know, for at that moment she pulled the trigger. He was no more than a metre from her when the bullet tore open a hole in his head equidistant between his two eyes. He dropped rather as a ripe apple might from the security of its tree. Remaining where she was, she waited. Seconds later, the remaining soldier came running out of the house, summoned by the shot from the pistol. With her legs firmly planted 400 centimetres apart, just as she had been trained, she again raised her arm and took aim. The distance between them favoured the rifle, a handgun being inaccurate at anything other than short range. Like his companion, he entered the yard from the house with his weapon still slung over his shoulder. However, with commendable speed he unslung it and while running towards her fired at Grace. The shot whistled past her head. She returned the fire, her first shot striking him in the right shoulder, the second in the chest as he fell. As if she were on the firing range with her instructor standing behind her, she took the bullets cradled in her left hand and calmly reloaded. The ubiquitous forces of destruction that is war had at last found her.

Entering the house, she cleared her small room in the garret of all personal belongings, hastily packing her case before returning to the scullery, where she took what food was available: some bread, cheese, and the two boiled eggs that had been prepared for her tea. Minutes later she was on her bicycle, leaving behind the farm and five bodies. It was important to put as much distance as she could between herself and the farm before darkness enveloped the countryside. There was no possible way she would be able to reach Thouars before the commencement of curfew. She had decided to return to the stable, if only for a few nights before her scheduled meeting with Dannielle. Tonight, though, she would sleep rough, in a barn if she was lucky.

It was midday before she eventually peddled down the narrow road that led to the stable in Thouars. The blinds were up on the top floor of the yellow house as she rode by. But as a further security measure, she would ride on a little, into the centre of town, before returning. With the key to both gate and house she let herself in. It was just as she had left it. There would be no bedding for her tonight; the place had returned to its abandoned state. She spent the next forty-eight hours hiding in the stables, eking out the food she had taken from the farm.

When it came time for her meeting with Dannielle, she left her bicycle behind and walked to the Place Saint-Medard. A cold, northerly wind held the town in its grip, and rain was on the way. They were to meet in a café. Walking along the

Rue Académie, she caught sight of Danielle going in the same
direction on the opposite side of the narrow road. She was about
to cross over and catch up with her when she noticed a man
ahead of her, on her side of the road, leaning up against a wall,
watching Dannielle from behind a newspaper. Further on there
was another pretending to look into a shop window. A car passed
slowly by. She was walking into a trap, and Grace could only
watch. It was all over in seconds. As the car drew up alongside
Dannielle, the two men, having moved into position, grabbed
her, one from behind, the other in front, and threw her into the
car, which then sped away. Those on the street who had stopped
and watched the arrest walked on as if nothing had happened.
To Grace it was the exemplification of a pacified nation and an
acceptance of the occupation.

Was she also under surveillance? If so, surely she would
have been caught up in the same trap. Why would they arrest
Dannielle and leave her free to wander the streets? What of
Gilbert? Had he already been arrested? Even if he was still free,
with Dannielle caught it was only a matter of time before they
would make her disclose all she knew about the network. Maybe
the stable was already compromised; dare she risk going back
there, if only for her cherished bicycle? No, that was one place
she could not return to. They had arranged to meet in a small
café off the Place-Saint-Medard. Out of security, Dannielle
would not have mentioned it to Gilbert. To her knowledge, only
she and Dannielle knew of their meeting.

On approaching the café, a boy was casually kicking a ball
up against a wall; it was Pierre, one of her other cut-outs. She
had never had any contact with him at the café and so assumed
that he too had witnessed the arrest and had come to warn her.
Having made eye contact with him, she walked on past the café
to the park where, days earlier, she had met Gilbert. A short

while later the boy entered the park, seemingly in pursuit of an errant ball. Retrieving it, he then threw it into the air, where it landed at her feet. While recovering it, he dropped a key at her feet, uttered an address on the Rue Rivière, and then ran off in pursuit of his ball, having kicked it across the park with youthful energy.

The house was in one of the narrow medieval streets sandwiched between the seventeenth century chateau and the river. It was raining by the time she found the address, and she wanted nothing more than to find somewhere dry. How long was it since she had drunk something hot? Or, for that matter, eaten a decent meal? Instead she smothered the natural desire to search for sustenance and carried out a proper surveillance sweep of the area. She continually amazed herself at how often she drew on her training, extracting from that well of knowledge provided by her instructors in England. As with her reaction at the farm, she had only to let her training dictate her actions, overcome her emotions, ignore her natural instincts, and at times act counterintuitively.

The street was deserted. The house, which opened onto the street, was seemingly unoccupied. She walked past it without appearing to notice its existence, first one way, and, after a stroll away from the area, past it the other way. It seemed clean. At first the key didn't seem to fit, but after trying it a few times she managed to open the door, its hinges objecting noisily. Inside all was silent. In the crepuscular half-light the three small rooms that made up the ground floor appeared empty of furniture and, she thought, devoid of human habitation.

"Bonsoir, mademoiselle. I've been waiting."

Chapter Fourteen

<u>Angers, France</u>

Wilhelm Milch, real name Karl Oberhümer, one of the party of four that made up Operation Pickaxe, having been forced to the edge of the landing field at Angers by members of the Resistance, could only watch as the Hudson escaped into the night sky. The communists, members of the *Parti communiste française*, the PCF, had failed to show, leaving them at the mercy of the Gaullists. At the last minute, both Karl and Freda, to his surprise and Hans's horror, had attempted to re-board the aircraft and return to England. Perhaps the failure of the PCF to show had been the final straw, convincing them of the utter futility of their doomed mission. As planned, the Austrian venture had little chance of success, but dropping them into France was suicidal. They must have considered their options and preferred to face Colonel Ivan Dekanozov and forceful repatriation to the Soviet Union, with all that that would entail, rather than fall into the hands of the Gestapo.

As the sound of the departing aircraft faded away and the reception committee dispersed with the containers that had been delivered with the Pickaxe members, the four Austrians were accosted by a short, bald man.

"Why have you come to France?" he asked aggressively.

The four stood silent for a moment, and then the three men looked at their female companion; she alone had sufficient command of the French language to offer anything like a cogent reply.

"To help the people of France fight the Germans," replied Freda, real name Gertrude Eisner. To her the reply, given their circumstances, seemed more than adequate.

"Since when have you communists done anything that didn't further your own cause? Fighting for France? What absolute bloody rubbish!" Running a hand over his bald scalp, he continued. "Because your comrades, the PFC, haven't turned up, you have become my problem. As communists you are barely acceptable, but, as if that were not enough, you are BOCHE! I should have you shot, now, here in Angers. What do you say to that?"

A car could be heard starting up and driving off. Two men appeared out of the darkness carrying the baggage belonging to the four. Karl moved forward to prevent his wireless set from being thrown to the ground, but too late. The two resisters threw the baggage to the ground at their feet and then disappeared into the night. If the wireless set was damaged, as now seemed more than likely, they had lost all hope of fulfilling their mission, even if they could reach Paris. The British wireless set they had been issued with on arrival in England was robust enough to survive a certain amount of rough treatment, but the manner in which it had come into contact with French soil was probably too much for the more fragile components. Fortunately, Karl carried the valves in his coat pocket, but on their own they were worthless.

"What to do with you?"

Freda quickly translated what Monsieur Galtier had said. Throughout, the two men guarding them, armed with Sten guns, stood ready to shoot should they attempt to escape.

"Do these men speak French or English?" Monsieur Galtier asked, pointing at her companions.

"Their English is better than their French, I think." In truth, she had talked so little to them that she had no idea as to their language skills. Exile in Russia had taught her many things, one of which was to keep her own council.

"They have come to France but can't speak French! And how long do you think it will be before the Germans pick you up? What the hell was SOE thinking of, sending you people here! Have they gone mad?" Monsieur Galtier was not pleased.

The four Austrians stood silent while he glared at them and thought. He was not a man who liked to rush into things. After a while he spoke.

"You Boche will go into hiding until we can contact the PCF, then they can have you. Do you understand?"

He had spoken in English, a language he had done well in at school, attempting at the same time to supress his frustration with the situation. His first concern was for his network, the loyal men and women who risked their lives for France and not for the cause of international communism. The four individuals who stood before him were expendable, but for the sake of his relations with London he was bound to give them protection, for now. They had, however, the potential to put all their lives at risk. One step out of place and he would order their execution.

"We must leave. That aircraft was loud enough to be heard in Nantes."

It was not the first night Wilhelm Milch had spent sleeping in a barn, nor would it be his last. That his immediate future would be separate from the other three was something he had more or less decided upon, but he had yet to work out how that might be achieved and under what circumstance. Whatever happened, he had no intention of going to Paris. But what options did he have? Hiding out in France without help was impossible. With a great deal of luck, he might be able to make his way from

Angers to neutral Spain, where at least he could make himself understood, but it was a long way to travel, especially through a country occupied by the enemy. Without help he would be unlikely to last the distance. Might he join up with a communist group away from Angers and fight the good fight alongside those whose true allegiance was to the *International* rather than the Allied cause? It then hit him. Why was his mind caught in such a trap? Why on earth was he thinking this way? Before, when the operation was destined to take him to Austria, he had decided to break with Moscow and the whole communist movement. So why then was he even considering joining up with a communist resistance group? But, as an Austrian, would he be able to convince the Free French that he wasn't a German spy or someone who was attempting to infiltrate the Resistance? Whichever way he looked at it, the immediate future appeared grim.

A guard had been mounted outside the barn. Monsieur Galtier had left the four in no doubt as to what would be their fate should they try to escape from his care. They could expect to be there for at least a day or so while he made contact with the PCF and arranged for their removal. He would return their wireless set to them when the PCF came to collect them. Once the barn door had been closed and they were in darkness, Hans left no time in verbally assaulting Karl and Freda for their attempt to re-board the aircraft. He had assumed leadership of the group and explained to them that Colonel Dekanozov had given him permission to kill all three of them should they attempt to deviate from the mission. It was not for any of them to think beyond that which the Party had ordained. At one point he had produced a knife and held it to Karl's throat while screaming communist doctrine at the poor fellow. Milch had intervened to calm the situation, while

Freda looked on impassively. For Milch, Han's behaviour was further confirmation of his decision to break with them. The man was homicidal, something Milch had long suspected from their time together in Spain. Perhaps in the fast-approaching morning he would come up with a solution to his problem. Meanwhile, having managed to persuade Hans into a more level frame of mind, he would sleep.

Daylight came, and with it breakfast, if four half-filled bowls of gruel and a pail of water may be so described. Hours later the door was slid open and Monsieur Galtier appeared. Unaware of the leadership position Hans had assumed, he addressed his remarks to Freda, for her translation.

"Your friends in the PCF inform us they will come for you within a couple of days. Why the delay? I don't know. They don't seem to be in a rush to receive you. Till then you will stay in here. The guard will remain outside."

Since the team had been put together in the Soviet Union, there had been little communication between them. Only Milch and Hans, through their previous association, had anything to say to each other. Following Hans's threatening behaviour towards Karl the previous night and his claim that Colonel Dekanozov had given him permission to kill them all for any deviation, a claim that Milch thought to be true, there was little to bring them together, even the shared threat of capture. Now, in the barn in France, they had each sought refuge in their own shell, even separating themselves physically as much as the confines of the barn would allow. A less cohesive group it would have been hard to envisage, a situation that was not lost on Milch as he contemplated his future.

Mid-afternoon and the barn door was slid back just wide enough to permit the entrance of Monsieur Galtier. He stood observing the group. After a few minutes, pointing at Milch, he said, "You, come with me." His gesticulation left Milch in little doubt as to what was required of him.

As Milch rose from the wooden box on which he had been sitting he could feel the distrustful eyes of Hans boring into him. Both Freda and Karl ignored his exit.

Monsieur Galtier led him under a threatening sky across the cobbled yard to the farmhouse and to a small room that served as a kitchen. It was as primitive in its furnishings as any he had witnessed in the Soviet Union, consisting of a stone sink, an open fire, and a coal stove that was Napoleonic. A wooden table and two chairs completed the room. But it was the smell that most interested him: nitrate and glycerine. Not two odours one would normally associate with a kitchen.

"Sit. Your name? Nahmer?" he repeated.

"Milch, Wilhelm Milch."

"You are a communist?"

"Nein! Socialist." To emphasise the point he repeated, "A socialist, no communist."

"But you are with the communists."

"My country, Austria," he was struggling with his English, "is now fascist, I leave. To Spain and so to Russia."

"You fought in Spain?"

"Fight, in Spain, yes."

It was a statement upon which it was Monsieur Galtier's wish to ponder. The conflict that had erupted on the other side of the Pyrénées in 1936 had awakened in the most dormant of French minds the fact that times were changing, particularly in Spain. Monsieur Galtier's brother had been one of those who had gone to fight for the Republic, and from him he learnt much about the conflict. After a while he called out, "Claude." Immediately a man appeared from within the house. Words were exchanged, and the man left only to reappear minutes later accompanied by

Freda. As there were only two chairs in the room, she was left standing, along with her escort, who took up a position by the door that led onto the yard.

"His English is no good. You must translate."

"What do you want?" she asked.

He told her. Two German soldiers had been captured by the Resistance and were being kept in a forest camp close by. Both had been working for the *Funkhorchdienst*, manning radio detection vans and so were of interest to the Resistance. Since occupying France, the Germans had perfected the art of radio detection, which was why the average length of time an operator could remain free in the field was reduced to two weeks. Milch was to find out what they knew and why the *Funkhorchdienst* was so successful. He was then to return to the farm and pass on what he had learnt. Freda asked why the Germans could not be brought to the farm for questioning. It was a question Monsieur Galtier ignored. She then suggested that she interrogate the two Germans rather than Milch. Forcefully he explained that a woman would be unacceptable to his fighters in the forest. They were simple men, more used to seeing women as vestals of the hearth. As an aside, he added that he could not, even for one as unattractive as she, guarantee her safety among men who had not benefitted from the company of women in months.

Ignoring his insult, Freda told Milch what was expected of him. She was then escorted back to the barn.

Later, after a meal of vegetables and bread, Milch left the farm accompanied by two armed *resisters*. In light drizzle, taking first back roads and then crossing open country, they eventually came to the forest, just as the light was fading. They had barely entered before receiving their first challenge. A moment before the shadowy armed figure suddenly appeared in front of them, Milch heard the familiar click of a safety catch being removed.

Allowed to continue, following the exchange of, what Milch assumed, were passwords, they moved deeper into the forest. By the time they encountered their second challenge what light there had been no longer penetrated the trees. This time the sentinel appeared from behind them. His eyes now accustomed to the dark, Milch was staring down the short barrel of a Sten gun, a notoriously unreliable weapon, making him feel less than secure, particularly in the hands of a lad no more than fifteen. Again words were exchanged before they were allowed to continue.

Eventually they came to a clearing in the centre of which a small fire gave off a welcoming glow and limited heat against the gathering cold. Around it were a number of men, some sitting on the ground and others standing, all were armed and staring at Milch. To one side, away from the firelight, sat the two bound uniformed Germans. Milch and his escort were given a hot drink, the identity of which was open to question. It could have been tea or coffee; it didn't matter, after which he was taken to their captives. He felt the hostility of the resisters towards him, this new German. He was less than a heartbeat from joining the two hapless soldiers.

Crouching down beside them he found that both had been badly beaten, their faces swollen, their eyes having received particular attention. One of them, the larger of the two, was coughing blood. His left arm appeared broken. Both showed the early signs of the onset of hypothermia. They stared at Milch with fear and resignation. Both were young, no more than twenty-five. From the mood in the clearing, Milch knew that for the two Germans not only was their war over but shortly also their lives.

The initial shock of being questioned not only in German but in an Austrian dialect translated into a pathetic hope, a misplaced expectation on their part, that they might have their miserable lives spared. They weren't to know that Milch was in no position to offer such a guarantee. The steady stream of readily supplied answers to his unprepared questions, mainly from the smaller of the two captives, as the other obviously found speaking difficult, was further proof of their erroneous belief that if they cooperated they might not be killed. He had seen it before in Spain out of the mouths and on the faces of the condemned. Also, fear has a smell of its own, something else he had come across in Spain. As Milch listened to the flow of technical information he thought how much more suitable Karl, Pickaxe's wireless operator, would have been for this mission into the forest. The farmer had selected the wrong person for the job. Possessing little knowledge of wireless, he found much of what he was told gobbledegook. All he could do was try and memorise as much as possible. It would have made sense to write down at least some of what he was hearing, but he had not come equipped for dictation and neither was he disposed to ask for help from those gathered around the fire. Eventually he had exhausted his store of what he hoped were meaningful questions. Whether or not it was sufficient to satisfy Monsieur Galtier was something he wouldn't know until his return to the farm. He could only hope that his own survival didn't depend upon a satisfactory report.

On standing, Milch eyed the two pathetic figures huddled on the ground in front of him. One of the two Germans, the smaller of the two, asked if he would help them. He explained that they had served first in Poland, then in Russia, and now had no stomach for a return to the fray. Having been unwantedly seconded as wireless technicians to the *Funkhorchdienst*, by the Wehrmacht, they wanted an end to their war. They were not Nazis, they protested, merely soldiers fighting for their country and were willing to do whatever their captors wanted of them.

Their pleas for his intervention on their behalf became more urgent, more wretched, more pathetic, until one of the *resisters* stepped between them and pushed Milch away.

Rather than an immediate return to the farm, as he had expected, his hosts had made plans for him to spend the night with them in the forest. It put added pressure upon him to carry in his mind all that the two captives had imparted. What chance had he of remembering all that he had been told until he returned to the farm? Being in no position to refuse their hospitality, all he could do was make himself comfortable upon a bed of damp grass and leaves. The last thing he could remember hearing before dropping off to sleep was one of the German soldiers pathetically weeping for his mother.

He woke at dawn, stiff and cold, to find most of the *resisters* gone. Gone also were the two Germans. He wondered if they had already been killed. The two fighters who had remained in the clearing were finishing breakfast. They offered him coffee and some bread, after which all three set off for the farm.

Monsieur Galtier was less than pleased with his account of events in the forest. Milch would be the first to admit that his report was amorphous in its delivery and at times incoherent, particularly when it concerned matters technical, such as loop rotation antenna, radio frequency spectrum, condensers, transponders, and semiconductor rectifiers. Freda had been brought from the barn to translate, but try as she may could offer little through her translation that improved matters. However, Milch suspected that Monsieur Galtier knew even less than himself about radio direction finding. This begged the question, what had he hoped to achieve by sending him into the forest?

In his absence the PCF had unexpectedly appeared and taken Hans and Karl away. She had witnessed the confrontation from the barn door. There had been something of a standoff in the yard, with both the resisters and the communists pointing guns at each other. Monsieur Galtier had been adamant that not only was Milch not available to travel with them to Paris, but also Freda would be staying at the farm until he was ready to release her into their custody. The PCF were equally insistent that all four of the Pickaxe mission would go to Paris, and they would not leave without them. It took the arrival of more resistance fighters at the farm to convince the members of the PCF that it was in their best interest to depart without Freda and Milch. All this he learnt from Freda upon his return with her to the barn, notwithstanding her continued reluctance to communicate.

Chapter Fifteen

Tempsford, Bedfordshire

Following his penitential period on the Hudson, Sergeant Hodges was back on the Lysander. He had enjoyed flying with Anders Tosen and Bert Copperwood, his Hudson crew. They had jelled well as a team in the short time they were together. He would happily fly with them again if the powers that be so decreed. Until joining Coastal Command he had no experience operating as part of a crew. All his flying in Western Canada had been as a single pilot, and it had taken some adjustment on his part to include others in his operational thinking. Now he could slide easily from being part of a crew on the Hudson and back to flying single pilot on the Lysander.

That night, the weather both in France and England was not good. Over the field there was low cloud with heavy rain. The freezing level was low, just five thousand feet, cloud ceiling over the Channel was around four. It was anybody's guess what it would be like over the target. The field he was to operate into was three kilometres southwest of Champigny. This was not an SOE operation, but one laid on for the Alliance intelligence organisation. His passengers outbound were the Alliance's air advisor for the region, Christian Sabbe, who had been attending a course at Tempsford, and a René Foreau, one of the Alliance's intelligence officers. It appeared at one stage in the proceedings that the flight would be cancelled due to weather, but those responsible thought it was worth giving it a go.

Their flight across the Channel was uneventful and without the icing problems Gifford had anticipated. It wasn't until shortly after crossing the French coast that they encountered trouble. The engine cut. They were at 8,000 feet between layers, just east of Lisieux. The Lysander began to lose height immediately, forcing them into thick cloud. When the reserve tank was being carried, after take-off it was his habit to switch from the fuselage tank to the reserve tank, slung beneath the aircraft. At 6,500 feet, having changed the fuel cock back to the fuselage tank, the engine burst back into life. With the weather the way it was he would need all the fuel he had on board for the round-trip back to Tangmere to complete the mission. If the fuel in the reserve tank was contaminated, as he now suspected, he might have to do the entire flight on what was in the fuselage tank, making it a close-run thing. Water is heavier than petrol, and when present the former generally tends to collect at the bottom of the tank. Once on the ground he would attempt to drain off any water floating around in the bowels of the reserve tank, but it would have to be done without shutting the engine down. He had no wish to find himself unable to restart the engine.

At Saint-Calais he altered course, turning southwest to pass west of Tours. They were back at 8,000 feet in broken cloud when a night fighter suddenly appeared, possibly from the Luftwaffe base to the east at Châteaudun. He threw the aircraft into as tight a spiral dive as the Lizzie would go, seeking the refuge of thick cloud. It was not a manoeuvre for which the Lysander was built. The gyro horizon toppled. A stream of tracer bullets passed close by the cockpit window before they were able to merge with the elements. Levelling out at 3,000 feet he enquired after the health of his Joes.

"Everything okay down the back?"

"Yes, we are okay. You are making this trip exciting for us, Captain."

"We do try, monsieur. ETA in approximately twenty minutes, always assuming we don't get any more distractions."

Having shaken off the night fighter, the rest of the flight went as planned until they caught sight of the landing strip. This was made easy for them because the flare path had been erroneously lit before either those on the ground or in the air had identified themselves. Whoever was responsible had not been Tempsford trained, or . . . On passing over the field Gifford signalled the assigned code, letter G. Back came the correct response, the letter L. What followed was one of the heaviest landings he had inflicted on a Lizzie. In any other aircraft it would have meant disaster. He had miscalculated his round-out, pure and simple. So robust is the Lizzie's fuselage that a number of pilots had found themselves sitting in the cockpit of an otherwise serviceable but wingless fuselage following an overly heavy landing. Fortunately for him the wings of his aircraft had remained an integral part of his aircraft.

At the end of the short landing roll he turned the aircraft through 180 degrees and taxied back to lamp A and the reception committee, unsure of who was waiting for them. As he again turned the aircraft, this time ready for take-off, he saw several figures approaching, none of whom appeared to be in uniform, which, in itself, didn't mean that they weren't German. Even though to his knowledge the Gestapo never wore uniforms, it was still a good sign. He felt the fresh air that entered the cockpit as the rear canopy was slid back, allowing the offloading of the packages followed by the Joes. A beaming young Frenchman was waving to him from under the port wing. While the exchange was taking place he quickly left the cockpit to check the reserve tank for contamination. To leave the cockpit with the engine running while the Joes were alighting would earn him a reprimand from Tempsford, were they ever to find out, but needs must. It was his second time on French soil, but it was one he had no desire to extend.

The bung on the underside of the tank appeared stuck, and, try as he may, he could not unscrew the cap. Seeking the help of one of the *resisters* he gesticulated furiously his need for a hammer. Minutes later the man returned with something that looked like a stonemason's tool. Getting down on his knees in the wet grass Gifford gave the bung a couple of healthy hits, which loosened the cap sufficiently for him to unscrew the bung and allow the release of what he hoped would be that portion of the fuel that had been contaminated.

With the homeward-bound Joes aboard, along with the freight, he looked for the thumbs-up from the man off to his left, just visible beyond the wing tip. They had been on the ground five minutes longer than planned! With a torch in his right hand, the man shone the light onto the raised thumb of his left. Sergeant Gifford opened the throttle and they bounced into the air.

"Bonsoir, welcome aboard." He had no idea who was behind the bulkhead. The SOE form had simply said one male, one female. Before his departure it had been stressed that everything possible must be done to bring his two passengers safely back to England, as lives were at risk. Was that not always the case?

They were climbing to 9,000 feet in search of sufficient cloud to cover their return flight. What he didn't need was another brush with the Luftwaffe. Fuel management would provide all the excitement he required.

* * *

Earlier that day.

<u>Thouars, France.</u>

The voice had come from a dark corner of the room in the house sandwiched between the chateau and the river. She froze.

"We have to leave, mademoiselle. They are picking up our people all over Thouars." It was Gilbert.

"Monsieur Gilbert, what's happened? I saw them arrest Dannielle in the street."

"We've been betrayed. There's nothing to be done. In three hours we are to be picked up and flown back to England. Our work's finished, at least for the present. I've outlived my time in France, and with the network exposed it's only a matter of time before they pick you up. Nothing will be served by our being arrested, mademoiselle, and there is little we can do for Dannielle and the others."

"Who would have—"

"It could be anybody. We'll never know. Perhaps when the war is over some of those who helped the Germans will be uncovered, certainly not all, there are too many. We haven't much time. Our rendezvous with the aircraft is close, but we must leave now."

Grace did not ask how it was that a pickup had been so swiftly arranged but assumed that it had been laid on for Gilbert and that she had been lucky enough to be included.

They had been hiding in the field on the eastern edge of the town for half an hour before a small van appeared out of the darkness. Grace recognised it as one she had sometimes seen outside the red garage owned by Jean Badia in Pas-de-Jeu. As soon as it had come to rest the rear doors flew open and hands pulled the two inside. She would remember that ride as one of the most uncomfortable she had experienced. Not only was it cramped, but those with whom she shared that journey had only a passing acquaintance with soap and water. Gilbert, she was willing to bet, had not washed since their first meeting. Apart from their cycle ride together out of Montsoreau, this was the longest she had spent in his company, a man who had so deftly defied the odds and remained in the field longer than any other SOE wireless operator. Among the *resisters* he had become something of a legend, and the price the Germans put on his head rose by the week.

To Grace the landing strip near Champigny appeared small. It had tall trees at one end and dropped away into what she assumed was a riverbed at the other. The terrain didn't allow for any other interpretation. Monsieur Badia did not wait for the plane's arrival. Having dropped them at the field, he drove off with his men back to Pas-de-Jeu. Gilbert and Grace stood waiting beneath a large, leafless oak. Above them the heavens were obscured by cloud whose height she found hard to assess, possibly no more than 1,000 to 1,500 feet. A light drizzle began to fall. She wondered if the aircraft would find the field in such poor conditions.

Which one of them first detected the presence of others emerging out of the dark Grace could not be sure. She only knew that Gilbert pushed her to the ground at the same time, drawing a revolver from his raincoat pocket as he went into a crouching position. More figures appeared.

"Bonsoir, monsieur. I'm André. We were expecting you. You can put that away. The gun won't be necessary. We know who you are and the identity of your friend." The tall, gangly young man who addressed them held out his hand. He moved as someone who had limited control over his limbs, as if he were being controlled by an inexperienced puppeteer. He was part of the reception committee, whose immediate tasks were to prepare the flare path and gather the freight bound for England.

To Grace they didn't look particularly well organised. Men were running around in a disorderly manner. One tripped and fell, cursing loudly. Each had his own idea of how matters should proceed and called out his demands, oblivious to the need for security.

Gilbert confirmed her observations. "I'm not sure they know what they're doing. The sooner we get out of here the better."

To the northeast came the sound of an approaching aircraft. The flare path, having been set after several attempts in different configurations, was switched on. Suddenly the aircraft was overhead flashing a signal. Grace had done well on her course with the Morse code and easily identified the letter G. One of the reception committee had already sent their investigating signal. The small aircraft disappeared to the west, only to reappear through the drizzle minutes later, brushing the tops of the trees on the southern end before dropping onto the field and bouncing down towards the north.

Grace and Gilbert stood back and watched as the reception committee, rather chaotically, went about the business of offloading the Lysander and helping the two Joes down the short ladder affixed to the rear of the fuselage. The pilot then appeared out of the cockpit and disappeared under the belly of the aircraft. In his bulky flying suit, it was hard to identify him, but Grace thought that he might be the very aviator who brought her to France. It certainly looked like it could be him. He was motioning to one of the young men as if in need of something. Shortly after, above the sound of the aircraft's idling engine, she heard a knocking. Grace could just make out the pilot, on his knees, hammering at something under the aircraft. Then they were told to board the aircraft, first Grace and then Gilbert. Behind her Gilbert slipped on the wet ladder but quickly regained his footing. Inside it was only marginally warmer, but it was at least dry. The drizzle had turned to rain and she wasn't dressed for such weather; everything she had, including her warm coat, was back at the stable. Seated side by side and facing aft they felt the pilot re-enter the cockpit, then they were off.

Later, in the air, she asked, "Bonsoir, Captain, have we met before?"

"Do you know, I think you might be right. Have you bought a season ticket for these flights?"

"The government is paying, I hope."

"In that case we'll try and make it a comfortable trip. Is your colleague okay?"

"I'm fine, thank you, Captain," Gilbert answered.

"You'll find a thermos and something to eat on the bulkhead in front of you. I'm afraid the service leaves a bit to be desired."

En route, low and middle cloud had increased, blocking out what moonlight there was and obscuring any navigational waypoints on the ground. He was again having to rely on dead reckoning, using basic navigation, drift, speed, and time to work out his position. Thoughts of an earlier flight came back to haunt him, when things had turned decidedly nasty thanks to some wide-awake flack gunners. A depression was forming out in the Atlantic and was expected to move into the area over the next twenty-four hours. Its direction and intensity would dictate the winds, and Tangmere could expect low cloud with a strong southerly wind once the cyclone took hold. With luck they would be on the ground before the worst hit. He had aimed to cross the coast between Trouville to the east and Villers to the west, keeping well clear of Le Havre.

An hour into the flight there had been no repeat of the fuel problem that had plagued the outbound journey. He had avoided running the auxiliary tank dry before switching to the mains in case there remained some contamination. However, if push came to shove and he was short on fuel before reaching Tangmere, he would be forced to drain the auxiliary tank.

Below he could see whitecaps glittering in the weak moonlight. They had crossed the French coast. Now all he had to do was find Tangmere. Their homing beacon would assist. Half an hour later he caught site of another coastline, the cloud having lifted as they neared Britain's south coast. Minutes later, to his left he could just make out Selsey Bill. It was farther away than his flight plan had allowed, putting him somewhere between Littlehampton and Worthing, from which he could only assume that the beacon on which he had been relying was either incorrect or not functioning. Altering course to the northeast and reducing height, he scoured the terrain for some identification. There seemed to be only minimum cloud at lower levels. He was close to home. Having sighted the satellite aerodrome of Merston, which was south of Tangmere, he could breathe a little easier, but just as he approached his destination the engine began to falter. Was there contamination in the main tank as well as his reserve? Should he risk switching back to the auxiliary tank? At that point the lights were switched on at Tangmere, along with a light on the nearest windsock to his position. Electing to land to the southwest, the runways ran N-S and NE-SW, with height in hand he readied the aircraft for a possible dead-stick landing. With land flap and slats having been extended and landing lights on, Gifford's Lysander plummeted towards the runway. At that point the engine gave up generating what little power it had been producing. Furiously he attacked the trim wheel. All he could hear was the ratcheting sound of the trim wheel, the wind-milling prop, and the air rushing through the aircraft. All he could think of was the round-out; he could not risk a heavy landing that might damage his aircraft or endanger his passengers. At the last moment he pulled hard back on the

167

stick and held the aircraft level, allowing the speed to wash off to the point where, all lift lost, it sank onto the runway.

The runway lights were extinguished as his aircraft coasted down the runway before coming to rest.

"Everybody okay down the back?"

"We're fine, Captain," she replied. "A nice landing."

"It would have helped if the engine had been running. We may have to wait a few minutes before they come and tow us to dispersal."

Aware that he was blocking the runway, he considered breaking radio silence to inform the tower of their predicament. Instead he gave his Mercury engine a chance to redeem itself. It sprung into life and they taxied in to dispersal where they were met by two men in civvies and the squadron commander. As Gifford climbed down from the cockpit, waiting for him was his female passenger. A few yards away stood her colleague, along with the reception committee beside a waiting staff car.

"Hello, Captain, it was you who flew me to France, wasn't it? Thank you for a safe trip home," she said, extending her hand.

"My pleasure, madam." It was against all the regulations, not to mention standing orders, but Gifford knew that if he was ever to see this woman again, and that was something he now realised he wanted above all else, this was the time to speak and not so loud that his squadron commander could hear. "Do you think we should wait until your next flight before we meet again?" It was an audacious move, one that he hoped she would not misinterpret; on the other hand she might, but that would be okay.

"Do you say that to all your female passengers, Captain?"

"No, only those I want to see again. How about it? Can we meet again?"

"Gifford," his squadron commander yelled, "these gentlemen are waiting."

"You can reach me at the sergeants' mess at RAF Tempsford. Ask for Sergeant Ian Gifford. Leave a message if I'm not there."

"Yes, why not. I must go before that rude man yells again. Bye."

"Your name?" he called after her.

She stopped, paused, and turned. "Simone."

He watched her walk away towards the waiting group. In the restricted light of the car's blinkered head lamps she looked bedraggled. Her clothes and hair had been deprived of that attentive care a woman gives to her appearance. How had she survived in occupied France? What had she experienced, and, for that matter, who was the older man who had accompanied her across the Channel? But for her demeanour, she seemed just as she had when they first met, at one and the same time both strong yet vulnerable. There had been only a few times since his divorce that he had been so attracted to a woman. Mostly they had come and gone, liaisons of a temporary nature, some extremely brief. This one was different. But if she didn't contact him then, given existing security procedures, it was very unlikely that he would ever see her again, unless, by some miracle, she once more flew to France and he happened to be rostered on that particular flight, but what were the chances of that?

Chapter Sixteen

<u>Bedfordshire</u>

Adrian J. Padmore harboured disloyal thoughts while polishing his shoes, seated on his cot in the Abbey annex and pondering on how best he might sabotage Operation Pickaxe. To have had such notions within the confines of the offices of the SIS would have seemed seditious, but here, in rural Bedfordshire, they seemed less so. He wished no ill to either his employer or his country, but rather he wanted to save them from the evil of further communist infiltration, which, in his mind, was the logical outcome of dealing with the Russians. It was a known fact that communist *agents provocateurs* were active mainly among certain elements of the working class, often disrupting the war effort.

While deciding what would be the most effective way to put a stop to the flights, he also had to consider his future within the Foreign Service. The obvious method was to inform the general, assuming he didn't already know. Clearly the SIS would not take kindly to his interference, as they were, after all, implicit in its operation, and he was not willing to jeopardize all that he had worked for – his position and the financial and social security of his family. A way would have to be found that would exonerate him. The considered wisdom was that were the general to become aware of its existence the affair would quickly become history. But how to reach the general? Any attempt at written communication would be futile as it would never reach its intended recipient. SIS had, through the French Secret Service in Duke Street, a conduit to the general, but who could he trust to deliver his message? There was Colonel André Dewavrin (*nom de guerre* was Colonel Passy), head of the Free French Force Intelligence Agents, who might be the right individual. Surely he had access to the general, but how close was he to SIS? On the other hand, among the French there were so many communists, although it was unlikely that someone of Dewavrin's exultant rank would support Moscow. The matter required some thought.

The possible answer to his problem came the following day when, through a contact in the SOE, he learnt of the existence of a certain Colonel Jean-Guy Bernard of the Free French, currently ensconced at the Swan Hotel in Bedford. It seemed that the man was helping the pedantic Inspector Sim with his enquiries. Such a fellow might well serve as the messenger he required. Without foreknowledge of the colonel, he would have to rely upon his own judgement when he met him, to assess his loyalty and reliability. To question the Free French as to his suitability might alert those who were happy to keep the general in ignorance of Operation Pickaxe. Padmore prided himself on being a good judge of character, a talent which in the past had stood him in good stead. A visit to Bedford was called for.

The Swan Hotel dates back to the eighteenth century and overlooks the Great Ouse River in the centre of the town. Like all such establishments it was awash with servicemen and women, with many of the rooms requisitioned for the duration. He was informed by the receptionist, a vitrine of bosoms and cameo brooches, that the colonel was not available, but if he wished to wait in the bar or the front lounge he was welcome to do so.

It was early evening before Colonel Bernard put in an appearance. Although there were servicemen from many different countries, mostly American, Canadian, and Australian airmen, Bernard stood out as the only Frenchman that evening to grace the front lounge of the Swan. Such was the shine on his cavalry boots that Adrian J. Padmore was pleased that he had gone to the bother of polishing his own shoes the previous evening. In the large front lounge the noise from the main bar could be heard and was gaining in volume. He had thought about how best to approach the colonel. Perhaps he could introduce himself as someone involved in Sim's enquiries. That would seem the best move and one not too far from the truth. He hoped that the colonel's English was better than his French, for, in spite of his years within the Foreign Office and service abroad, he didn't trust himself to speak in anything other than his mother tongue in matters of a delicate nature.

The Frenchman had entered the lounge clutching a glass of red wine and positioned himself in an armchair near the fire, around which several ATS officers had gathered.

"Colonel Bernard?" Padmore enquired.

"Yes." He did not invite Padmore to join him.

"Adrian J. Padmore, British Foreign Office. May I have a word?"

"What about, Monsieur Padmore?"

"I believe you are interested in certain enquiries being undertaken by Inspector Sim of Special Branch, is that correct?"

"*Probablement.* What do you wish to know?"

"Perhaps we could find somewhere less public. May I buy you another drink?"

The colonel remained seated and for a moment Padmore wondered if he had heard or possibly not understood his invitation. Eventually the man rose from his chair.

"This will do," he replied, raising his glass. "Where would you like to go, monsieur?"

"Perhaps into another room and farther away from the bar. Those airmen are creating quite a noise, don't you think?" Anticipating the need for privacy, he had earlier surveyed the lower floor of the hotel and found an unoccupied, small, unheated lounge off the main reception area to which he now led the colonel.

"Are you sure I can't buy you a drink, Colonel."

"This room is cold, is it not? Coffee might be more appropriate, that's if it's available."

"I shall see. Please, give me a moment."

The hotel having reluctantly supplied, what in late 1942 passed for coffee, Padmore opened the batting.

"I think you would agree, Colonel, that even during a war the death of any man is to be abhorred, particularly of one who has sought sanctuary in a country, wanting only peace from the ravages that may beset his country." Had he struck the right note with the colonel? He was perhaps being a little melodramatic, but Frenchmen were known romantics.

"If you are referring to Monsieur Bonoteaux, then 'sanctuaire' is not perhaps the appropriate word. What is it you want, monsieur? I have had a long day, and it would be best for us both if you came to the point. Is that possible?"

"Very well." Since first sighting the colonel, Padmore had been consciously trying to evaluate the man. Could he trust him? Clearly, he was every inch a career military officer and perhaps one who would look to the general first and politicians second. As with previous moments in his life, Padmore felt moved to play his hand. He would trust his instincts and reveal his mission.

"What I have to tell you has little if nothing to do with the death of Henri Bonoteaux. At least not as far as I know, but perhaps I may be wrong. I wonder, Colonel, if you have heard of Operation Pickaxe?"

"Operation Pickaxe? I don't think so." Padmore had closely watched the face of the Frenchman as he replied. Had he lied? He thought not.

"It is important that what I am about to tell you is relayed to your general, General de Gaulle, and to nobody else. Do you understand?"

"Go on."

Padmore paused. Should he continue without the man's assurance that he would do as asked? It wasn't too late to turn back. Could he trust this man? *Damn it all! Operation Pickaxe had to be terminated!*

"My government, in an act of utter stupidity, I might say, has entered into an agreement with the Russians to drop their agents, communist agents, into France, not only France, but also the Low Countries and even Austria, ostensibly to help the resistance movements in these countries, but we both know that the Russian agents' true mission is to establish covert cells so that when the war ends the communists will be in a position to seize power. Operation Pickaxe is a Trojan horse, Colonel, and a secret known only to a few. Many within the British government are unaware of its existence, as are all our allies. Most of all, your general doesn't know of it."

"Monsieur, may I see your identification?"

It was not the reply he had expected. He felt deflated. Fumbling for his identification, Padmore tried to recapture his vehemence.

"The general, once he hears of the arrangement between the Russian NKVD and our SOE, will want it stopped, immediately. Surely, you must agree, Colonel?"

The colonel paused before replying. "On whose orders do you tell me of this Operation Pickaxe? Who has told you to do so?"

"I act alone in this, Colonel. I'm not under orders, as you put it. The Foreign Office knows nothing of my approach to you." He paused. "You should know that my father was killed in Russia, at the hands of the communists. I have watched for years how they have infiltrated our unions, British industry, and our institutions. Your own country is infested with them, is it not? They have to be stopped. Operation Pickaxe has to be closed down, and once the general is made aware of it, then the Russians will be sent packing!"

"I see. I will not ask how you know of this operation, but tell me, how are these agents delivered to France? Are they dropped from the skies, or perhaps they arrive by boat?"

"Some are delivered by plane, by the same people who brought Monsieur Bonoteaux to England and who deliver your Free French agents to France. It is an SOE operation, Colonel. Your people have only to ask."

"Thank you, Monsieur Padmore. Was that all?"

"Isn't that enough!" The response he had received was not the one he had expected. Where was the shock, the surprise at such a revelation? "Don't you at least want to know how many have been dropped into your country?" Growing within him was the realisation that he might have done the wrong thing confiding in the colonel.

"You have the number?"

"Well no, but I'm sure it is not inconsiderable."

"Hundreds?"

"Perhaps not that many, but surely the numbers aren't important. It's the fact that it's going on at all. They are like rats. It only takes a few to spread the plague. The general would agree. He must be told."

"Monsieur Padmore, what you have told me, if correct, is a secret that was not yours to tell, I think. If I were to pass this 'secret' onto the general he might like to know where it came from, and where would that leave you with your superiors if, as I suspect, the 'secret' was not yours to tell?"

Scrambling to recover from the colonel's ambiguous reply, Padmore added, "Naturally I had hoped, Colonel, that it would remain between us that the general, once he heard of its existence, would be interested only in closing it down." It was all going wrong. This was not how he had envisaged the encounter.

"I think, monsieur, that you are not a stupid man, possibly naïve, but not stupid. However, you have allowed your dislike . . . No, that is not strong enough, your hatred for the communists, understandable in the circumstances, to cloud your judgement. You assume to know where my loyalty lies, and you are correct. It is the general who has my loyalty, but I have also a loyalty to France. All of France. Do you understand?"

No, he didn't. What did the colonel mean by 'all of France'?

"I think we should consider this conversation at an end, Monsieur Padmore."

"Do I have an understanding from you, Colonel, that you will deliver this information to the general?"

"I will think about it. That is all I will say. Good evening, monsieur."

Padmore could only watch as the Frenchman, into whose hands he had entrusted his career, left the small lounge. The room suddenly seemed even colder.

Chapter Seventeen

<u>Bedfordshire</u>

Sergeant Hodges was not a man to act unilaterally when working in tandem with a colleague, be he above or below his rank. Full cooperation between members of an investigation was the only way to proceed, as far as he was concerned. It was with this principle in mind that he had told Inspector Sim of his interest in talking again to Sergeant Ian Gifford, the pilot who had brought Bonoteaux to England. There was everything to be gained and nothing to lose from such a meeting since, if they were to be honest, the investigation into Bonoteaux's murder had not progressed very far. And so, with the approval of his inspector, Sergeant Hodges went in pursuit of a particular sergeant of the Royal Air Force, while his superior did battle over the phone with his own seniors and the SIS in London.

He found his quarry in the sergeants' mess, a requisitioned Georgian farmhouse not far from RAF Tempsford. Alone in the lounge, he was slouched in a large overstuffed armchair, his left leg slung over the armrest, his battle dress jacket unbuttoned, his face hidden behind a copy of the *Illustrated London News*. Al Bowlly could be heard on the wireless in another room, appropriately crooning 'Time on My Hands.'

"Sergeant Gifford, Sergeant Hodges of the Met. We met at Tempsford."

"That's right. What brings you here?"

"You. I wonder, could I have a word?"

"Sure. Is it okay here? As you see, we're not very busy. Being the only pilot in the mess, I pretty well have the place to myself during the day. All the other NCOs are off greasing the wheels, if you get my meaning."

"'Ere will be fine. I thought it might be beneficial to go over that flight again, the one you did with Bonoteaux."

"Why not, although there isn't much more I can tell you. You've heard just about all there is to tell. Take a seat. Why don't I see if there is some tea around here? They've only just stopped serving breakfast, so with luck the mess lads will still be in the kitchen."

"I'm fine, thank you. I 'aven't long 'ad breakfast myself. Let's go back to when Bonoteaux first appears on the ground in France." Were Inspector Sim present, he would not believe that his sergeant had actually turned down the offer of a cup of tea.

While Hodges took notes, Gifford again went through all he could remember concerning that flight. From memory it seemed to Hodges that there would be nothing new when he came to compare the two interviews. However, what followed was not only revelatory, but, in view of what the two smarmy gents from the SIS and the Air Liaison Officer at Tempsford had said, was also an abnegation of what they had all vehemently denied.

"Let me see if I've got this right, Sergeant."

"The name's Ian."

"Right, Ian. You flew a party of four communists, Germans—"

"Austrians."

"Sorry, Austrians, into France, where they were to be met by the communist resistance, who failed to turn up. Is that correct?"

"It's probably not something that I should be talking to you about, but it seems to me, having given it some thought, that as they were here, in the area at the time your Frenchman had his throat cut, it may be of interest. What do you think?"

"It's certainly worth considering."

"Would I be right in assuming that nobody else has told you about the Austrians?"

"You would be right."

"I thought so. That's why I've stuck my neck out and mentioned it."

"You say there were four of them."

"That's right, three guys and a woman."

"Rather a lot to get into one of your small planes, isn't it?"

"The Lizzie? No, I took them across in a Hudson. As I said, a couple of them wanted to come back with us, but I had a return load and there wasn't room, even if I had been willing to take them, which I wasn't."

"Right. Thank you, Ian. You've been a great 'elp. I 'ope we won't need to bother you again."

"That's all right. As I said, I'm not sure I should have talked to you about the Austrians, the Official Secrets Act and all that, but if I hadn't mentioned it you probably wouldn't have found out about it. It being hush-hush and all."

"You're right. Nobody needs to know where we got the info from, okay?"

"That's all right by me."

"Was that the first group of communists you've flown to France?"

"As far as I am aware, but how would you know?"

"Exactly. I don't suppose you could tell me where the group were accommodated before the flight?"

"No idea, but SOE would have all that info. You need to ask them. It was their show."

"Thanks, I will." Hodges rose to leave. "Tell me, when it's all over, do you plan to return to Canada?"

"Absolutely. If it weren't for Hitler I wouldn't be here now. The longer I spend in this country, the more I'm convinced that nothing short of a revolution will change things. No offence intended. When this war's over, you see, the same old crowd will still be running the show. I guess it's all right if you're one of them, but I'm not, nor do I want to be. You know what I mean?"

"Yes, I do, Ian." They held similar pessimistic views on the future of the country, two men but of one mind with regard to social justice.

"Canada's more open. A lot of this stuff just isn't there, at least not in BC. You can be or do whatever you want."

"Sounds invitin'."

"It is. You know, Sergeant, instead of your daughter returning to England after the war, why not join her in, Toronto, wasn't it?"

"Yes. I'll give it some thought."

"You could join the Mounties."

"I think I'm a little too long in the tooth for that, besides, I don't quite see myself on a sledge in the frozen North. Thanks for your 'elp, Ian."

"Any time."

Inspector Sim viewed his morning as one might who had backed the third horse across the line in a three-horse race. There was little to shout about, although he had unearthed a nugget of information that might lead somewhere, quite where that would be he wasn't sure. It was possible that they had found the motive behind the murder. Earlier, before speaking with SIS on the phone, he had told himself not to become agitated. There were few things these days that upset him. He had reached that stage in life when he was able to look on most things dispassionately. Matters that once may have sparked within him a fervent response no longer did so. Not now. But dealing with SIS seemed to set him off and awake within him something that normally lay dormant. Today's encounter had been no exception, although he liked to think he had remained totally in control of his emotions. Whether the SIS were of the same opinion he would never know. First, he had spoken with his superiors in Special Branch, from whom he had gleaned one salient fact. Henri Bonoteaux was suspected of being a double agent, and at the time of his death SOE was about to be told that he would not be returning to France, as scheduled. Why Special Branch had not informed the inspector of this development was not explained. And, when Sim attempted to confirm the suspicion surrounding Bonoteaux with SIS, they wouldn't comment. It had been an SIS flight that had brought him to England, and, presumably, it would have been an SIS flight that returned him to France. Sim may not have been sufficiently important, in the grand scheme of things, to have been told of the distrust surrounding the French agent, but SIS would certainly be high on the list, that's if they weren't the first to be alert to his treachery. He was, after all, their agent.

If Bonoteaux was working for the Germans, then it fell within Special Branch's purview. SIS did not have the power of arrest, neither did Five. Why had London failed to pass on to him this important piece of information? The more he thought of it the more he became convinced that SIS was aware of Bonoteaux's duplicity, if not before his arrival in England, then certainly since. It was even possible that the two SIS wallies he had met at Tempsford, Padmore and colleague, knew at the time of their meeting about Bonoteaux's treachery. This development put the case in a new light. It was now more than likely that the man was murdered because of the double game he was playing. As to which side was responsible for his death was anybody's guess.

He was finishing lunch, a vegetable soup accompanied by fresh home-made bread, when the sergeant returned to the hotel.

"Sergeant, you're back. Have you had lunch?"

"Not yet, sir. What's on the menu?"

"Soup of the day, and it's not bad. Vegetable, I think. I would order now, before it all goes. By the way, you've had another phone call. Someone still trying to contact you. They didn't leave a message."

"Thank you. I can't think who it can be. The Met know I'm 'ere, at least I suppose they do." He hoped that nothing had happened to his daughter in Canada but reasoned that, if that were the case, whoever called would have left at least a contact number, if not a message.

Not wanting to disturb his sergeant's appetite, Inspector Sim waited until he had finished his lunch before breaking into his news of the day.

"I rang our superiors and SIS this morning." Looking around to make sure they could not be overheard, he continued. "It seems our Henri was playing a double game. They thought it would help with our enquiries if we knew."

"You mean 'e was working for the—"

"Quite. His return ticket had been cancelled and no refund."

"And nobody thought to tell us till now!"

"It would seem so. This particular piece of news came from Special Branch. I can only presume that both SIS and SOE have since been informed. SIS had no comment to make, as you would expect."

"Do you think those two smarmy gents from SIS, the ones we met at Tempsford, knew about 'enri's little game when we talked with them?"

"Possibly. After all, he was their agent. However, as I said, when I challenged them earlier today they wouldn't comment. There's something about the SIS that sets me off, Sergeant. What is it, do you think?"

"I couldn't say, sir, but I 'ad noticed."

"At least we now have a possible motive for the murder."

"And we 'ave a suspect or suspects."

"Really? What have you learnt, Sergeant?"

"Do you remember, both the Air Liaison Officer at Tempsford and our two smarmy gents denied any official contact with the communists?"

"Yes. They seemed affronted that we should even suggest it."

"Well, it seems SOE has been working with the Russians."

"What?"

"Yes. Dropping communist agents into France."

"Where did this information come from, Sergeant?"

"Sergeant Gifford, the pilot who brought 'enri over from France. 'E recently delivered four agents, Austrians, took 'em over in an 'udson. Apparently they weren't too 'appy about it either. Two of 'em wanted to come straight back."

"Do you know, was it an SIS or an SOE operation?"

"SOE, sir."

"And they were here at Tempsford at the time Henri was murdered?"

"That I can't say, but SOE could tell us if that's the case."

"Are you saying that it could have been one of the communist agents who did poor old Henri in?"

"It's possible. It's a bit of a long shot, but you never know, do you, sir. If they left from Tempsford, which they did, then they were billeted somewhere close by before their flight. But if it was one of them, 'ow did they know 'e was 'ere, 'enri, I mean, in Milton Ernest? They 'adn't been long in the country. To pull it off they would've 'ad to 'ave someone in SOE working for 'em, someone who knew where 'e was staying." Sergeant Hodges did not elaborate, but it was at that point that an intriguing thought first crept into his mind, one that he would prefer not to think about and certainly one he would not share with his inspector, at least not at this time.

"True. Although, if the Russians are involved, we can't discount the participation of their security people working from their embassy in London. They would know, through SOE, where Henri was billeted. Odd thing to do, though, drop Austrians into France, don't you think?"

"I suppose so. Do you think that we should find out from SOE where these Austrians were at the time of 'is death?"

"That's if they'll tell us. And, in view of what we now know of Henri's duplicity, I think it might be a good idea to have another chat with that French colonel. Perhaps we'll do that next. What was his name?"

"Jean-Guy Bernard, sir, 'es staying at the Swan in Bedford."

"Well done, Sergeant. Let's get started. What did you think of the soup?"

"Not at all bad, sir. The 'ome-made bread was a bit of all right. Where do you think 'e gets the flour from?"

"Don't ask, Sergeant."

Chapter Eighteen

Angers, France

Monsieur Galtier's farm was sufficiently isolated that ample warning could normally be given, should either the Germans or Vichy approach. As for fellow resisters, it was a little more complicated. Screening such visitors at a distance was problematic. Even those who were known to his group as loyal Frenchmen could have changed sides. The communists, who were periodically active in their area, felt free to come and go as they pleased, given to pushing their weight around, always challenging. For them it was all-out war against the occupation, their actions being driven by principle rather than consequence, as a result of which many innocent lives were lost through German reprisals. To them it mattered little that for the murder of one German soldier twelve local townsfolk were put up against a wall and shot. Following his last encounter with them, when they had come for the four Austrians and had been forced to depart with only two, he had expected a further visit from the *Parti communiste française*, the PCF. When they did appear, it was late one evening during a winter storm, and not the sort of weather in which to make a social call. The sentry in the wood behind the farm had been taken by surprise, being more interested in keeping dry than sentinelling. He had, however, fired off a warning shot before being bludgeoned with the butt of an old muzzle-loader. Galtier, seated in front of his fire in the farmhouse, couldn't be

185

sure that what he heard was a rifle shot, what with the sound of the pelting rain on the kitchen roof and the wind in the trees. Being a cautious man, he rose from his chair and called his small group together.

Shortly after the departure of their comrades and Milch's return from the forest, he had allowed the two Austrians to take up residence in the house. Galtier, although remaining suspicious of their intentions, had taken pity on them, the barn being no place in which even communist Boche should spend too many winter nights. Freda had broken away from her afferent behaviour and would openly discuss politics with her captors in fractured French and English, although that was not how either now viewed Galtier. He had become to them, just as he had been from the beginning, their protector. Neither were interested in joining forces with the PCF, and both were aware that their best chance of survival rested, for the present, with Monsieur Galtier and his men.

They were in the upstairs portion of the house when they were made aware of hurried movements on the stairs and men calling out below, followed by the sound of a breaking window and the splintering of a door, then the discharge of a revolver. Both looked at the other and sat motionless. More raised voices. More loud footsteps on the uncarpeted stairs. Suddenly the door to their room burst open, blowing out the lamp. The drenched figure of a man stood in the doorway, pointing a rifle at them.

"*Partons!*" he yelled. "*Maintenant.*"

Neither of them moved.

"*Kommen!*" he repeated. "*Schnell!*"

Downstairs they found the small kitchen crowded. Galtier and four of his men, all disarmed, were lined up against a wall, facing six armed members of the PCF, menacingly brandishing their assortment of weapons.

"*Là-bas*," one of the communists said to them, gesturing towards the damaged door with his rifle.

Freda and Milch moved cautiously across the crowded room. Galtier had four disarmed men against six armed of the PCF; it was an uneven match. Missing from the gathering, Milch noticed, was the short bald man who had been given the task of feeding them when they were in the barn. A heated discussion now erupted between the usually reserved Galtier and one of the communists. The exchange concerned Milch and Freda, who, Galtier was attempting to point out, had no wish to depart with the men of the PCF. It was a view she must have passed on to Galtier during their discussions, but it was one lost on his protagonists. They were leaving with the communists, whether they wished to or not. Their value to the cause was no longer relevant; it was a point of honour. The verballing ended when a shot was fired into the roof, showering everyone in plaster and at the same time extinguishing the lamp, plunging the room into darkness. A moment of silence followed before chaos ensued.

"*Sortez! Maintenant!*" yelled the man who had fired the shot.

Milch pushed open the door that hung broken on its hinges and thrust Freda out, quickly following her into the windswept pitch-dark night of the yard. The storm, far from abating, had intensified, and horizontal rain squalls propelled them away from the house. Behind them men were spilling out of the kitchen into the driving rain and onto the slippery cobblestones, their raised voices lost in the wind. It was not a night in which to be out and about, and Milch was unsure of the farm's geography. Freda, on the other hand, seemed to know which way they should go. Taking his arm, she directed him towards some small huts, the outlines of which came into view as they ran hunched against the elements. Ignoring the nearest, she shoved him through a small aperture into the second, quickly entering behind him. The hut was no more than one and a half metres high, forcing them to crouch. It smelt of pig. Both remained silent, the rain and wind on the tin above them providing all the acoustics. But it was dry, and by edging their way farther into the hut, away from the entrance, they would be free of the penetrating wind. There was no physical evidence of the hut's previous occupants, only the strong odour exuding from the straw beneath them. Freda, in a rare moment of communication, explained in a whisper that, during Milch's abortive trip into the forest to interrogate the two German soldiers, Galtier had taken her on a guided tour of the farm, explaining, among other things, how he had slaughtered his pigs and sold the meat rather than have it requisitioned by the Germans.

In the early hours of the morning, the rain ceased and the wind lessened. At dawn a weak wintery sun decided to shine on their portion of France, exposing the damage wrought by the storm. Milch and Freda carefully made their way back to the farmhouse, at one point clambering over a fallen tree. There was no sign of the communists. Entering the kitchen, they found Galtier making coffee.

"*Bonjour*," he said without looking up.

"*Qu'est qui s'est passe?*" Freda enquired.

"Your French is improving, madam. Any better and we can stop speaking this damnable English, although you, monsieur, you must try harder, or do you intend to stay silent till the end of the war? Yuck! You both smell of pig! No need to ask where you spent the night."

"It was not very comfortable, monsieur," Freda replied.

"My pigs never complained. Our communist visitors decided to leave us in peace, after a little persuasion. I don't think they'll be returning for you. Pity France if they should take over after the war. The man who was keeping watch in the forest was badly injured by them. We will not forget. It is possible that they will sell us out to the authorities. We will have to be careful." Galtier poured thick black acorn coffee into two chipped cups, putting them on the bench for Milch and Freda to help themselves.

Taking a cup, Milch asked Freda to translate for him. 'When we came down to the kitchen last night one of your men was missing. The man who fed us when we were in the barn. Was he the one injured in the forest?'

Freda quickly passed on Milch's inquiry.

"Gaston!" Galtier spat out the name and then, as if to emphasise his feelings, spat onto the floor. "No. It was Gaston who helped the communists through the woods. He has become a traitor. We were together at school. Of all my men, I thought he could be trusted. War does strange things to a man."

Chapter Nineteen

SIS HQ, Broadway Buildings, St. James Park, London

Adrian J. Padmore didn't have to wait long before the consequences of his discussion with Colonel Jean-Guy Bernard of the Free French became apparent. Summoned to the fifth floor by his department head, Padmore entered and was invited to sit. Others in the room, along with the head of his department, Walter Maurice Cavendish-Brown, were the director representing C, and a secretary. Padmore nodded to both men, neither of whom returned his greeting. The secretary, a middle-aged spinster of no known parish, didn't look up from her pad.

"I'll get straight to the point, Padmore. You have been interfering in matters that are not of your concern. You recently met, in Bedford, with a Colonel Bernard of the Free French. Is that correct?"

The subject of the question was not unexpected. After his meeting with the French colonel he had returned home to London and that evening told his wife, Emma, who had attended St Leonards, of his visit to Bedford. He had done so believing that whatever happened from then on could greatly affect his career and so the rest of his family. If the worst happened, he would be unable to hide the outcome from Emma. He reasoned that if Emma was forewarned the storm that may follow would be less severe. Once her dander was up she could be fearsome.

Barely had he left the Swan Hotel before realising that what he had just done was probably the most foolish thing possible. Whatever made him think that the colonel would react as per the script he had envisaged? He had received no assurance from the man that he would pass on to the general the information concerning Operation Pickaxe, and yet Adrian J. Padmore had placed his career on the line. It and the not unpleasant life his family was able to enjoy, in spite of the war, he had placed into the hands of a complete stranger. What had he been thinking of? There would be an almighty stink if his superior were to hear of his indiscretion, something which he now knew, as he left the hotel, was more than likely. And now thought had become fact.

Emma, unknowing of his work, had sat frozen to her seat when he explained. The man to whom she was married was not the career climber she had hoped he would be, but what he had now done was to risk what little progress he had made within the FO. She was not amused. Those within her circle of acquaintances, whose husbands were not fortunate enough to work for the FO, would be similarly unimpressed if it all went bad, something which Adrian seem to think was more than probable. And how would she face other FO wives that she met from time to time at the bridge club? Having married and given up a promising career in children's publishing, she was reliant upon Adrian for her position within wartime London society. What had he been thinking of? The evening had ended with Adrian sleeping on the couch.

"Yes," he confessed. "The colonel and I met at the Swan Hotel in Bedford."

"Yet you chose not to write a report on the matter, or inform your superiors."

"I can explain—"

Walter Maurice Cavendish-Brown silenced Padmore with a dismissive wave of his hand.

"Was this meeting at your behest, Padmore?"

"Yes," again.

"And what was the purpose of this meeting?"

His boss knew the purpose, Padmore could feel it. The director knew also. Only the secretary was in the dark, though possibly even she had been informed. What was their point in pretending otherwise? Perhaps if he were allowed to explain why, he might be able to salvage something from the meeting. After all, he had spoken to the colonel out of concern for his country. He had nothing to gain personally. Had he acted out of concern for his country, or was it more out of his hatred for communism? Patriotism was his best defence.

"I thought that General de Gaulle should be made aware of Operation Pickaxe, sir."

"I see. And on whose authority did you approach the colonel?"

"I used my initiative, sir. It seemed the right thing to do. Of course, I realise that in so doing I may have put my esteem within the service at risk."

"Loyalty to country before the Foreign Service, is that how you see it, Padmore?"

"Yes. I suppose I do, sir." Given that he had no other defence, it wasn't bad.

"Some may think that admirable, but I do not! Any officer with divided loyalty is no good to the service." After a pause, he continued. "What did you hope to achieve by your action?"

"I thought that once the general knew about Pickaxe he would bring an end to it, sir."

"And you thought it your place to act unilaterally, without authority?"

"I have always thought that personal initiative was encouraged within the service, sir."

"You have, have you? Tell me, what makes you think the general doesn't already know about the operation you were so keen to see terminated, assuming such an operation exists?"

"Well, sir, I believe that if he had known about it the operation would have been closed down, it being not in the interest of France."

"You know that for a fact, do you? You know what is best for France?"

"Well, no sir. The communists—"

"Your feelings about communism," Cavendish-Brown interrupted, "are known to me, Padmore." At this point he consulted some papers that lay before him. "I see from your file that your father was killed by the Bolsheviks, something that may have coloured your thinking and influenced your judgement. Be that as it may, let me tell you something about how we as a service stand with the Soviets. In the days ahead, it might help you to understand the damage you have attempted to inflict on HMG, albeit unwittingly. As a service we have insubstantial contacts in the Soviet Union. Much of the information we receive comes to us through SOE's mission in Moscow. Their contact with the NKVD is priceless to our understanding of what is going on in Russia. I take it you know of the position the NKVD holds within the Soviet Union. Apart from Stalin and a few of his cronies, they control all life in Russia. No Russian can so much as pass wind without their knowing. SOE is the only British organisation the NKVD recognise and will have any dealings with. Central to this is the agreement the SOE has with the NKVD. If that agreement were to flounder, then not only we in SIS but also HMG would suffer a loss of much-needed intelligence. I'm aware that were such an operation to exist it would not be universally popular, particularly with some of the country sections within SOE, in particular the French section. That's not our concern. Nor should it have been yours! You have acted in a disloyal manner to the service, Padmore, and that is reprehensible. Do you have anything to add?" he said, looking at the director.

"No, I don't think so, except to say, 'He who meddles in a quarrel not his own is like one who takes a passing dog by the ears." Silence ensued. It was a euphemism lost on all other than the deliverer.

"Thank you for that. What about you, Padmore? Do you want to add anything more to this pitiful mess in which you find yourself?"

What was he to say? Principle, he would stand or fall on that. What else did he have? Clearly Walter Maurice Cavendish-Brown wasn't impressed by his argument, but if only to save face he would continue to push it for all it was worth.

"I hope, sir, that, if I were confronted with a similar situation I would make the same choice, as a matter of principle. My country above all else."

"Yes, yes, yes. We know all about your principles, Padmore, and look where they have got you. Loyalty, that's what the service expects from its officers, and you have displayed a lamentable lack of that particular quality. Enough. This is what is going to happen. You are suspended from the SIS as from today, and I shall do my utmost to see that you do not return. Clear your office and be out of this building by lunchtime. Personnel will contact you. Fortunately for you the manpower shortage in the FO means that you can re-muster with them. I understand they have a position in Birmingham, in their General Department, dealing with the Ministries of Supply and Economic Warfare. I suggest you take it. You shouldn't get into too much trouble there. May I remind you of the documents you signed when you joined the service. You will not utter a word ever, to anyone, about your work or that carried out by the service. Do you understand?"

"Yes, sir."

"Good. Your card is marked, Padmore. Remember that. You're dismissed."

After he had left and the secretary had returned to her office to type up Padmore's suspension, Cavendish-Brown and the director lit up their pipes and sat back in their chairs. A full four minutes elapsed before the silence was broken by Cavendish-Brown.

"Can't stand disloyalty."

"I know what you mean, Walter." After a pause, "Padmore, strange chap. Oxford, wasn't he?"

"I believe so." After a further pause, he continued. "The FO's General Department is a good place for him."

"Do you know what? I think I knew somebody who used to work there, not in Birmingham, you understand. Whitehall. Might still be there. Haven't seen him at the club for ages. Donald Maclean. He was Cambridge, though. Married an American woman, as I remember. Got into some trouble with his ambassador while serving at the embassy in Paris, just as the Germans marched in. Wasn't invited into the new French Department when they set it up. Ended up with the General Department. Getting back to Pickaxe, SOE's man in Moscow. Bit of a worry."

"Absolutely. Far too sympathetic towards his hosts. Needs to be watched. I take it—"

"Absolutely, Walter, it's in hand. What are you doing for lunch?"

One hour later, Adrian J. Padmore left Broadway Buildings for the last time. What he had feared the most had happened and all because – because of what? His personal crusade against communism? This was turning out to be one of the darkest days of his life, and it was just about to get darker. He had yet to face Emma, who had attended St Leonards. She would not like Birmingham!

Chapter Twenty

The Swan Hotel, Bedford, Bedfordshire

It was early evening by the time the two policemen took up space in the lounge of the Swan Hotel. The bosomy receptionist had been unable to tell them when the French colonel would be returning. However, since taking up residence at the Swan he had been a regular at the dinner table. Both men settled down to wait in armchairs, each clutching a glass of ale. The close proximity of other patrons excluded any discussion of the case, leaving both policemen free to think their own thoughts. Across the reception hall, in the front bar, bomber aircrew from local airdromes were assembling and beginning to warm up for an evening of rowdy relaxation.

It was 18.30 before the colonel put in an appearance.

"Good evening, Colonel. I hope we're not imposing upon you, but something has come up that requires some clarification." Nicely put, thought Sergeant Hodges, although quite how the military gent in the jodhpurs was going to take the news that a fellow countryman was a double agent was open to question. "Is there somewhere we can talk?"

Minutes later the colonel had escorted them to the same small unheated lounge where, on another day, he and Adrian J. Padmore had spoken.

"How may I help you, Inspector? We are both busy men, so let us hope we can conclude this meeting as soon as possible."

Sergeant Hodges wondered what it was that kept the colonel in such a state of busyness? What did he do apart from walking around England looking like an actor who had just left the set of *Beau Geste*? But he did agree with the colonel concerning the need to keep their meeting brief; the room was cold and the springs of the worn armchair in which he sat were punishing.

"Henri Bonoteaux. We understand that he was not only working for us but also for the Germans. He was a double agent. Quite when this disturbing news became known to our security people I can't say, but, at the time of his death, the British authorities had cancelled his return flight to France. Were you aware of this?"

"Who has said this, or is it speculation?"

"I'm afraid it is not speculation, Colonel. Would you mind answering the question?"

"Which was?"

"Did you know that Bonoteaux's was a German agent?"

"No."

To Sergeant Hodges, even Marcel Gillier, the waiter, was a better liar.

"But if I did know, would that make me a suspect in your enquiries?"

"Not necessarily, but if you had known, I'm sure you would have had your own good reasons for not telling the sergeant and me. But I ask myself, who else knew? It could mean we now have a motive for his murder. Wouldn't you agree?"

"It's possible."

"When we last spoke, you thought that it could be a rival resistance group who had killed Bonoteaux."

"Did I say that? You must have misunderstood me, Inspector. If what you say is true, then maybe we cannot rule out the Boche. Maybe he was going to tell all to British intelligence."

"That is a possibility, I agree." Pause. "What do you know about Russian communist agents being dropped into France by SOE?"

The Frenchman sat back in his chair and examined the two policemen. Withdrawing a cigarette case from the flap pocket of his tunic, he asked, "Do you mind?"

"No, not at all, Colonel."

Studiously affixing a Gilanes Brunes to the end of a gold cigarette holder, he then lit his cigarette. After a while he replied, "Until a few days ago I knew nothing about the Russian operation. Then a man, who I think you know, Inspector, came here to this hotel and told me about these agents. I believe they are part of something called Operation Pickaxe."

"That's interesting. Why do you think he came to you, Colonel?"

"He believed that if General de Gaulle knew of this secret operation he would stop it."

"And he wanted you to tell your general?"

"Exactly."

"And the name of this man that you met here at the hotel?"

"Padmore."

The two policemen exchanged glances.

"And did you pass this information on to the general?" Sergeant Hodges enquired.

"That is of no interest to you, Sergeant." The slap down was not the first Hodges had experienced in his career when dealing with those who thought themselves superior. It was something of a relief to know the caste system was alive and well among the French as well as among his own tribe.

"At around the time Bonoteaux was killed," the inspector continued, "four Russian agents may have been billeted close by. If so, it is possible that one of them was the murderer. All

199

four were later flown to France by our air force from RAF Tempsford. They were not the first group of Russian agents to have been flown into France. And you claim to know nothing about these operations?" The inspector's tone bordered on being accusatory.

"I have already told you. Until this man Padmore told me, I knew nothing about Operation Pickaxe."

"So you say."

"I am not used to having my word doubted, Inspector."

Pause.

"I'm having trouble trying to understand how it is over there. We must assume that these Russian agents are met on arrival in France by fellow believers, communist resisters, but yet these airfields are run by our SOE, with whom, I would presume, your people cooperate. And you're saying that the Free French know nothing of these flights? I'm sorry, Colonel. I'm finding that hard to believe."

"If you knew how matters stand in France, you would not find it so hard to believe. The communists do not always cooperate. No, I will say that they never cooperate with us. Your SOE and SIS also run their operations without consulting us. There is little liaison between the Free French and your people. There are many parallel lines, seldom do they converge, Inspector."

"May I ask, Colonel, what is your opinion of Operation Pickaxe? Do you approve of the dropping of Russian agents into France to help fight Germany?"

"My opinion is of no importance, Inspector, but, since you ask, no, I do not approve. The communists would like to take over my country when the war is over. They have made no secret of it. If these agents are trained by the Russians, it is not to fight the Germans but to act as political agents, to spread their message of revolution among the French people."

"So you believe that if the general knew about Operation Pickaxe he would have it stopped?"

"That is not what I said. Speculating on whether the general would or would not approve will not help you, Inspector. It has nothing to do with the death of Henri Bonoteaux."

"I'm not so sure about that, Colonel."

"I cannot say what the general would do if he knew, that is assuming he doesn't already. I know that the *Comité français de Libération nationale,* the CFNL, would not have given their approval."

"I see. Is it possible that the CFNL may have known but not the general?"

"I think not, Inspector."

"So, we may assume that neither the CFNL nor the general knows of the operation. Thank you, Colonel."

"And am I right to think that without the Russian agents you have nothing? No one else is in the frame. Isn't that what the Americans say?"

"I wouldn't say that exactly. There are other possibilities."

"Really? These four Russian agents of whom you speak, I think, Inspector, that is all you have. They were Frenchmen?"

"Austrian."

"Austrian. That is interesting. Why would the Russians drop four Austrian agents into France?"

"I have no idea, Colonel, unless they were to pretend to be part of the occupation."

"Why don't I believe that? Can you tell me when and where in France they were dropped?"

The inspector looked to his sergeant, who could only shrug his shoulders. He should have asked Sergeant Gifford, but such questions had not seemed sufficiently important at the time.

"No matter. Perhaps your friend Mr. Padmore could have provided me with the answer. I will make some inquiries. Was that all?" the colonel said, reaching for his kepi as he stood to leave.

"I think so. Do you have anything you would like to add, Sergeant?"

"No, I don't think so, sir." There was much he would like to have asked the colonel, but he knew his place.

"Then I wish you all the best with your search for whoever killed Bonoteaux, Inspector. I will be returning to London soon. Let us hope we are successful. Please keep me informed."

With the departure of the colonel and having no wish to spend any longer than was necessary in the cold lounge, not to mention the discomfort of Sergeant Hodge's armchair, both men moved back to the warmer front lounge and thoughts of food. Across the reception area, in the front bar, male voices were lustfully offering up the second verse of 'Once There Was A NAAFI Girl.'

"What do you say to dinner in Bedford, Sergeant? We should be able to find somewhere to eat. By the time we get back to Milton Ernest we'll have missed the boat."

"We could always 'ave dinner 'ere, sir. What do you think?"

"No, I don't think so. We'll run into the colonel if we do, and I would rather not. Let's see what's on offer in Bedford, and tomorrow we'll find out what SOE has to say about our recent visitors from Russia."

As the colonel mounted the stairs to his room, leaving the two policemen to do whatever such men are driven to do in pursuit of the truth, his immediate surroundings, the faded décor and worn carpet, reminded him of another hotel in another town and the momentous events of that evening.

Chapter Twenty-One

The Hotel Normandy, Bordeaux, France

Early hours of the 17th June 1940

Minutes before, the youngest general in the French army, Charles de Gaulle, known as The Constable of France, had preceded him up the same stairs. He was grateful to have found a bed for the night in a city that, like the rest of the country, was falling apart. Packed with refugees as well as remnants of both the French and British armies, with the government of France thrown in for good measure, the city was in chaos and covered by a pall of smoke trapped beneath a cloud cover of low stratus, removing any chance of moonlight. Lawless elements were out on the streets, eager to use the situation to their own advantage. Twice on his way to the Hotel Normandy, while pushing through parked vehicles stacked high with the worldly possessions of displaced French families, he had been forced to draw his revolver, once to dissuade a group of drunken matelots from attempting to break into a jewellery shop, the second to ward off two British soldiers intent on robbing some refugees sheltering for the night in a doorway.

When Charles de Gaulle, returning from London, landed at Mérignac Airport, twelve kilometres west of Bordeaux, at 22.00 hrs the 16th June, Major Jean-Guy Bernard, having been forewarned of his arrival, was there, not to meet him but to observe his arrival. His self- appointed mission was to protect the general from falling into the hands of the defeatists, those who wanted to throw in the towel and surrender to Germany. The general's safety was only assured as long as he was a member of the government, but once that legal nicety vanished, that appeaser, General Weygand, the commander in chief, would pounce.

A little while later, at 22.30 hrs, Pétain, the hero of Verdun, became head of state, just thirty minutes after de Gaulle had stepped back onto French soil. From that moment the fate of France and the general was sealed. Pétain brought into his cabinet a cabal of traitors, including Laval, Weygand, Darlan, and Bouthillier. All talk of a Briton redoubt, a last-ditch stand to halt the German advance, was replaced with calls for an armistice, something Weygand had been promoting for weeks. France was now both politically and militarily defeated.

General de Gaulle was met at Mérignac by his head of military staff, who told him of Premier Reynaud's resignation, which effectively meant that the general was no longer a member of government, a position he had held for all of ten days. Through an aide, Bernard had heard of the French premier's resignation prior to leaving for the airport, which meant that de Gaulle could be arrested at any moment, now that he was stripped of his immunity. While waiting for the general's aircraft to land, he had stood in the shadow of a large wooden hangar ruminating on the events that had led up to the perilous situation his country now faced and what his own future would be.

Unlike de Gaulle, he had not attended the Saint-Cyr military academy but had gone to Saint-Maixent-l'École, where NCOs were trained for higher rank. At twenty-five, he had been commissioned and posted to an artillery unit, first in Valence and then in Douai. Like de Gaulle, his mentor had been Emile Mayer, a military theorist who also advocated for a strong air force. Such a need was obvious to Bernard but a blind spot in de Gaulle's thinking. For all his failure to see the need for air superiority, de Gaulle influenced the younger Jean-Guy Bernard with his writing: *Vers l'armée de métier, Le Fil de l'Epée,* and, most important of all, *La France et son armée,* to the extent that he saw de Gaulle as the one man within the French military establishment with foresight, who had not only seen the need for reform but how it should be carried out. The French high command, however, didn't agree with de Gaulle, a man who was possibly the greatest theoretician in Europe on the tactics of armoured formations. The army was simply unwilling to accept change. If they failed to grasp de Gaulle's theories on tank warfare, as expressed in his writing, such was not the case in Berlin, where they were avidly digested. Before the war he had called for the establishment of armoured divisions within the army, but when the first shot was fired France was without one armoured division. The Germans, who had taken de Gaulle's pronouncements to heart, had six.

For Bernard it was imperative that the general should realise his destiny and go on to save his country, no matter that those who had served under him would run a mile rather than repeat the experience. It was known throughout the army that the general was not an easy man with whom to work, as many in London were about to find out. Bernard had never been directly under his command, so had been spared the man's arrogance and idiosyncrasies.

Later that evening, at 23.00 hrs in Bordeaux, de Gaulle met with some of his supporters before calling on the soon-to-be-replaced Premier Reynaud in a villa requisitioned by the government. Bernard found himself the observer yet again, this time from across the street under a tall oak. For the next half hour he stood watching civilians and military personnel coming and going from the building. At one point a lorry containing military policemen slowly drove by. Had Weygand sent them to arrest not only the general but possibly also Reynaud? They drove on. The rear lights of their vehicle had barely disappeared when the night sky to the north, towards Blaye, suddenly lit up in a momentary blaze of flame and light. A fuel dump had been set ablaze to prevent it falling into German hands.

At just before midnight, de Gaulle, accompanied by one other, left the villa and walked to the Hôtel Montré, with Bernard in pursuit. Following them into the hotel, he observed a meeting in one of the hotel's reception rooms between the general, Sir Ronald Campbell, the British Ambassador, and the corpulent Sir Edward Spears, Churchill's appointed personal representative with the French government. Retreating to a small alcove beneath the main staircase, from where he could not be seen and yet watch, Bernard wondered if this was how he was to spend the night. Less than an hour later, de Gaulle and the man who had accompanied him from the villa, someone who he later identified as Lieutenant Geoffroy Chodron de Courcel, left the Montré and walked to the Hotel Normandy, where both men spent the night. It was on their way to the Normandy that Bernard had been forced to draw his revolver. Throughout their nocturnal perambulations neither the general nor his lieutenant seemed to be aware that they were being followed, both strangely oblivious of the tumult that surrounded them.

With all rooms occupied, Bernard was forced to spend what was left of the night on a lounger in a reception area crammed with as many as could fit into the small space. The city was filling up with those who mistakenly thought that where their government was there also was safety. The next three days would prove them wrong. At six o'clock, the general and de Courcel left the Hotel Normandy. Had it not been for a Zouave major dropping a dispatch box onto his head, Bernard would have slept in and missed their departure.

The two men returned to the hotel Montré a little after seven o'clock but not before stopping en route at the offices of the prefecture, from which they emerged with two large boxes. Waiting for them outside of the hotel was Spears. Bernard watched as the large boxes and a number of cases were loaded into one car. De Gaulle, de Courcel, and Spears climbed into another with its owner behind the wheel, de Courcel sitting in the passenger seat and the general in the rear. Since arriving in Bordeaux, Bernard had acquired a 500 cc Peugeot motorcycle, one of the first models produced by Peugeot after it had absorbed Automoto. The machine proved its worth on the overcrowded roads, and he had little trouble following the shrouded lights of the two cars. At first he thought they were heading for the port, possibly to board a ship for Algiers or England, but then it became clear that the destination was the airfield at Mérignac. There they were stopped at the gate by a guard, who after a few minutes let them pass. Bernard had no such problems and was quickly waved through. The airfield was in a state of disarray and confusion with abandoned vehicles and masses of people milling around, most hoping for a flight out that would never materialise. A number of aircraft, most of which were unserviceable, were parked on the hard. Off to the northern end of the grass cross runway a Dewoitine D.520., a French-built fighter introduced into service that year, lay on the grass with its wheels retracted. Engineers were attempting to raise the aircraft using a makeshift crane, a Heath Robinson affair that had little chance of success. To Bernard, the damaged Dewoitine signified at one and the same time all that was right and all that was wrong with French air power. It was a good aircraft, one that could hold its own against Germany's best fighters, but at the outbreak of war only thirty-six had been put into service. Since nationalisation of the aircraft production industry in the mid-thirties, only a dribble of modern combat aircraft had been produced. In the spring of 1940 the French air force consisted of only 550 aircraft, of which the majority were obsolete.

The two cars had come to rest beside a biplane of the Royal Air Force, a Dominie, or DH89, in civilian life a Dragon Rapide. Its pilot, who had spent the night in the aircraft, was pointing at the baggage being unloaded from one of the cars. As Bernard sat on his motorcycle some distance away he saw Lieutenant de Courcel leave the group and run over to a hangar. Spears began pacing back and forth, clearly disturbed by the delay, and he kept glancing towards the road leading to the operational area. While the pilot loaded the baggage into the aircraft, the general was like an aurochs, unmoved by the events taking place around him. Eventually de Courcel reappeared, running between the parked aircraft clutching a ball of twine. The pilot ran to meet him. Minutes later, with the baggage now safely stowed, de Gaulle boarded the plane. As he stepped up into the aircraft he slowly turned around and, looking directly at Bernard, nodded before disappearing into the cabin. De Courcel and the pilot followed. The two Gipsy Queen engines, each able to generate 200 hp, burst into life and the aircraft began to taxi while Spears returned to his car. As the Dominie neared the end of the runway, Bernard saw, out of the corner of his eye, his attention having been on the taxiing aircraft, a military police vehicle fast approaching the dispatch area. Quickly he started up the Peugeot and roared across the grass, weaving around parked aircraft and assorted vehicles to intercept the military police. Having reached the approach road, he turned to face the oncoming military police, who bore down on him with discomforting speed. It came to rest inches from his front wheel. Two armed men jumped out and menacingly confronted him.

"Who the hell are you? Get out of our way unless you want to be arrested."

"And what gives a sergeant-chef the right to arrest a major?"

"What?"

"I am Major Jean-Guy Bernard."

Over his uniform Bernard wore a long brown leather coat. Unaware whom he was addressing, the sergeant-chef instantly appeared unsure of his position.

"We're under the orders of the commander in chief himself, General Weygand, to arrest someone, Major. You're blocking our way."

"And who have you come to arrest, Sargent?"

"That's our business, Major."

"Oh really." At that moment the noise of two Gipsy Queens could be heard opening up for take-off. Seconds later the three men watched the Dominie fly into the air and disappear to the north.

"Go about your business, Sargent, and carry out the commander in chief's orders." With that, Bernard pushed his motorcycle to the edge of the road, allowing the military police to proceed, something about which its two occupants now seemed less enthusiastic. To further block their now fruitless mission, Sir Edward Spears pulled up in his car. Winding down his window, he beckoned Bernard over.

"I don't know who you are, but on behalf of the general, thank you. Can I be of any assistance?" he said in accented French.

"No, I don't think so."

"Well, if I can be of any help to you I'll be at the Hotel Normandy until later today. France owes you a debt of gratitude, whoever you are."

Chapter Twenty-Two

<u>Northern France</u>

The routine double operation had gone as planned. Their rendezvous was over the small town of Pierrefitte-sur-Seine on the river Sauldre, northeast of Salbris. The field was to the south and a few miles north of Ménétréol. Gifford had been the first to land, clearing the trees on the western edge by a few inches. Minutes later, with three Joes crammed into the back of his Lizzie, he was airborne and climbing away to the north with the other Lysander lined up on final approach.

Minutes earlier, the changeover had been textbook, with everybody on the ground knowing what had to be done. However, the agent in charge, who had worked in a circus before the war, seemed to view the whole procedure as something of a carnival, running first this way and then that around the aircraft, gesticulating energetically and urging his crew on. With the massive propeller churning away on his stationery aircraft, Gifford was concerned that the clown would fall victim to one or more of the idling blades.

Five years earlier he had witnessed one such accident in Ocean Falls, south of Klemtu. A member of the local Squamish tribe had walked into the rotating blade of a Pratt and Whitney S3-H1 radial engine. It powered an almost brand-new Norseman, Canadian built, designed specifically for bush flying. Not that such details would have been of interest to the poor fellow who wouldn't have known what hit him. The fabric fuselage and wings became instantly covered in his blood and parts of his brain. It had taken a few hours and several swigs of the local hooch before Gifford had sufficiently composed himself to fly back to Vancouver. It wasn't to be the only surprise of his day. He had arrived home to the small wooden house, with its view of forest and sea, unprepared for the second, although he shouldn't have been.

After scraping together enough money for a deposit, he and Maggie had bought the clapboard bungalow on the edge of town shortly after he had started flying for BC Wings, a bush operation that, from its main base in Vancouver, covered almost the entire coast of the province. It was expected of pilots that they be prepared to operate for weeks at a time from smaller bases often hundreds of miles from home. This separation, along with Maggie's shifts as a nurse at the city's main hospital, meant that they would often go weeks without seeing each other, and when they did it was a continual time of adjustment. That evening before his flight to Ocean Falls they had sat up late, drinking and smoking, trying to make sense of the relationship they shared, just as they had done on other gin-soaked evenings. It wasn't that they had grown apart. It was more that they had never grown together. There was nobody else involved. Each had remained faithful to the other, but it was clear to them both that since neither was prepared to give up their job to save the marriage. It had run its course.

She had left a letter on the plain pine table in the room that had served them as kitchen, lounge, and study, Maggie having recently enrolled in an advanced nursing course. In her letter she had clinically itemised the points that each had made the previous evening, magnanimously addressing her own selfishness and unwillingness to change. If he was in agreement, her brother, a lawyer in town, would take care of the legal side of their parting. There was no mention of a trial separation or the possibility of their ever being together again. She had made up her mind, and that was that. No hard feelings.

The return flight from Ménétréol had gone well, with one exception. He had had to tell his three passengers to either sing quietly or desist from vocalizing all together. It seemed incredible that their combined voices could drown out the roar of his 860 hp Bristol Mercury XX radial. They were a distraction and contributed nothing to the navigation of his Lizzie over the darkened French countryside. Not that he had anything against music, although his first choice would not be for the romantic *chanson*, interspersed with the *Marseillaise* emitting from the cabin.

On arriving at Tangmere, they were met by the usual SOE and RAF brass, after which he had breakfast in the mess before flying onto Tempsford. Whenever he breakfasted at Tangmere he was assigned a room off the kitchen, since no allowance had been made for a sergeant pilot to dine at the officers' mess. It was while working his way through a welcomed plate of eggs and bacon that he was joined by a perfumed civilian, a tall willowy personage with long hair that trailed over his collar. He wore a finely tailored, woollen suit and identified himself as a member of the Security Service but gave no name. He wanted Gifford to understand that their little chat was totally unofficial, and he was convinced that Gifford would grasp its significance in the war against the Hun. He had also guaranteed that they would not be interrupted, all of which left Gifford wondering just what it was that had brought the effeminate London apparition into the little room off the kitchen, interrupting what, up until then, had been a damn fine breakfast.

"Earlier this month you brought two lovely passengers back from Thouars, a man and a woman. Am I right? My dear boy," he said, laying a hand lightly on Gifford's arm, "of course I am. I bet you remember all your passengers." He spoke with a slight lisp.

Gifford looked down at the manicured hand that rested on his arm and then at the dissipated face of its owner. He was in his fifties, with liquid eyes that spoke of drink. The hand was slowly removed, but not before it had squeezed the limb on which it had rested.

It would be some time before he would forget that flight to which this individual referred, if ever. Simone had stubbornly remained in his thoughts. Barely a day had gone by without him hoping she would make contact. Perhaps he might find a way of reaching her through this dissolute individual, someone who gave all the appearance of 'rowing from the Cambridge end.'

"Yes, I remember them."

"I thought you might. How clever of you. We would like to know if you spoke to either of them, in particular the man. Do you remember?"

"Not that I recall. I did speak to the young woman, Simone, but I can't remember her surname. What was it—"

"So you don't remember talking to the man at all, not on the ground in France or back here in England? Perhaps during the flight? I understand you can communicate with your passengers in the air, am I right?"

"Yes, there's an intercom system, but I didn't speak to the man."

"I see. Before they joined you in your little plane, did you see him arrive at the airport?"

"As I remember they were already there waiting for our arrival. That's normally the way of it. The less time on the ground the better. Once we had landed I was too busy getting the operation back into the air." He didn't volunteer the information that he had removed himself from the cockpit with the engine running, against standing orders, to check for fuel contamination.

"I'm sure you must have been frightfully busy, my dear boy. How brave you flying fellows are. All those nasty Germans. It gives me palpitations just thinking about it. How did they seem, the two people you brought back to England?"

"How did they seem?"

"Yes. Were they euphoric? Escaping from the Germans is rather special, wouldn't you say? Or did they seem detached? How would you describe their mood?"

"Since you ask, they appeared exhausted and in need of a bath."

"Yes, I'm sure. I—"

"Look, what is all this about? I'm not sure what it is you want to know. They were there on the ground when I arrived. They boarded the aircraft, and once we were underway I spoke to Simone over the intercom. On the ground, back here at Tangmere, I spoke to her again and then they took off in a big American car with the CO and some London guy. I don't remember exchanging one word with the man. Does that help?"

"Absolutely, my dear boy, absolutely. The young lady, you say you spoke to her in the air and on the ground, here at Tangmere. What about?"

"What about?"

"Yes. What did you speak to her about?"

"I can't remember exactly. I think she thanked me for the flight and that was about all."

"Are you sure that was all, Sergeant?"

"If you must know, and it's against regulations, I asked if I could see her again. Not that I ever will with this bloody war going on."

"You may be sure, Sergeant, I will not mention to anyone your little indiscretion. *Semel insanivimus omnēs.* Did she say anything at all about her companion?"

"No."

"Thank you, Sergeant. I'm sorry to interrupt your breakfast."

As the man from the Security Service rose to leave, Gifford asked, "If you should see—"

"My dear boy, I understand perfectly." Resting a limp hand upon the sergeant's shoulder, he said, "Rest assured that if I should see the young lady I will pass on your, shall we say, affection?" With that he squeezed Gifford's shoulder and minced out of the room.

Chapter Twenty-Three

Office of the SOE, RAF, Tempsford

Major Arthur L. Satterthwaite had no experience in dealing with the police. As a regular army man he never had cause nor need to accommodate such people. When he did think of them it was as persons who were quasi military, and in so doing he hoped he might find common ground on which to communicate. His briefing from SOE HQ at Broadway Buildings, St. James Park, in London, was both amorphous and ambiguous. When the SOE was first established, the Minister of Economic Warfare, Dr Hugh Dalton, called it The Fourth Arm, or The Secret Army. Since joining, Satterthwaite had become accustomed to a certain level of opaqueness in the way orders were disseminated. It was not how his army did things. An order should be clearly defined so that it may be efficiently and effectively executed. But he understood, as much as he was able, that the war had to be carried out in ways that he did not always comprehend or like.

While studying for his major's exam before the war, he had read Wellington's account of the Peninsula War and of the three young Catalans who gained admission to the fortress of Figueras and let in the guerrillas to destroy the large French garrison. Although it was not part of the curriculum, he had also read of George Washington's use of irregulars, men, who it was said, had saved the American Revolution. Washington's British-style army had proved they were not up to the task of defeating the king's soldiers. At the time, Washington had referred to his militiamen as 'an exceedingly dirty and nasty people [evincing] an unaccountable kind of stupidity in the lower class of people.' It was a view he felt sure he would have agreed with had he stood beside Washington. The major was not a supporter of irregular warfare, but if both Wellington and Washington saw the need for such forces, who was he to doubt their usefulness. However, if he were running the show, SOE would have nothing to do with the Bolsheviks. In the war against the Hun, this business with Operation Pickaxe was a step too far.

He looked at the two men who sat opposite him. Shielded by his metal war department desk he felt secure, protected from civilian contamination, albeit of the quasi military variety, a detective inspector and a sergeant. What did such ranks mean? Was an inspector equal to or higher than a major? Where did they stand in the hierarchy of Scotland Yard? And Special Branch, what was that all about? He had, of course, heard of them but never come face-to-face with the animal. Special Duties Squadrons operated from Tempsford, so it was probably fitting that Special Branch should be investigating whatever it was they were here to investigate. It was just a thought.

"Major, the sergeant and I would like to know, as much as you are permitted to tell us, about four Russian agents who were recently flown to France from Tempsford. We have spoken to the station commander and the pilot who carried out the flight. As it was an SOE operation, we were hoping that you would be able to enlighten us."

"Yes, well, it's all rather hush-hush, don't you know. Not to sort of thing to talk about with—"

"Major, we're investigating a homicide. Both the sergeant and I have all the clearances necessary to carry out the investigation, and your help would be most appreciated."

"I'm sure it would be, Inspector. But I don't know that I can. Help you, that is."

"Perhaps you can start by telling us where the four were billeted before flying to France."

"Ah, possible, possible," he said, opening a thin mauve file in front of him.

On entering the office, Sergeant Hodges had immediately seen how much the major resembled Colonel Blimp, the *Evening Standard's* cartoon character. He wondered if the inspector had also seen the likeness. Although the cartoon normally appeared in black and white, Sergeant Hodges always thought of the colonel as being rather pink, as well as fat. Certainly the person opposite was fair-haired and rotund, with a ruddy complexion and an untidy Kitchener moustache. Unlike the cartoon character, he was not wrapped in a bath towel. They were, after all, not in a Turkish bath, but Hodges could easily envisage such a sight.

"It's here somewhere." The few pages that existed in the file were being thrown about as if a wind had suddenly developed. "Here it is. Ridley House, Kimbolton. Never been there myself, but I suspect it's not too far from here, wouldn't you say? Was that all, Inspector?"

"Thank you. Who runs the house, is it SOE?"

"We billet the agents in a number of country houses around the county, you see. Ridley is one of them. I suppose the staff who run such places are recruited locally, domestic affairs, not my concern, don't you know, but SOE would have a presence when they're being used. Damned if I know why you should be interested, though."

"Is there anything else you can tell us about the four? Three men and a woman. Their names, for instance?"

"Wouldn't do you much good, even if I were to tell you their names. No value at all, you see. You don't think for one minute, do you, that such individuals go around using their real names, and anyway, we probably issued them with new ones when they arrived in the country. No, their names won't help you."

"Even so, what names do you have for them?"

"I can assure you it isn't going to help you, Inspector. Let me see. Here it is," he said, recovering a sheet of paper off the floor. "Wilhelm Milch, Karl Wenninger, Hans Kotze, and Freda Volkmann. Damned if they sound Russian to me. Part of their disguise, I suppose."

"They were Austrian."

"Austrian? Are you sure?"

"I take it you personally had nothing to do with them, Major?"

"Me? Heavens no. Bloody Bolsheviks! Wasn't here, actually. Just returned from a spot of leave, you see."

"How convenient! The SOE officer who was on duty when they flew out, do you have his name? And where we might find him?"

"Can't help you there, Inspector. You'll have to go through official channels for that."

"Anything else we should be made aware of, Major?"

"You seem to know more than I do, Inspector. Austrians, you say. Would you believe it! Typical Bolshevik trick, sending Austrians to France. The blighters are not to be trusted. Anyway, what's all this about? Why so much interest in these four Reds?"

"We think that at least one of them may have been involved in a local homicide before flying out of Tempsford."

"Do you mean a murder? Wouldn't surprise me. Bloody Bolshies, capable of anything. Can't trust the blighters, don't you know."

"Thank you for your time, Major. Before we go, do you happen to know if Ridley House is being used at the moment?"

"Yes, I believe it is, but you won't find any Bolshies in residence."

"Thank you."

After the policemen had departed, Major Arthur L. Satterthwaite sat at his metal desk looking out of the dirty window at the wet Bedfordshire countryside. What to make of it all? Damn funny war, cosying up to the Reds, continuing to help the French in France after they had thrown in the towel while parts of his own regiment were fighting the Frogs in Mesopotamia, losing Singapore to little yellow men on bicycles, and now he had the police to contend with. He liked to think that he was broadminded enough to encompass within his world the likes of Inspector Sim and his sergeant, but they weren't army, and that was all there was to it. What would his father have made of it all?

The late Major Enoch Dexter Satterthwaite, Arthur's father, had fought in the first show with the 2nd Battalion of the Oxfordshire and Buckinghamshire Light Infantry, the Ox and Bucks, and was one of the few officers remaining after the battle of Loos, 25th September to 8th October 1915. Later the brave captain saw yet more action, along with his battalion, taking part in the battles of Havrincourt, Canal du Nord, and at Valenciennes before being invalided home as a major, his war over. He was something of a reclusive chap, not the sort of fellow you could have a chat with over a drink in the mess. Only Arthur's mother knew how to handle his moods, particularly towards the end of his life.

Early in 1939 Arthur's own war had all the signs of being equally as adventurous as that of his father's when the 4th Battalion of the Ox and Bucks, of which he was part, left for France as members of the BEF. Later they were involved in the defence of Cassel, Nord until the 29th May 1940, when they were eventually surrounded near Watou and forced to surrender. The battalion had split into two groups with the aim of reaching Dunkirk, but of the men of the 4th Ox and Bucks that had left Cassel only four made it to the beach. Not that Lieutenant Arthur Satterthwaite was one of them, in fact, he never left the United Kingdom. All set to leave with the 4th, he went down with tonsillitis, followed by a septic right toenail. In the end there didn't seem much point in sending him to France, the situation having deteriorated to the stage where the lieutenant would have added little to its defence. Those of the Ox and Bucks who had made it off the beaches of Dunkirk were sent to Northern Ireland, where he eventually caught up with the reconstituted 4th Battalion. Unable to boast or even talk of active service, he found his time in the mess with his fellow officers difficult. And yet, being unmarried, wherever he was stationed the mess was his home, the place where he wanted so much to be accepted, to belong. It was not that he was considered a malingerer, rather, he just wasn't taken seriously. It wasn't his fault that he had been left behind, unable to share in the battalion's ventures.

It was unfortunate but true that among his fellow officers Captain Sattersthwaite was thought of as something of a joke, foisted on them by someone in the Ministry of War with an infantile sense of humour. Yet it was loneliness, not humiliation, that he experienced. What did he have to do to be accepted by his contemporaries? Then, to heap one thing on top of another, due to a misdirected instruction from the War Office he was seconded out of his regiment, the Ox and Bucks, into SOE, where his bumbling incompetence went unnoticed. That he would survive the war ending up as a Lieutenant Colonel, when others within his regiment, more brave and competent than he, had either been killed or spent years in POW camps, was perhaps the cruellest joke of all for those in the British army who knew him.

As they walked back to the main gate, the inspector asked, "So what did you make of Colonel Blimp, Sergeant?"

"I wondered if you noticed the resemblance, sir. With all due respect, I don't see 'im as much of a threat to the Third Reich, do you, sir?"

"No, not really. Where do they find these people? You will have noticed that he pretended to know nothing of Henri's murder, when surely the entire SOE staff here at Tempsford must have been made aware of it. Having met the major, one could be excused for thinking that SOE wants us to desist in our hunt for Henri's killer. At least that's one interpretation one might put on it. It makes you wonder, Sergeant. Have we been sent on a wild goose chase?"

"You may be right, sir. Bit like last year at Bletchley Park."

"Exactly. Fancy a drive to Kimbolton?"

"Why not? Always assumin' ACW Little 'asn't run off with a military policeman."

ACW Little had not absconded with a 'Red' or a 'White Cap' but was waiting dutifully beside her Humber. Lurking under the low roof of the guardhouse, on the small veranda, was the hunched figure of a tall hooked-nosed flight sergeant of the Royal Air Force Military Police, glaring threateningly at the female driver. Behind him stood a suitably chastened corporal. It was a picture that required no explanation.

"Everything in order, ACW?" Inspector Sim innocently enquired.

"Yes, sir," came the meek reply.

"Good. Can you find your way to Kimbolton?"

"Yes, sir. It's near Staughton."

"Then we'll depart. We'll ask directions for Ridley House when we get there."

The secluded, thirty-room, early Victorian building that was Ridley House had extraordinary chimneys. Beyond that there was little to recommend it architecturally. It was a house in the country rather than a country house. Set in fifteen acres of woodland, it offered the privacy demanded of it, and yet it was only an hour from London. They had been met first at the main gate by two aged members of the Home Guard who, after diligently checking their identification, let them into the grounds. At the house a young lieutenant took them to a large office on the ground floor. The room had once been the main parlour of the mansion, with its mixture of Gothic and Rococo furniture replaced now with government-issue utilitarian desks and metal chairs, which clashed mercilessly with the faded Acanthus wallpaper and a large, yet to be requisitioned Rochester Brass chandelier hanging from the ten-foot-high decorated ceiling.

"Tempsford rang, so your visit isn't unexpected, Inspector. How can we help?"

"We're after information concerning four people who were billeted here recently before flying out from Tempsford. They were Austrian, if that helps."

"I see. You should speak to the SOE rep. I only look after security at Ridley. My contact with the guests is on a-needs-must basis. Give me a minute and I'll try and find the person you need to see."

After the lieutenant had left in search of SOE, Sergeant Hodges rose from his seat and walked over to a plate glass window, minus anti-blast tape, that looked out onto a long, sloping lawn flanked by conifer trees. Two young women and a man in shorts and singlets were engaged in callisthenics, under the watchful eyes of a similarly attired muscular instructor, heedless of the cold winter drizzle that had begun to fall. The instructor suddenly put a whistle to his lips and blew a clear, shrill note, at which all four set off at a run down the lawn.

The door opened and in strode a person clutching a brown file. Sergeant Hodges initially identified the individual as male but then changed his mind. Of medium height, between thirty and thirty-five, with a ramrod straight back and short black hair cut in a pageboy style, she wore a dark suit and light blue shirt with a deep red tie, her sensible shoes clicking their way across the parquet floor. She had a long face devoid of any makeup, with deep-set, intelligent eyes. She had about her a blend of intellectual prominence and social assurance but also a level of sadness that, since the beginning of the war, had become all too familiar to Sergeant Hodges. So many people had lost loved ones, and he had had more than his fair share of having to inform them. He saw no rings on either hand, so he assumed she had lost a close friend or maybe a family member.

"I'm Margot Taylor, the resident SOE officer here. How may I help?" Her voice belied her appearance, being incongruously feminine but at the same time commanding.

"Inspector Sim, and this is Sergeant Hodges, we're from Scotland Yard."

"Yes?"

"We understand that you recently had four Austrians as guests at Ridley House, three men and a woman."

"What about them?"

"Do I take that to mean that they were here?"

"That is correct."

"At last we're getting somewhere," Sergeant Hodges interrupted.

Casting a critical glance at the sergeant, she continued, "We have a number of people passing through Ridley. Why are they of particular interest to you, if I may ask?"

"It's in connection with our enquiries into a local homicide."

"Interesting. And you think one or more of the Austrians may be implicated in this homicide."

"It is possible. That's all we can say at this stage."

"I've confirmed that they were here. The matter is on record. What more would you like to know, Inspector?"

"How closely were their movements monitored while they were at Ridley House?"

At this point, the SOE representative opened the file she had been holding and quickly scanned its contents while balancing the file at such an angle that neither policeman was able to read it.

"The four you mentioned were here as part of an operation about which I can tell you little, and that applies to all our guests. Our instructions were that while they were with us they were specifically to be kept separate from the others, eating and sleeping away from all the other guests. Their time with us was brief, three days, during which they never left the house and grounds without an escort."

"To your knowledge."

"We don't chain our guests to the wall, Inspector, if that's what you mean."

"Is it possible that one of them could have left the premises and returned without being missed?"

"Possible, but unlikely. During the day we try to keep them busy. They had a full programme while they were with us. Their absence would have been noticed. As I said, we don't chain our guests to the wall, but they are regularly checked. The grounds are well patrolled throughout the night."

"When they went out, with an escort, where did they go?"

"According to the file there were no daytime excursions. In the evening they were taken to a local pub a couple of times.

Morale among them is recorded as being low, unusually so. Visits to the local pub was one way of lifting their spirits. Most of our guests are highly focussed and enthusiastic. The four in whom you are interested did not seem to fit into that pattern."

"The dates of those visits, would you give them to my sergeant?"

Quickly she wrote them on a piece of paper and handed them to Sergeant Hodges.

"Thank you. Did they receive any visitors while at Ridley House?"

"You mean apart from their contact with SOE personnel?"

"Well, yes."

Referring again to the file, she replied, "It seems not."

"I see. On their evening visits to the pub, how well would they have been supervised? After all, there were four of them. One escort, if that's all there was, would be hard-pressed to keep an eye on all four all the time. Wouldn't you agree?"

"According to this," she said, tapping the file, "they only ever went out with one escort, a Corporal Bernard R. Cunningham, German linguist on loan to us from Bletchley Park."

"Would it be possible to speak with the corporal?"

"It would if he were here, but he's returned to Bletchley."

"I see. Is there anything else you can tell us about the four?"

She again referred to the file. "What might be of interest to you, Inspector, is a note about one of the four by his PE instructor. During some unarmed combat exercises, one of them exhibited a level of violence beyond what was considered commensurate with the exercise. He injured his instructor. Read into that what you will. But I should add, the people who come here aren't being sent away to harvest flowers, if you see what I mean."

"Understood. We were given four names by your representative at Tempsford. I wonder if they correspond with those in your file."

"I don't see why they shouldn't, if they were given to you by SOE at Tempsford."

"It might help if you were to name the combat enthusiast you just mentioned."

It was a request on which she sat and contemplated for a few minutes. "You appreciate, Inspector, here names are somewhat ephemeral, nomenclatures in which one shouldn't put too much trust. However, since the individual has, shall we say, moved on, I see nothing wrong in giving you the name in the file, Hans Kotze. Does that help?"

Inspector Sim looked at his sergeant, who, after checking his own notes, nodded. "Thank you, Miss Taylor. It is, miss?"

"That is correct, Inspector. Would you like me to show you out?"

"No, please don't bother. I'm sure the sergeant and I can find our own way."

The young lieutenant was waiting for them in the cavernous hall, ready to escort them off the premises.

"Everything in order, sir?" he asked.

"I think so, Lieutenant. Tell me, Corporal Cunningham, to your knowledge, is he still at Bletchley Park?"

"Corporal Cunningham? Ah, the German linguist, yes, as far as I know. He was only on secondment to us for a few days."

"Thank you, Lieutenant."

"Where to now, sir?" queried ACW Little as they drove out of the main gate of Ridley House.

"The Queen's Head for a spot of lunch, I think. That all right with you, Sergeant?"

"Sounds fine, sir. Bletchley Park this afternoon, is it?"

"It might be easier if we arranged to meet the corporal away from the park, if it's at all possible. That way we don't run the risk of meeting that tiresome doctor from last year. What was his name?"

"Doctor Townsend, as I recall, sir."

"That's right. The linguistically challenged doctor. No, we can do without running into him. Did you notice those dates the lady gave you?"

"I did, sir. It could fit." Sergeant Hodges lowered his voice. "So, you think it possible that one of the four, possibly this fellow 'ans, leaves the pub while out for the evening with the group, without 'is escort noticing, goes to the 'ouse where old Henri is stayin' and does 'im in, after which 'e re-joins the others at the pub and no one is any the wiser. Is that 'ow you see it, sir?"

"That's about it, Sergeant. You have to admit, it's a possibility, if he had transport, somebody to take him to the house and return him to the pub. Can't be more than a ten-minute drive both ways, wouldn't you say?"

"That's all very well, sir, but surely the escort would 'ave noticed 'is absence for that length of time, and why would somebody drive to the pub, pick up this 'ans character, drive 'im to the 'ouse, and then, after the business, drive 'im back to the pub? Why didn't whoever was doin' the drivin' kill Henri himself?"

"Are you being difficult, Sergeant, or just trying to put me off my lunch? Maybe the driver wasn't the sort who liked slitting throats. Who knows? We have a motive and an opportunity. The dates fit. What more do you want? Anyway, at the moment, we're a bit short of suspects, even if we now have a motive."

Chapter Twenty-Four

Angers, France

Gertrude Eisner, alias Freda Volkmann, and Karl Oberhümer, alias Wilhelm Milch, half of Operation Pickaxe, were no longer interested in reforming the world to conform with the dictates of the Comintern, the Communist International, if they ever had been. Both had been members of Austria's Social Democratic Party before the war. For them, as with others, there was a clear distinction between socialism and communism, but it was one lost on the Heimwehr, Austria's fascist militia, from whom they had fled.

The situation in which they now found themselves was one neither could ever have envisaged when volunteering to work for the NKVD, the USSR's premier security service. With Operation Pickaxe they were to be returned to their mother country as agents to help defeat the Third Reich. That they had ended up in rural France, hiding out at the farm of Monsieur Galtier, left them with a future that at best was thwarted with few possibilities, none of which was without risk. Occupied France was, for two Austrians, one of whom spoke little or no French, dangerous ground on which to walk. As if the presence of German troops and the Vichy police were not enough, they must live with the possibility that the local communists would denounce them to the authorities in revenge for their aborted raid on the farm and the refusal of them both to join the communist resistance.

In spite of Allied victories in North Africa and Soviet advances in the East, the war showed little sign of finishing soon. Since arriving at the farm, Milch had toyed with the idea of setting out for Spain, where he had served during its civil war. In Spain he could sit out the war and at least make himself understood, but getting to the border when he spoke little French would be almost impossible. If caught by the Germans he would probably be shot as a deserter from the Wehrmacht. A similar fate would await him should he fall into the hands of the Resistance. It was unlikely they would check with London before shooting him, and besides, who would believe such a story as his. Staying at the farm under the protection of Galtier seemed, for the moment at least, the safest option, though there was always the possibility that they would be denounced to the authorities, for it was not only the communists who might denounce them. From what he had observed, there seemed to be little solidarity among the French in their fight against the Germans, and there was no shortage of collaborators.

With every day, Freda approached her life on the farm with alacrity, helping out wherever and whenever she could. Milch noticed how close she and Galtier were becoming. Personal survival aside, was it possible that she found the short, bald Frenchman attractive? He held their lives in his hands; it was something Freda would treat with the utmost circumspection. She hadn't exactly bloomed since taking up residence on the farm but had certainly opened up to Galtier, practicing her French whenever the opportunity presented itself, this from a woman who had barely uttered a word from Archangel to when they left for France. It was made easier by Galtier's loneliness, having been widowed early in life. That he should find the physically unappealing Freda pleasing was living proof that there was indeed no accounting for taste.

On evenings when Galtier would leave the farm on resistance business, Milch would attempt to engage Freda in conversation, attempting to solicit from her just where she thought their future lay. Were they to stay at the farm until they were eventually denounced, something that seemed inevitable, or had she some idea that they might, for example, join up with one of the partisan groups that, according to Galtier, were forming in the Massif Central? If so, was there a place in such a group for two Austrians? But try as he may, she would not be drawn on what they should do. Perhaps she had already written him out of the equation; in the future it would be only Freda and Galtier. Was that why she was so keen to improve her French? In which case, could he trust her? He had never put total faith in the other members of Operation Pickaxe; trust, like truth, did not prosper in the USSR. More and more he felt isolated, unable to communicate, and totally at the mercy of the farmer.

Galtier's small group of fighters was affiliated to the Alliance network, not that the farmer regarded the relationship as anything more than loose. Being a cautious man, he distrusted the network. There had been too many betrayals. Too many men and women had simply gone missing or been picked up by the police or the Germans. Neither did he accept the offer of a wireless operator into his group, something London as well as others within the Alliance had been pushing. Again, too many operators had been exposed by the *Funkhorchdienst*, some lasting only a few days after being airlifted into France. Once captured they were either turned or tortured by the Gestapo to reveal all they knew about the network to which they had been assigned. Rather, Galtier preferred to use couriers, men and women, sometimes children, people he could trust, moving around the country delivering messages and informing him of intended drops by the SOE.

But things were changing within the Resistance. A semblance of order was being imposed upon them from London, and Galtier, like others, would find himself becoming more of a cog than a wheel.

Occasionally shadowy figures would pass through the farm, sometimes staying for one or two nights in the barn. When this happened, Milch and Freda were expressly forbidden to have any contact with the strangers and during the day would either spend their time in the house or take to the forest with one of Galtier's men. There was, however, one exception. It was after midnight on a foul night with freezing rain, and Galtier and his men had been out since nightfall. On their return to the farm they had suddenly entered the house, catching Freda and Milch by surprise. Galtier had not been expected until around two or three at the earliest. The two had been crouching over the only fire in the living area, trying to gain some warmth before retiring to the frozen bedrooms up the narrow stairs. Along with Galtier and four of his men were two rain-soaked elderly individuals, both short, each clutching a small leather suitcase. The room quickly filled with the pungent smell of wet wool on unwashed bodies. The dirty windows steamed up, cutting out the miserable weather outside. Galtier ushered the two strangers in front of the fire, at the same time instructing Freda to make coffee. Milch retired to the stairs, from where he sat and watched. After everyone had been given a hot drink, Galtier dismissed his four men and motioned Milch to join the small group now seated around a reanimated fire.

"These two will be with us for a few days until they can be moved on. The weather was against us for a pickup this evening. It will take time to set other plans in place." Turning to Milch, he said, "They will take your room. You can sleep down here," indicating the chair on which he sat. Galtier then addressed the two strangers in rapid French that even Freda found impossible to understand. He then reverted to English.

"Our guests were rescued from a deportation train some days ago. They were going to Poland, we believe. London has asked that they be removed from France as soon as possible. The Germans are out looking for them. To London they are important. We must be careful how we handle this situation. Do you understand?"

Freda and Milch both nodded.

"They know that you are Austrian. That is all. They speak some English, maybe even some German."

At this Freda asked, "*Guten Abend. Wie lange bleiben Sie hier?*"

Both men looked at each other before one of them hesitantly replied, "*Pardon, wir spreche nicht Deutsch.*"

The gloomy room in which they were gathered, illuminated as it was by just one hurricane lamp, gave Milch little chance to view the visitors in detail. They were elderly and in their seventies, dishevelled and soaking wet. This was all he could immediately discern. But as he studied them more closely by the fire he saw more. Both were Jewish, on that he would stake his life, which made their claim of not speaking German odd. The European Jews he had met in Vienna spoke Yiddish, originally a German dialect, both high and low German being not too distant from Yiddish. Perhaps Yiddish wasn't spoken among the Jews of France? One was not well and seemed to have trouble breathing. From time to time he would pull a soiled handkerchief from his coat pocket and cough into it, a rattling cough that would disturb the squeamish. Milch wondered what it was that made these two unprepossessing individuals so important to London. Perhaps they were scientists in possession of knowledge that might shorten the war. Maybe they were financiers with friends in high places. That they were important to London was enough for Galtier. He felt it his duty to look after them as best he could until they were sent on their way. If, as the farmer had warned, the Germans were hunting for the two, then there was an added risk to both Freda and himself remaining at the farm.

The next morning dawned wet but a little warmer. The rain was no longer freezing. Milch had spent an uncomfortable and cold night on a chair in front of dying embers. He had woken early when Galtier made his appearance at five o'clock to relight the fire, something he did every morning before leaving the house to check on and provide a hot drink for the poor fellow who had been given the job of night sentry. Two hours later Freda appeared and started to prepare breakfast. It wasn't until nine that the first of the two visitors descended the stairs. He was clearly disturbed. A quick conversation ensued between host and guest, after which Galtier explained.

"The other visitor, he is sick." At that point his English failed him. "*Il a de la fièvre, poussée de fièvre*," he added. What followed, as best as Milch could understand, was a three-way discussion between Galtier, the visitor, and Freda about calling for a *docteur*, something that would have ramifications beyond attending to the sick man up the narrow stairs. Did Galtier have access to such a man or woman, one whom he could trust, Freda asked? Galtier shrugged his shoulders. In the end a solution was arrived at which clearly did not meet with the approval of the elderly man, who stood leaning against the stone sink clutching a cup of coffee.

Freda explained, "Galtier will send for a doctor tomorrow if the man's health has not improved. He doesn't want to risk bringing one here to the farm unless it is really necessary."

Later Galtier explained that since the occupation they had never had cause to call on the services of a doctor at the farm. One time one of his men accidentally shot himself while on patrol in the forest. They had taken him to a nearby nunnery and left him on the imposing stone steps in front of the big oak door on which they banged loudly before making a hasty retreat. The 'ladies of mercy' had asked no questions, removed the pellets from the unfortunate foot, and the following day left the injured man beside the roadside. A repeat performance at the nunnery involving the man upstairs was, given his poor state of health, not possible.

All day and most of that night Freda acted as nurse, taking drinks up to the sick guest and attempting to reduce the high temperature he was running. Galtier had left to inspect a landing field for a drop and pickup should the weather improve, making little secret of the fact that he wanted his latest guests gone as soon as possible. Milch spent the morning chopping firewood and replenishing the wood supply in the kitchen. At one point, while passing through the kitchen, Milch observed an argument between Freda and the elderly man. Again the subject seemed to be the need for a *docteur*. Galtier returned at nightfall and was brought up to date with news of the patient.

Throughout the night Freda sat beside him, his companion having joined Milch, sleeping as best he could on an upright chair downstairs. At three the next morning a tired looking Freda informed Galtier, Milch, and the guest that the man she had been attending had died. His companion offered no recriminations but seemed to accept the fact. He had tried to persuade Galtier into calling a doctor but had failed. There was now nothing that could be done.

They buried him that morning in a clearing deep in the forest, with a promise that after the war the body would be given a proper Jewish burial. Later Galtier explained that, weather permitting, the remaining guest would be flown out to England by Lysander that night. Freda, Milch, and Galtier debated whether a message should be passed, via the pilot, to SOE that half of Operation Pickaxe was hiding out at the farm. In the end it was agreed that once their location was known to London someone might inform the USSR Embassy, and that they did not want. Both wanted to distance themselves from all things Russian. They would let sleeping dogs lie, at least for the present.

Two days after the departure of the remaining guest, a courier arrived at the farm in the early hours with instructions from the Alliance network. Galtier had waited for the morning and the completion of his matutinal rounds before sharing the news with Milch and Freda. It had been decided to mount an operation to free a number of Resistance fighters being held by Vichy in a local jail. The prisoners were to be moved, under guard, from the central prison in Auxerre to Paris, where they were to be delivered into the hands of the Gestapo. The instruction was that under no circumstances were they to reach Paris. Milch wondered why he and Freda were being made privy to such sensitive information.

Galtier explained, "The network knows you are here at my farm. They see a use for you, Milch. You are to help free the fighters. The operation is planned for early tomorrow morning. A man will come and explain your part in the operation. After it is done you will not come back here. You understand?"

"You mean I am to become part of the Resistance?"

"If that is how you see it, yes."

"I want to know what they want me to do before I agree to it."

Galtier turned to Freda and spoke exasperatingly in French, after which he left the house, waving his arms in the air.

Freda left no time relaying Galtier's pithy reply. "He says you have no choice. You must do as they say. It is that simple. He suggests I cut your hair and you should shave. You do not look sufficiently like a German soldier, and then you must get some rest. You may be up all night."

It was mid-afternoon when he came to the farm. Milch had been mending a broken fence in the field that separated the farmhouse from the forest and saw him enter the barn, where Galtier was working on a damaged plough. Moments later Galtier appeared and summoned him to the house. Freda was on hand to translate. On entering the living area, Milch could hear someone moving around upstairs. Freda sat at the table, and Galtier stood by the door, as if to prevent Milch from escaping his fate. The visitor descended the stairs with a Wehrmacht officer's uniform draped over his left arm. In his right he carried a soft fatigue cap. Since Milch had observed his arrival without baggage, he assumed the man must have worn the uniform under his outer clothing.

It wasn't hard to work out that they wanted him to impersonate a member of the occupying forces. To masquerade as a German officer among members of the Resistance was about as dangerous as walking into a lion's cage smelling of lamb. Even if the ruse were to succeed, whatever the ruse was that he was expected to execute, he was doomed. What trust could he put in those who were to carry out the operation? And, assuming it was successful, what then? Galtier had said he would not be returning to the farm. What did they have planned for him? If things did not go as intended and he was captured by the Vichy or the Wehrmacht the best he could hope for was a firing squad. All in all, his prospects were not exactly bright, but he was, as he had been from the day they had arrived at the farm, completely in the hands of others. But if he had learnt one thing from his experience in Spain it was not to think too far ahead but to concentrate on the immediate future and seize whatever opportunities were presented.

The man returned just before nightfall. Milch had been told to wear the uniform under his day clothes and to take nothing else with him but be ready to leave upon his arrival. It was odd that Galtier was not there to see him leave. He had left the farm earlier on other business and had not even left a message. Freda, who had been sitting in front of the fire, looked up, coldly wished him luck and returned to the mending of one of Galtier's winter coats. He had already been written out of the script.

Milch followed one of Galtier's men through the forest, with his escort bringing up the rear. Rather than feeling part of whatever lay in store, he felt more like a prisoner being led to the slaughter, albeit with a cropped scalp and cleanly shaven. Was that how it was? After all he had been through in Spain and Russia, was this to be the day it all ended? Eventually the trees petered out into flat farmland that seemed to stretch into the evening's infinity. Shortly after, they came upon two bicycles. Milch turned to say farewell to his last contact with Galtier, but the guide had already vanished.

After cycling along back roads for an hour avoiding Vichy roadblocks, they came to a hamlet and a two-storied house that sat in darkness. In its large courtyard stood a covered German army vehicle in the back of which sat four men in uniform clutching rifles. Behind the wheel Milch could make out another, also in a Wehrmacht uniform. The lack of alarm or even caution by his fellow cyclist was indication enough that, whatever the reason for the appearance of an enemy lorry in the yard, it was not unexpected.

"*Aus gehen*," someone said, from which he assumed they wanted him to dismount. Milch obeyed and, after removing his outer clothing and packing them under his arm, was ushered into the front seat of the lorry to sit beside the driver, who barely acknowledged his presence. The door to the house opened, revealing a tall figure silhouetted by a dim light. He walked casually over to where Milch sat.

Chapter Twenty-Five

France & England

Sergeant Ian Gifford took off at 20.00 hours in a Lizzie that, until a few hours earlier, had been deemed unserviceable. The inner slats on the Lizzie are chain-linked to the flaps, and as the slats go out, so do the flaps. It was this linkage that was the cause of the problem, but thanks to sterling work by the squadron's engineers his machine had been made operational in time for the arrival of two Joes, accompanied by the usual SOE minders. Respect for those who kept the aircraft in the air was something that had been drilled into him throughout his initial training. Without their expertise nothing would happen, but since joining the Royal Air Force he had found the attitude among many of his fellow pilots towards aircraft engineering ground staff condescending, though less so among NCO aircrew. To Gifford it was yet a further manifestation of the British class system. After all, how could you maintain an aircraft and keep your hands clean? *Ipso facto*, dirty hands equalled manual labour, i.e., those of a lower order.

Weather over much of the British south coast and northern France was far from ideal: low and middle cloud accompanied by moderate to heavy rain with a more-of-the-same forecast. Icing was also something he could expect, a condition to which the Mercury engine was particularly susceptible when met, and so he would be keeping a close watch on the carb temperature gauge. Flying the Lizzie was meant to be a VFR (visual flight rules) operation, that is to say, maintain visual contact with the ground, a rule that he and all the others within the squadron ignored. The weather over northern Europe was such that to achieve any chance of success it was often necessary, particularly in winter, to fly between layers of cloud, thus losing sight of the ground. Often he found himself in cloud and engaged in instrument flying, using a limited flight panel. It was a skill he had tried to develop while flying off the coast of British Columbia. Frequently he had purposefully flown into cloud, first making sure that he had sufficient altitude in which to recover should he become disorientated. Like all such skills it was one that required continual practice. Now that time spent in cloud off Canada's West Coast was proving its worth.

Once airborne Gifford moved the throttle from FULL fine to COURSE to prevent over speeding beyond its 2,650 rpm max climb limit, setting the prop to just below 2,400 rpm and setting course in the climb for Cabourg, the point at which he hoped to cross the French coast. Climbing through various layers of cloud he reached his cruise altitude of 8,000 feet, with just the odd glimpse of the night sky above. He then moved the mixture control to weak and power back to 2,200 rpm to reduce his fuel consumption to 30 gallons per hour. The round trip would take just under five hours, if all went well. However, he had enough experience under his belt to know that things seldom went as planned.

He would cross the coast at Cabourg, then go south to Lisieux, giving a wide birth to a new flack battery at Vimoutiers that had suddenly appeared two days earlier, catching a Hudson crew by surprise. On then to Mortagne. The field was ten kilometres east of Nogent-le-Rotrou, one he had used before. It was an

SOE operation, something he had started taking an interest in since his meeting with the two policemen from Special Branch. It made little difference to him whether the Joes were SOE or SIS, but his brush with the policemen had made him cautious. Things had a habit of coming back to bite you when you least expected it, e.g., Henri Bonoteaux.

Over the Côte Fleurie he caught a glimpse of Le Havre through cloud, off to his port, and not a light to be seen. The Germans, as in most things, were efficient in their imposition of the blackout. For the next thirty minutes he was between layers of altostratus before a solid line of thicker cumulus type cloud appeared ahead. During his preflight met briefing there had been talk of the possibility of a front developing. With no way through and unable to out-climb the cloud in search of clear air above, he was forced to either turnabout or descend and hope that he could battle through underneath. There was, of course, the possibility that the cloud extended right down to the deck, in which case he might have to divert to the east or west and find another way through or terminate the operation and return to Tangmere. The weather had recently been such that the squadron was completing only one out of four sorties. They had also lost two pilots, presumably to bad weather. They had simply been posted as 'missing.' Bomber Command was experiencing similar problems with their operations. Once back in British Columbia, never again would he criticize its weather. Putting the British social structure aside, its weather, summer or winter, was enough to tell him he had made the right choice moving out to BC.

He was now down to less than 1,000 feet above ground level in reduced visibility and still unable to see through the bank of cloud ahead. Diverting to the east and searching for something that would confirm his position he sighted a river. It had to be the Risle. If so, he was further east than he thought. A railway line on the other side of the river would confirm his suspicion that it was indeed the Risle. A railway line came into view. Also, it looked as though the cloud to the east, towards Evreux, had lifted a little, and by following both the river and the railway he might yet be able to get through to the target east of Nogent-le-Rotrou. Minutes later a fairly large town came into view beneath him. It had to be L'Aigle, but with no light from the moon it was almost impossible to confirm the observation. Ahead lay high ground. The map strapped to his left leg clearly showed the need for him to climb or he would fly into something solid, but low cloud precluded such an act. Now was the time to make a decision, before exposing himself and his passengers to unnecessary risk. He was aware of the 'press-on syndrome,' the tendency to keep going rather than abort the mission and admit defeat. After all, nobody likes to fail, and there was always the possibility that you might win through. 'It was always hard to act decisively in the absence of certainty.' How many times had he been faced with this very scenario in his relatively short flying career?

Reluctantly he turned about and applied climb power but too rapidly. The engine cut, what was known as RICH-CUT, another idiosyncrasy of the Mercury engine on the Lizzie. To avoid such a thing, it was necessary to advance the throttle progressively over four or five seconds. With less than a thousand feet to spare it was not the best of times to lose an engine. The nose dropped. Dark shapes loomed up beneath him. Checking that the elevator trim was halfway between the TAKE-OFF and FULL-UP marks and putting the mixture into max rich, he quickly restarted the engine. The massive three-bladed prop had barely stopped moving before it spun into life and the aircraft started to climb away. To the north, as to the south, the weather was deteriorating quickly, and unless he wanted to join the others in that big hanger in the sky it would be prudent to beat a hasty retreat and call the operation off. As they say, 'There are young bold pilots but no old bold pilots.' Now was the time to bring his instrument flying skills to the fore. Often a pilot with no instrument flying experience has only a few minutes before disorientation sets in and he or she loses control of the aircraft. Keep the scan going: attitude, altitude, and airspeed, 'the three A's.' It took all of his concentration and experience to get through the next ten minutes of flight while climbing in cloud to 9,000 feet, on a heading of 330 degrees. He should talk to his passengers, who, he assumed, were sufficiently familiar with the operation to guess what was happening, injecting as much *bonhomie* as he could muster.

"*Bonjour* gentlemen." He had failed to communicate with them on the outward journey, something he should have done, but he had simply been too occupied with the flight. "*Comment allez-vous?*" His command of French remained primitive.

"*Qu'est-ce qu'il y a?*" came the reply.

"Sorry about this, my friends. We're returning to England. The weather doesn't agree with us. Have you on the ground in a couple of hours. There are sandwiches and a flask stowed in front of you. They were for the return trip, but you might as well help yourself."

"*Merci*, Captain."

Given the conditions, he felt sure that the return flight would not be without incident. He could ignore any threat from the Luftwaffe; they were too smart to be flying in such weather, but getting into Tangmere might be a problem, assuming he could find the place.

It was impossible to tell at what point they had crossed the French coast, if in fact they had, not having caught sight of land or water since commencing the climb at L'Aigle. Navigation was by dead reckoning. It would have to suffice, using time, airspeed,

243

and a heading. Of course, airspeed did not equate to ground speed, but it would have to do in the absence of any visual contact with the ground.

"Messieurs, let me know if you see anything below. We should be out over the Channel, *la mer*."

"*Hippo*, Captain, below is *hippo*, land."

Suddenly the aircraft was caught by first one and then a second beam of bright bluish light. The cloud beneath them had become sufficiently broken for their Lizzie to be picked up by a battery of coastal searchlights. Far from being over the Channel, they had yet to clear the French coast.

Throwing the Lizzie into a dive and at the same time banking steeply first to port and then to starboard, he attempted to shake off the lights, knowing that seconds later his aircraft would attract flack. Were he to pull negative G a lean-cut would quickly follow, but it was a risk he had to take. Just as violently he pulled the aircraft into a steep climb and back into cloud, losing the interrogating beams of light. The speed was right back to 60 mph, something that should only be performed if necessitated by operational consideration. At such a speed should he experience an engine failure the nose would drop and he would lose at least 600 feet before he would be able to regain control, in which case he would probably be picked up again by searchlights. Also at 60 mph in a steep climb he risked stalling the aircraft, although the stall in a Lizzie was delayed, except in an exceptionally large angle of attack, something he was fast approaching. Were it to enter a stall a wing would drop very sharply, and control would be entirely lost until he could regain sufficient speed, and in all probability he would lose at least 1,000 feet.

At 7,000 feet he levelled off and settled down to concentrate on his instrument flying. The Lizzie was a stable platform from which to indulge in the art of flying on instruments. His thoughts on the operational performance of the aircraft that the air force had entrusted him to fly were that in pitch and roll the Lizzie was heavy and sluggish. Pitch stability was high, but roll stability lower. And, with an external tank fitted, overall stability was low. The rudder sensibility was high, and the forces were light, so there was the propensity to over-control in the yaw, particularly when an external tank was fitted. In this operation he was without an external tank. Enjoyable as it was to fly, whoever said the Lizzie was not for beginners was correct.

By now they should have been out over the Channel. Whatever the wind was doing it was not as forecast. There was more headwind and considerably more drift than anticipated. Following such violent manoeuvres, it would take time for his compass and the horizon indicator to settle, putting yet more pressure on his instrument flying skills. In spite of poor cockpit heating, an outside air temperature of 31 degrees Fahrenheit, and ice starting to build up on the leading edge of the wings, he found himself sweating. Flying is all about experience, the pilot assessing each situation with what has gone before. Sergeant Gifford had been in tighter situations, but nevertheless adrenalin kicked in, coursing through his system, increasing the excitement and stimulating him to a level from which he knew it would take time to calm down.

Unable to think of anything other than keeping his aircraft airborne and safe, he left his passengers to their own devices, hoping that neither of them had sustained any physical damage during his erratic manoeuvres. Ice was becoming a problem. He would have to find some clear air before the ice on the leading edge of each wing built up to a point where it endangered the flight. Below he caught glimpses of whitecaps on a sea into which he would not want to ditch. While stationed in Cornwall he had heard various accounts of pilots who had been forced to ditch their Hudson's into the Atlantic – an experience he could do without. He was sure that putting something like a Lizzie, with its fixed undercarriage, down into the Channel would be every bit as traumatic as ditching a Hudson in the Atlantic. At least with the Hudson you could belly-flop onto the water. With a non-retractable undercarriage, the Lizzie would nose-over the moment it hit the water.

Tangmere proved to be less of a problem than he had feared. Its cloud base was alternating but not dropping below 300 feet. Once on the ground, having passed his Joes over to SOE and delivered his operational report to the duty operations officer, he booked into the sergeants' mess for what was left of the night. In the morning he assumed that he would be on call for another attempt at delivering the Joes of the previous evening, but instead, after a much welcome breakfast, he was instructed to fly back to Tempsford, where, on arrival, he was to be given three days' leave. Quite why he had become the recipient of such largesse he neither knew nor cared. How would he spend the next three days of freedom? The answer came from an unexpected though hoped-for source.

At Tempsford, before returning to his room, he did what he always did and checked his pigeonhole for mail, never expecting any communication of a private nature, but there it was, a personal letter, something he immediately assumed must be from his mother, in Devon. The writing on the envelope was that of a female, but not that of his mother, whose idiosyncratic writing style he would recognise immediately. It was from Simone. He had given up hope that he would ever hear from her again.

Dear Sergeant Ian Gifford,

I thought I should write and thank you for delivering me safely home, for that is how I now see England, home. No doubt you are continuing to lead an exciting life. My own has become a lot less exciting. Since we last met I have returned to work at my aunt's hotel in Bristol, although it may not be for much longer.

If you would like to contact me, you may do so at the above address, and that would be nice, but you will have to ask for Grace Harris.

Regards,

Simone.

Presumably this Grace Harris and Simone were one and the same. Such subterfuge was hardly surprising. Didn't she work for SOE? From her letter she would appear to have left that secretive world behind, but, then again, maybe her release was only temporary. There being no time like the present, as his mother would say, he would phone the hotel in Bristol and ask for Grace Harris.

By midday he was on his way. He had phoned the hotel but had been unable to contact Simone; it was her day off, and she had left the hotel to go into town. He would travel to Bristol and surprise her. Having secured a travel pass, visited the bank, and packed a small bag, he had caught the train from Bedford, changing at Swindon for Bristol Temple Meads.

It was late evening by the time he stood outside the four-storied tenement hotel and went in. Behind the small reception desk a middle-aged woman, her hair wrapped in a knotted scarf, was leafing through a copy of *Picture Post*.

"Can I help you?" she asked.

"Is Grace Harris available?"

"I don't think she's returned yet. Who shall I say called?"

"Would you tell her Sergeant—" But before he could finish he felt a gentle tap on his shoulder. On turning he looked into the open face of a woman to whom he would have given the world, at that moment, were it within his power.

"Hello," she said.

Dressed in a warm, grey, woollen coat and a matching felt hat with a red rosette attached to one side, her appearance differed starkly from the bedraggled creature he had last seen on the tarmac that night at Tangmere.

"Simone, or should I have said Grace?"

"Grace will do. What a surprise. You obviously received my letter. This is my Aunt Irene, who has been kind enough to take me in."

Introductions complete, the aunt tactfully withdrew to the office that abutted the reception desk.

"Why didn't you ring? It's my day off and I was in town shopping," she said, lifting a paper shopping bag as proof.

"I've been given three days' leave. It was unexpected, so, here I am. I did ring but—"

"I see. Do you have somewhere to stay?"

"No, I haven't thought that far ahead. I wasn't sure that you would be free."

"I see. Perhaps—"

"Room twenty-one is empty," interrupted a voice from the office. "It offers a panoramic view of the neighbour's outdoor privy, but I'm sure the sergeant won't mind."

"There then. It's all settled, you can stay here. What would you like to do?" To Gifford, standing in the foyer of that faded Edwardian provincial hotel, her voice possessed a bell-like quality more suited to a convent. He detected just the hint of an accent – French? It was as if English were not her mother tongue.

"Well, why don't we go out for a meal somewhere?"

Again, the voice from the office. "The Royal Greyhound has game pie under the counter. Tell them I sent you."

The next two and a half days were among the most enjoyable he could remember since arriving in England. Aunt Irene proved to be very helpful, allowing Grace as much time off as she wanted. It was made possible because the troublesome Irish maid, Maureen, had been replaced by two Polish girls who were proving to be quite the most efficient members of staff Aunt Irene had been able to attract to work at her modest establishment. The escape of the two girls from Warsaw, off a Soviet merchant ship in Dublin harbour, was a story he would hear in due course but was nonetheless thrilling for the delay. Thanks to the two girls from Warsaw, since returning to the hotel Grace had found herself to be more of a guest than an employee.

However, throughout their short time together in Bristol, she appeared to him to be distrait and restless. Maybe it was her normal personality. After all, what did he know of this woman to whom he was so attracted? He had first met her under unusual circumstances, and perhaps her behaviour was the result of her dangerous time spent in occupied France?

Chapter Twenty-Six

<u>Bedfordshire</u>

To the casual observer, Inspector Sim of Special Branch would seem to be of a rather somnolent disposition. His sergeant knew otherwise. Whether it was his years spent working for the British Raj, or simply the way in which he viewed things, Inspector Sim could not be rushed or, for that matter, pressured, traits that his sergeant found agreeable. If at times he failed to exude overt enthusiasm for the task in hand, which was more often the case, Sergeant Hodges put it down to the man's personality and his advanced years. Also, he remembered something he had read about a French government minister in the eighteenth century, addressing his diplomats before they left for their respective postings on how they should deport themselves when representing France. "Above all, gentlemen, no zeal!" He liked that.

"I suppose we should be on our way, Sergeant."

"That sounds like a good idea, sir. Bletchley Park, is it?"

They had finished a satisfactory lunch at the Queen's Head and were ready to take on the rest of the day. ACW Little had arrived with the black Humber and was awaiting instructions. It had stopped raining. It even looked as though the sun might put in a wintery appearance.

"Bletchley Park it is, well almost. I made a phone call before lunch. Our Corporal Cunningham was just going off duty. He's happy to meet us away from the prying eyes of the park. We're to meet up with him at his billet in Ridgmont, wherever that may be."

ACW Little knew Bedfordshire like the back of her young hand and had no trouble in delivering them in front of a cluster of Nissen huts parked incongruously on the village green, clearly a wartime exigence. A number of soldiers in greatcoats were kicking a football about. On seeing the Humber arrive, one of them left the game and walked towards the parked car.

"Inspector Sim?" he asked. The tall, thin, bespectacled character in his mid-twenties looked more the academic than the warrior, which was no doubt why the army had found fit to station him at Bletchley Park with those of a similar ilk. The army was not always so accommodating.

"Corporal Cunningham. Thank you for seeing us. This is Sergeant Hodges. Where can we talk?"

"We're a bit short of somewhere to entertain, I'm afraid. Something the army neglected to include when constructing our camp." The educated voice of the corporal left Sergeant Hodges wondering what part of the United Kingdom Corporal Cunningham could call home. He liked to pigeonhole people, to classify them. It helped him to understand how they functioned, essential in police work. Of course, he knew that such a technique was superficial and open to misinterpretation, but it helped. If he were asked, his assessment of the corporal was that the man was university educated, though possibly from a working-class background. The standard English he used was acquired. That he worked at Bletchley Park and was a linguist only helped to reinforce his observation.

"There's a tea shop in the village, sir. I saw it as we drove in," ACW Little offered.

"Right, that's where we'll go then. Jump in, Corporal."

ACW Little remained in the car while the three men sat in the small tea room, an enterprise that had been on the verge of closing until saved by the influx into the area of so many servicemen and women.

"How may I help you, Inspector," he asked.

"You were escort to a party of four Austrians staying at Ridley House." They had waited until the café's owner, a large, sour-faced woman of middle years, had taken their order and retreated to the kitchen.

"That's correct, Inspector. I think we went out twice, to the local pub. They weren't the happiest people on this planet, as I recall."

"The lady at Ridley House made the same observation. Why do you think that was? Why were they like that, do you think?" It was a question that had little bearing on the case but was of interest to the inspector.

"I couldn't say. Being at the park I don't have much to do with what goes on at Ridley House, but from what I hear the people who pass through there are normally highly motivated and highly focussed on what they've been trained to do, whatever it is. You understand that I wasn't made party to the purpose of their mission. It's not my business. But if I was to describe their attitude towards whatever it was they were going into, at least for three of them, it would be reluctant. One of them, Hans, he seemed unaffected by whatever it was that didn't suit the others, although the woman was hard to read. She spoke very little, if at all. A proper killjoy."

"I see. And you were with them all the time they were away from Ridley House."

"Yes. We were taken to the pub and brought back in transport provided by SOE. I don't drive, you see. The only time they were out of my sight was when one or another of them went to the toilet. There is one thing I should mention. I suppose they told you about the man who spoke to Hans during one of our visits to the pub? I did report it at the time."

"You tell us."

"It was on our second visit. I was getting the drinks in, at the bar. In a mirror behind the bar I could see my group. A large man entered the saloon, walked over to where they were sitting, and spoke to the four. More accurately, he spoke to Hans. The others didn't seem at all pleased to see him. And then he walked out. When I returned to the table they pretended nothing had happened. I told them I would have to report the incident, which I did."

"The man who spoke to them, or to Hans, what did he look like? You said he was a big man."

"Yes. I was too far away to catch what was said, but I think that he may have spoken to them in Russian, certainly not German. He had a Slavic look about him. And his clothes. They looked Russian, if you know what I mean, the way they were cut and the poor quality."

"You're familiar with that sort of thing?" Sergeant Hodges asked sceptically.

At that point the tea arrived. Only when the woman had returned to the kitchen did their conversation continue.

"Before the war I spent two years at university in Heidelberg. I was completing my doctorate in eighteenth century German literature, until Hitler put an end to that. While I was in Heidelberg a group of us took a couple of weeks away from our studies and went to Leningrad. It was damned hard getting the visas. The Soviet Union doesn't exactly encourage tourists, but eventually they let us in for a week. It was damned interesting. We were carefully supervised wherever we went. We only saw what they wanted us to see. But, as I say, it was very interesting, particularly coming as we did from Fascist Germany. For what it's worth, I don't think either fascism or communism has much to offer."

"That's reassuring," Inspector Sim added.

"Neither do I think that you have to be a master tailor to tell the difference between a Russian and a German or for that matter an English suit." The remark was aimed at the sergeant, who was suitably chastened.

"Thank you, Corporal. They made no mention of this man again. Not on the way back to Ridley House or later?"

"No, in fact, as I remember it, they didn't exchange one word on the way back. As I say, I reported the incident because I thought it was important. Naturally I asked myself how it was that this man, whoever he was, knew that we would be at the pub that evening and at that time, unless he was with SOE."

"And that was the conclusion you came to. That the man was from SOE?"

"It seemed the obvious explanation. Wouldn't you agree?"

"Quite. What time was it when this man appeared, and what time did you all return to Ridley House?"

"I suppose it would have been about nine p.m. when he came in. He was only in the room a few minutes. By the time I returned to the table he had gone. We left the pub at ten, closing time."

"I see. When you reported it, what did they say at Ridley House?"

"That was the thing. They didn't seem at all interested, which rather confirmed my suspicion about him being from SOE."

"And you can't think of anything else about the four? This chap Hans, what did you make of him?"

"A violent type. Not at all the sort you would like to spend any time with. The interaction between them was interesting, though. This Hans character was the dominant one among the four. He got on well with one of the others. Milch was his name. You appreciate it's anybody's guess what their real names are or were. I did get the impression that Hans and Milch had known each other for some time."

"And you wouldn't 'ave 'eard what 'appened to them after they left Ridley House?" Sergeant Hodges asked.

"No. The day after they left I returned to working at Bletchley."

"Is there anything else you feel we should know, particularly about this Hans character?"

"I don't think so, Inspector. I was only with them a few days, and only then for part of the time."

"I see. Anything you would like to ask the corporal, Sergeant?"

"What are you going to do after the war, Corporal?" Sergeant Hodges enquired.

"Complete my doctorate, if I can. I don't suppose I'll be able to return to Heidelberg, but you never know."

On returning to the Humber, Inspector Sim instructed ACW Little to drive back to the Queen's Head.

"It's time we sat down and examined what we know, Sergeant."

"That shouldn't take long, sir." Hodges replied dejectedly.

"Buck up, Sergeant. We could be on the verge of a breakthrough. What did you think of our Corporal Cunningham?"

"A very observant young man, 'e'd make a good copper. Funny that business about the Russian comin' to speak with the group, don't you think?"

"More peculiar is that they didn't mention it at Ridley House."

"Maybe they just forgot."

"Possible but unlikely, don't you think? It must have been included in that file she was so secretively holding. If the corporal is to believed, our Hans didn't leave the pub to do the dirty deed, and he couldn't have done it later because, if you remember, Mrs. Huntington-Brown said that her husband discovered the body between eight and nine. So, I'm afraid, that rather let's Hans off the hook, wouldn't you agree?"

"You're right, sir. So if 'e didn't do it, who did?"

"Well, it wasn't the butler in the library with a lead pipe."

"Sorry, sir?"

"Nothing, Sergeant. Why not the big man who came to the pub? Well, it fits. Corporal Cunningham said that he came into the pub at around nine. Ample time for him to have killed Henri and driven to the pub. We could have a new suspect, Sergeant."

"If 'e did kill Henri, why would 'e do that? Drive to the pub afterwards, I mean?"

"Quite. Perhaps it was to tell this Hans fellow that he had carried out the deed. But then, why do that? We need to do some serious thinking. The question remains, who would benefit from killing Henri?"

"Just about everybody, if you ask me." Again the feeling came back to Sergeant Hodges. Maybe the inspector was approaching the same conclusion but, like himself, was not yet ready to admit it.

After a pause, during which the sergeant continued to admire the driving skill of ACW Little, so different to the death-defying technique of LACW Adler in her Hillman Minx, the inspector offered, "What do you think the Queen's Head has laid on for dinner, Sergeant?"

"Bubble and squeak? My mother used to make a fine bubble and squeak, sir. Of course, with 'ers there was meat."

"There's a war on, Sergeant. What would you really like for dinner?"

"A steak and kidney pie."

"I would settle for that."

As they entered the hotel a receptionist called out to them.

"Sergeant Hodges? A phone call for you. I'll transfer it to the booth."

"You're a popular fellow, Sergeant, either that or someone is very keen to get hold of you," the inspector commented.

Hodges entered the phone booth that stood to the right of the reception desk. Closing the folding door behind him, he picked up the phone.

"Hello, Sergeant 'odges speakin'." He heard a click as reception closed her connection.

"Alan, it's Bert Ashcroft from the Southwark nick."

It had been years since he had heard the voice, yet it was readily identifiable. Unlike himself, Ted was not an East Ender, and he wasn't even a Londoner. Bert had originally hailed from Wales and, in spite of his years in England, still carried the Welsh accent, though the dialect had been supplanted by the sound of East London.

"Yer an 'ard bugger to get 'old of. Are they keepin' you busy up there?"

"'Ello Bert. Long time since I've 'eard that voice. 'Ow are you?"

"Can't complain. I'm still at Southwark. Look, somethin's come up which might interest you. It's to do with that case you're workin' on."

"'Ow did you know about that, and, while we're at it, 'ow did you find me?"

"Never mind about that now. What I've got to tell you is probably best said to your face. Can you come down to the smoke, just for a day? It won't take long. What do you say?"

There was no reason why he couldn't excuse himself and head into town for a day. It was, after all, to do with the enquiry, if

Bert was to be believed. He was sure that the inspector wouldn't object.

"That should be okay, Bert. 'Ow are you placed for tomorrow? And where would you like us to meet up?"

"I've got the day off, so that should work well. I don't 'ave a garden to work in anymore. No more 'aving to dig for bloody victory. Tomorrow would be fine. What time do you think?"

"How does one p.m. sound? I should be able to catch a train down to London by then."

"One it is. Come to the Southwark nick. You'll have no trouble finding it again. It's just about the only complete building left standing in the street. The Luftwaffe did a good job of clearing away all those dreary Victorian tenements. We'll find somewhere more private to go to from there."

As he had thought, Inspector Sim had no objection to his decamping for London the following day, especially as it might shed more light as to who murdered the double agent Henri Bonoteaux.

Chapter Twenty-Seven

Auxerre, France

Milch sat in the front of the lorry next to the mute driver. He was cold in a Wehrmacht uniform that did not include a winter coat. They were six in all, five of whom were members of a resistance group that had coerced him into an operation to free important members of the Resistance held in Auxerre central prison and due to be transferred to Paris. The plan, as all the best of plans are, was simple, although one to which Milch remained in partial ignorance. Rather than attack the prison, they would wait until the French police had released them into the hands of their escort for transportation. Timing was all. As the gates of the prison opened and the vehicle carrying the prisoners drove out onto the *Rue Alsace,* they would appear and, with fraudulent documents, insist on taking over the transfer of the prisoners. The French escort, it was believed, when faced with an order from the Wehrmacht would be sufficiently intimidated that they would acquiesce. After all, were they not the occupying force? It was unknown how many prisoners were being taken to Paris, but it was believed to be no more than six. The exact number would not be decided upon by the prison authority until minutes before the transfer. Only two were of importance to the Resistance, they being in possession of knowledge that, were it to fall into the hands of the Gestapo, would be extremely damaging. Their informant was certain that the two of interest would be among those being moved. The fake documents Milch had been given did not specify the numbers involved, but as they were in German it was assumed the French police would not study them too closely. They would then be driven away into the countryside, where another group of resisters would help them disappear. Milch was to simply play the part of an arrogant German officer, thrust the documents into the face of whoever was in charge of the escort, utter a few contemptuous words in German, and leave the rest of the talking to the driver, who was dressed in the uniform of an *Unteroffizier* and who would affect a German accent to his native French. That was the plan.

Twice on their way into Auxerre they were forced to slow down at roadblocks manned by the gendarme, and on both occasions they were waved through. They had left with time in hand for the drive to the prison and found themselves to be early as they drove through the outer suburbs. Few people were out and about at that hour, and those who were did so beneath a threatening sky that looked capable of producing a lot of precipitation, even snow. It seemed that every other wall in the town was covered with posters, a few defaced, but most admonishing the populace to remember the slogan of Marshal Pétain's National Revolution: Work, Family, Fatherland.

With time to kill they parked by the roadside just short of the *Rue Alsace* and less than half a kilometre from the prison. Just as they were to resume their journey, a Mercedes 170V Kübelwagen carrying two SD officers and two men in civilian clothes drove slowly past, stopped, and then began to reverse, only to then drive away. What would they have done had the officers shown a deeper interest in the innocuous lorry parked by the road? The operation would have been over before it had begun.

As they turned into the narrow *Rue Alsace* they saw the Kübelwagen parked just short of the main gate, which had started to open to allow a blue Renault police van to depart. As the gates closed behind the van the two civilian occupants of the military vehicle, wearing long black overcoats and large felt hats, got out and stood in front of it, blocking its path. Words were then exchanged between the two civilians and the driver of the van. The two SD officers remained in their vehicle.

"Gestapo," muttered the man seated beside Milch. What had been a simple plan of abduction now had all the hallmarks of becoming a firefight or an ignominious withdrawal; the Gestapo, with their pre-emptive move, left them no other choice. Unable to converse with the driver, Milch could only sit and let things unfold as they may. Their lorry came to rest behind the Kübelwagen, which more than suggested that, regardless of the Gestapo, their operation would go ahead, if not quite as planned.

The driver produced a pistol from within his tunic and dropped it into Milch's lap, then, turning around, he issued rapid instruction to the four resisters in the rear. Milch looked at the weapon he had been given, a Mauser C96 semi-automatic. The last time he had held such a weapon was in Spain. He had liberated it from a dead fascist in Alcázar only to lose it to an officious French border policeman when he had sought refuge from the war, six months prior to Franco taking power.

"*Kommen. Du sprichst,*" the driver said. With that he indicated that they would now leave their vehicle and approach the Germans. The Gestapo was not in the script, and Milch was unsure what part he now had to play. Clearly he was still the arrogant German officer, but one without any identification and with a set of documents that might have fooled the Vichy police but not the two men in black coats. He felt as an actor might who was auditioning for a play he hadn't finished reading through.

The Gestapo were engaged in a heated discussion with the driver of the police van as Milch and his companion approached. Unbeknown to all save the police driver, the van that had just left the prison was empty, a fact its driver was having trouble explaining to the two Gestapo men. Behind him the French fighters had surrounded the Kübelwagen as if it had been part of the original plan. His driver nodded at Milch, as if to say, 'Well, what are you waiting for?'

Hoping that his delivery was sufficiently militaristic, Milch asked them what was going on. Why were they preventing the transfer of the prisoners whom they had come to escort to Paris? Did they know they were interfering with a Wehrmacht order?

Looks first of incomprehension, and then puzzlement, followed by suspicion crossed the faces of the two Gestapo men, whose attention was not on the man addressing them clothed as a German officer, but on the wooden-soled farming sabots of the Frenchman standing beside him. Seated at night in the lorry, Milch had not noticed the driver's boots; now it was screamingly obvious. No German would wear such things, let alone an Unteroffizier. Glancing at him, Milch could now see that in the light of day it was unlikely his French partner would pass as a German soldier, even with the correct footwear. There was something distinctly unmilitary and very French about him. Much the same could probably be said for the other four. Any Vichy policeman would have to be severely harassed and intimidated, as well as visually impaired, to accept their disguise.

"*Was machen* . . ." screamed the shorter of the two men from the Gestapo, pulling a pistol from his coat pocket. At that point they were all distracted by the brake-screeching arrival of an ancient Citroen lorry, out of which tumbled several men and two women armed with an assortment of weapons. Having earlier identified the Gestapo, Milch's driver now uttered one more word, "Communists," before falling with a single bullet to the side of the head, fired by one of the men in black coats. The shooting and the unwelcome arrival of the communists coincided with a sudden and continuous downpour. The heavens had opened, instantly drenching all in front of the prison. Milch turned and ran back to the lorry, passing the Kübelwagen, the doors of which were now open. The two Sicherheitsdienst (SD) officers were being dragged from the car. Everybody seemed to be shooting wildly. He heard French voices shouting above the discharge of various weapons as the unrelenting rain fell. He had almost gained the safety of the lorry when he slipped on wet cobblestones and fell heavily to the ground. Possibly his left arm was broken. It certainly felt like it. He had also sustained a bullet wound in the flesh of his right shoulder, which he hadn't felt until that moment. Painfully he crawled around to the back of the lorry, making himself as small a target as possible. He lay cold and wet, wondering what he should do. Dressed in a saturated Wehrmacht uniform with no weapon to defend himself, having dropped his pistol when he fell, unable to speak French, and in front of a group of hostile communists who, he assumed, were on the same mission as themselves, his situation seemed even more perilous and now somehow ridiculous. The whole operation had suddenly been turned on its head. Weapons continued being fired and French voices raised, while the rain persisted. And then it all fell silent, broken after a few minutes by the sound of the ancient Citroen lorry starting up and driving away. The rain abated.

Slowly and not without pain, Milch rose to his knees, shaken, cold, and very wet. Poking his head around the rear of the lorry he took in the scene. In the foreground the rear doors of the Kübelwagen were open and below each an SD officer lay. Beyond, the two Gestapo men had been shot in front of the French police van, whose driver knelt by the front right wheel shivering with fear. Also stretched out on the wet cobblestones were one of the resisters and two of the communists, one of whom was female. There was no sign of the remaining four resisters. They had either driven off with the communists, an unlikely possibility, or they had simply melted into the surrounding side streets, leaving him to fend for himself. Had the communists taken off with the prisoners? Such a concern was no longer of any importance to him, if indeed it ever had been. His own survival was now all that mattered.

The tall heavy doors of the prison were beginning to reopen, and people were leaving the safety of the surrounding terraced houses with their shuttered façades and coming out onto the narrow street, ignoring the rain. He needed to get away from the area and then decide what to do. Rising to his feet, he began to walk unsteadily around the lorry. There was no sign of the pistol he had dropped, but he did recover his field cap. If he was to continue impersonating a German officer, and that seemed the obvious thing to do until he could work out an alternative plan, the more authentic his appearance the better, albeit in a uniform that was not only saturated but torn and filthy. On reaching the driver's door he was relieved to see that the keys to the lorry's ignition were still in place. The lorry was his best option. To have taken the Kübelwagen would have meant first moving either the police van or the lorry, and, anyway, he could not be sure that the keys for the wagon were not in the pocket of one of the two prostrate Gestapo men.

Fortunately, the wound to his right shoulder didn't seem to impair his ability to operate the gears of the lorry, although blood had run down his arm, making his hand wet and sticky on the lever. With his foot firmly on the accelerator, Milch shot away with no idea where he was going, scattering a number of startled watchers. It was enough to separate himself from the prison and the hostile crowd that was beginning to gather. He turned right into the first street he came to, leaving the *Rue Alsace* to the French and German units who were descending on the area, alerted by the prison and the gunfire. After a few more turns he slowed down and took stock. His first concern was petrol. How much longer could he drive the lorry before the tank ran dry? The gauge was of no help; it appeared to be unserviceable, it being many months since it had last indicated anything other than mechanical zero. If he had to dump the lorry it would be better to do so away from a built-up area. He had to leave Auxerre and drive into the country. It was then that he remembered the small bundle of clothing sitting next to him on the floor of the cab. He had left it there after changing into the uniform of a Wehrmacht officer. Once he had been forced to leave the lorry he would change back into civilian clothes. Until then he would drive until he ran out of fuel. But then what?

What were his options? They were just as they had been from the time he landed in France. If he were to stay in France it would only be days if not hours before he was picked up. He would have to try and either go east and try to enter Switzerland or travel southwest and cross into Spain. Both options presented the same difficulties: distance, his inability to communicate, no documentation, and no money with which to buy food. If he were to head for Spain he might then be able to move on into neutral Portugal, but Spain was not only a long way off, it was also in the hands of fascists, those whom he had fought against. To be able to cross half of France and Spain without being caught seemed the height of optimism. If he were to head east to cross into neutral Switzerland, not only would he be able to make himself understood once over the border, but with luck he might just be able to traverse the country and enter his native

Austria near Innsbruck and go on to his uncle's farm high up in the Nierdere Tauern. It would be a return to his original plan, which, when he first conceived the idea en route from Russia, had seemed so straightforward, though not without risk. Now it was even less likely to succeed. He could dismiss any idea of joining the Resistance after being left behind outside the prison. He could trust nobody but himself.

Fortunately, he had always possessed the ability to tell his position relative to north. More than once in the confused fighting in Spain, with quickly shifting front lines, it had saved his life and that of those fighting beside him. He would head east for Switzerland, and, as if his subconscious had preceded this decision, he found himself already driving east, in the direction of that neutral nation.

Chapter Twenty-Eight

<u>London</u>

It took Sergeant Alan Hodges almost as long to cross the city as it did to travel by rail from Bedford to the smoke. It had only been a matter of days since he had left the place, and he hadn't missed it one bit. After the peace and quiet of Bedfordshire, London seemed as frantic, as dirty, and as noisy as ever. But with a sense of pride he marvelled at the resolve of the city and its inhabitants. Surely few places around the world would have ridden the storm so well, what with the bombing night after night and the fires. He wondered if the people of Berlin were as stoic.

"Sorry I'm late, Bert. Blasted traffic and the train was 'eld up just north of St Albans."

The firm handshake of the man he hadn't seen in years brought back the last time they had met. It was something he would have preferred to forget, one of those occasions in his career that were best left to rest.

"Good to see you again, Alan. It's been a long time. A lot's 'appened since then, eh? Look, I thought we might just buy some lunch somewhere and 'ave it walkin' beside the river, if that's okay? The rain looks like it might 'old off for a while. I would 'ave invited you back 'ome, but we was bombed out last year. Lost everythin'. We're livin' with the missus sister in Clapham. 'Er old man's away in North Africa. Our kids find it a bit cramped, but it won't be forever, I 'ope."

They walked beside the Thames eating sandwiches, each needing a beer with which to wash down the dry bread with its unpalatable filling.

"Just before you get on to what you 'ave to say, Bert, 'ow did you know I was in Milton Ernest? Did the Met put you onto me?"

"It's something of a coincidence. We 'ave a mutual acquaintance, you and me, namely the landlord of the Queen's 'ead. I've 'ad some dealings with 'im in the past. I 'ad cause to ring 'im the other day over a spot of business and 'e mentioned that 'e 'ad these two gents from Special Branch staying at the Queen's 'ead, and 'e mentioned your name. I won't tell you what our business was about. It's got nothing that need concern you, but you might call it very fortuitous, my callin''im when I did."

Nothing changes, he thought. Bert was still up to his usual nefarious dealings, no doubt something to do with the black market. He was right. It was nothing that need concern him. Sergeant Bert Ashford was not the only bent copper to cross his path. He was, however, the only one to whom he was beholding, and now he was to put himself further in his debt.

Bert continued. "I 'appen to know that you and your governor are currently lookin' for whoever murdered a certain foreign gent in Bedfordshire. I ask you, of all unlikely places, Bedfordshire. Am I right?"

"Yes, but 'ow did you know?"

"Let me finish."They walked on in silence for a while; it was as if Bert had suddenly developed second thoughts about whatever it was he had to tell. After a few moments he continued. "This bloke I know used to be assistant governor at The Scrubs (HM Prison Wormwood Scrubs). All the convicts and screws 'ave been moved out of there, as you know. It's now used by, well, let's just say the 'ush-'ush brigade, shall we? This bloke I know who is now workin' at The Ville (Pentonville Prison) says 'e prefers The Scrubs. Barnsbury is too far away from 'is favourite pub. At The Ville they 'ad under lock and key a particularly nasty type, 'uman junk, you might say, awaiting execution for the murder of a woman and child. You remember the Grace and Alice murders, mother and daughter, in Paddington?"

"Right. Now let me think, Fred Webster, wasn't it?"

"That's the one. You may remember, 'e's also wanted in France for a couple of murders 'e carried out before the war. The man is an 'omicidal maniac. God knows 'ow many other poor souls 'e's 'elped on their way. The other day, well, it was in the dead of night, a couple of gents in civvies roll up to The Ville, and our villain is taken away, without any notice. All legit, proper papers and all. This is where it gets even more interestin'. This bloke I know reckons that 'e, that's Fred Webster, was moved to The Scrubs. 'E got that bit of info from the driver of the paddy wagon. The next day 'e leaves The Scrubs under guard by car. Forty-eight hours later, again at night, 'e's back in 'is cell on A Wing at The Ville. No questions asked, no answers given. But 'e grasses to one of the guards, doesn't 'e. 'E couldn't resist a boast. Not very bright, our Fred. Said 'e was taken to a village north of the smoke where 'e carries on 'is trade, so to speak, but on behalf of HMG. 'E called it 'is legitimate murder, would you believe? 'E told the guard that in exchange for doin' the business, so to speak, 'e wouldn't 'ang but would be released and sent abroad after the war."

"What 'appened to 'im after that? Is 'e still at The Ville?"

"That's the other funny thing. Shortly after 'e grasses to the guard 'e goes missin'. 'Is cell is empty. Nobody saw or 'eard a thing, and nobody seems to know when 'e was moved or where 'e went. Nor, for that matter, are they interested. This bloke I know doesn't want to ask too many questions, you understand. You've got to admit, it's all very fishy, wouldn't you say? Now I'm not sayin' 'e is your man or that it was 'im who did your foreign gent in. It could 'ave been someone else, but it's a bit of a coincidence, don't you think?"

"What date was 'e taken from The Scrubs?"

"The twelfth of November. Needless to say, Alan, this conversation never 'appened, okay?"

His journey back to Milton Ernest was tedious, with the train stopping for long periods between stations for no apparent reason. He shared the dimly lit, unheated carriage with soldiers of the Gordon Highlanders, most of whom were sleeping off a few days of drunken revelry in the smoke. Those that were awake conversed in a language he assumed was English but could not be sure, since, to his Sassenach ear, it was no more than staccato grunts of various length. They did, however, offer him a wee dram from one of two hip flasks being passed around. Not wishing to appear unsociable, he obliged, the amber liquid warming the very depth of his being.

Bert had confirmed for him something that had been gestating since they first met the two smarmy gents at Tempsford, a suspicion that had grown stronger with each day. He remembered having said, right at the beginning, 'It had to be an inside job,' and so it had proved to be if Bert was telling the truth, not that he had any reason to doubt his word, but he would give a week's pay for five minutes with Fred Webster. He was also aware of the pagan mistrust in which he held the establishment, a prejudice that coloured his attitude, making him only too willing to believe the worst of such individuals as the smarmy duo and those they represented. The labyrinth within which the various elements of the British security services coexisted, MI5, SIS, and this military identity known as SOE, was another reality to this simple policeman from the East End. His experience of last year at Bletchley Park, and now Bedfordshire, left him yearning for the transparent world of everyday policing. The opaque environment in which he and his inspector now moved had little appeal, and yet, if he were honest, he rather enjoyed the country and working alongside the easy-going Sim. Leaving London had proved to be something of a tonic.

By the time he returned to the Queen's Head, Inspector Sim had gone off to bed. There seemed little point in disturbing the man at such a late hour. What he now knew could wait for the morning. The kitchen was closed, but in reception he ran into the landlord of the hotel, who volunteered to make some sandwiches and a pot of tea to take up to his room. It crossed his mind to mention his trip to the smoke and his meeting with their mutual acquaintance, but he thought better of it. Whatever was going on between Bert and this innkeeper was their business and not something he wanted to become involved with. However, that the man had identified them as Special Branch to Bert was of interest. When the inspector had registered at the hotel it was as a police officer from the Met. Nothing more. Clearly *mine host* had influential friends within the police establishment with whom he maintained regular contact, or had someone at Tempsford spoken out of turn? Perhaps in the morning he would have a few words with the man, but only after first speaking with his governor. Before that he had something of much more importance to report.

Chapter Twenty-Nine

France

He was approaching the end of his downwind leg and, having signalled his reply to the correct identifier from the reception committee, it was time for the pre-landing checks – the prop to fine pitch, airspeed about 100 mph, height approximately 1,000 feet above ground level, the field was 500 feet above sea level, check mixture normal, pitch to fine.

As the aircraft had decelerated through about 115 mph the outer slats had moved off their stops, the inners following at about 105 mph. Carb heat was fully out and the throttle almost closed.

Turning onto his base leg he checked his speed, 95 mph. He took a quick final look around before he put his attention onto the final approach into a field he hadn't used before. But for the forward view over the big Mercury engine, the cockpit of the Lysander offered the pilot good vision. This was a definite advantage for clandestine operations at night, and from the lights laid out on the ground he had no trouble ascertaining the direction in which to land. The strip was known for its downward slope to the south. He would be landing uphill.

Speed was 85 mph as he made his left turn onto final approach. Flying can be hours of boredom interspersed with moments of stark terror. Since moving to Tempsford he had not experienced any of the former and his fair share of the latter.

However, this evening the outward trip had been trouble-free, with scattered stratus over the Channel, little cloud at altitude, and bright moonlight, giving the Luftwaffe ample opportunity for an intercept, but they hadn't as yet put in an appearance.

Cowl flaps open, he was aiming for 70 to 75 mph across the threshold with small power increases on the approach to offset drag, but not too much, otherwise the flaps would retract. A normal Lysander approach should be carried out at twice the stall speed, something that had been impressed upon him during his conversion. Approaching the threshold, he checked that the tail actuator was in the full-up position even as he pushed forward on the control column. As the throttle is closed before landing and as the tail-plane effectiveness is reduced, all available back stick is required to arrest the descent rate and so achieve a three-point landing. It was a characteristic of the Lysander and something that had caught out many a pilot converting onto type.

Such was the slope of the strip that he found on landing, after a very short distance, he had to apply an unusual amount of power to keep the aircraft moving. Applying the right brake he spun the aircraft around to taxi back to where the reception committee was waiting.

The target had been easy to locate. It was between Segré and the Mayenne River. He had picked up the Mayenne just south of Laval and followed its shimmering moonlit waters south before turning right in search of the strip. On such a night it would be easy to forget that there was a war on, but then he had to ask the question of himself: 'What the hell was he doing flying an unarmed, obsolete aircraft at night, into a strip he had never flown into before, while keeping a watchful eye out for enemy aircraft that wanted to shoot him out of the sky?'

For Sergeant Ian Gifford the war had disproved beyond any doubt the presumption that human beings have absolute power over their destinies. And the sheer unpredictability of life during war, coupled with the slender thread from which his own life hung, night after night, made any thought of the future seem a pointless exercise. It was sufficient to live each day as it came and enjoy whatever was available. Shirley presented one such opportunity.

It was shortly after his return from Bristol and the pleasant few days with Grace that another female came into his life, this after a dearth of feminine company that had lasted almost a year. She arrived at Tempsford in a recently overhauled Lizzie.

Their paths crossed that morning quite by accident. Having been summoned to an intelligence briefing on some new strips the squadron would be operating into, he was leaving to return to the NCO's mess when she walked into the operations room carrying in her right hand a parachute and in her left a canvas overnight bag. She was tall, slim, and fair-haired, and had an uninhibited presence about her. Nebbish she was not. On the shoulder of her smart, tailored blue uniform she wore two gold stripes, one broad, the other narrow. Later she explained to him what rank she held in the Air Transport Auxiliary. She was a 2nd officer, which meant that she held a Class 4 qualification, allowing her to fly advanced twin-engine aircraft. He had the rest of the day to himself. The ATA taxi, a three-seater Fox Moth, was not due for a couple of hours to pick her up and deliver her back to Hatfield airfield, the ferry pool from which the women of the ATA operated. He beat the other men who were beginning to gather about her like flies around a honeypot by asking if she would like to spend the time away from Tempsford at a local tea shop. To his utter surprise, and the chagrin of all the other males gathered about, she willingly accepted. There was, however, one problem. How would he transport her to the tea shop? Around the base he used an ancient but reliable bicycle. It wasn't built for two. On an impulse he asked her to leave her gear in the ops room and walk with him to the hangar, where he planned to ask one of the sergeant engineers if he could borrow his car, an Austin Seven.

Fifteen minutes later they were seated in the café exchanging experiences, as pilots do. He found her incredibly easy to talk to, not at all repressed. Unlike many of the young women of the ATA, she had not come from a wealthy English family but had learnt to fly a Spartan C2-60 on her uncle's farm in New South Wales, 600 miles east of Sydney. Being in England when war broke out she was unable to return to Australia and so, anxious to do her bit for king and country, had approached the ATA. It was a history that in part mirrored his own.

There was one distinct difference in their aviation careers. Since joining the RAF and following his wings course, he had flown only the Hudson and then the Lizzie. Since volunteering for the ATA, Shirley, on the other hand, had flown over twenty-five different types and sometimes six different types in one day, including Wellington bombers and Spitfires, accumulating 400 flying hours. When flying a particular type for the first time, pilots of the ATA were armed with a set of white notes setting out any peculiarities, such as with the Spitfire's tendency to swing on take-off. They also carried a pocket-sized *Ferry Pilots Notes* containing information on all types of aircraft. Often, with no experience on the types they were to fly, they were expected to sometimes work fourteen days without a break. They flew VFR from one end of the country to the other, often in atrocious weather, normally for thirteen hours a day, to be followed by two days off. He had never met a female pilot before and had wondered what to make of the species. There had been one rumoured to be flying on the coast of BC, but they had never met. It was known that Russia even used women as combat pilots. Although she had not met any Russian women in the ATA, it was, she said, like being in the Foreign Legion. Women from all over the world had joined up to fly, the largest foreign contingent being American. One, a Pole, had flown with the Polish Air Force before escaping the German advance into her country. Another was from Argentina, having learnt to fly in Patagonia at the age of seventeen.

They were together for only a few hours, at the end of which he felt he had known her a lot longer, yet there was so much more he wanted to know about her. The Australian had made a big impression on him. On returning to Tempsford he watched as she climbed into the Moth, after first stowing her parachute and bag. Before disappearing into the cabin, she turned and waved. With much noise and smoke the biplane started up and taxied out. Within minutes it was a speck on the horizon. Would he see her again? It was doubtful, unless, as with Grace, she contacted him and then he could track her down. At least with Shirley there were no security problems to overcome, and Hatfield was not all that far away. In his war so many people had passed through his life, from the Joes he carried into and out of France, other pilots, some of whom had gone from his and everyone's life forever, and now two new arrivals, both female. His war was looking up. They were as different as two women could be. The one a creature of Europe, gentle, urbane, and vulnerable, someone whom he had an innate desire to protect. The other was from down under, self-assured, outspoken and confident, exuding health. When he allowed himself freedom of thought he would ruminate on their dissimilarity and fantasise about them both.

He had brought in two Joes for the SIS and was to pick up two for the Alliance, SOE operatives. Being Tempsford trained, the reception committee was swift in the execution of the Lizzie's turn-around. Within minutes, the incoming baggage and agents were offloaded and his outward consignment aboard. From the trees at the end of the strip he could see in the moonlight that the expected wind change was two or three hours in advance of the forecast. The strip faced northwest to southeast, and he had landed uphill with all of ten knots on the nose. Now the wind had picked up and veered around to the east, giving him a crosswind of twenty knots and rising.

Off his left wing tip, behind the figure giving him the thumbs-up by torchlight, he could see in silhouette other members of the welcoming committee running about, some taking up defensive positions with weapons raised. Above the sound of his idling engine he heard gunfire. It was time to leave. The security of the pickup zone had been compromised.

Making sure not to circumvent the four-to-five-second rule in opening the throttle from idle to full power, to avoid backfire or rich heat, he released the brakes and the Lizzie shot forward and upward. At the same time he applied right rudder and aileron sufficient to keep the aircraft straight. On take-off the object of the exercise is to transfer cleanly and definitely from the ground to the air. In a Lizzie this happens a lot quicker than in most types of its size, particularly from its three-point take-off position. Once clear of the ground he turned the aircraft into the wind and climbed steeply away at 70 mph, which he maintained to 200 feet above ground level before pushing the nose forward. At 110 mph he set the prop pitch to course and throttled back slightly to put the aircraft into a steady climb to 9,000 feet.

He would return the way he had come, via the Mayenne and Segre Rivers, crossing the coast between Blonville and Deauville. Just as with the outward flight, he could expect gin-clear conditions all the way, but there was a chance of radiation fog at Tangmere, which could present a problem. Once the fog has formed overnight or in the early morning it requires further heating before it will clear. Being winter, when the sun did appear it would have little strength, insufficient to burn off the thick fog until much later in the day, in which case he would have to think about diverting to another field.

"*Bonsoir*, gentlemen. *Accueil*. We'll be on the ground in about two and a half hours, depending on the wind. The *vent?*" Perhaps when the war was over, before returning to Canada, he would come to France and seriously set about learning the language, until then his Joes would have to put up with his pigeon French.

"Coffee and sandwiches are somewhere in the back, help yourself. Let me know if you see any German night fighters."

"Thank you, Captain. It's nice to be a guest of the Royal Air Force." His perfect if heavily accented English caught Gifford by surprise. "We were lucky to get away. A little later and we would have been guests of the Gestapo, not the RAF. Someone betrayed us."

"The public weal requires that men should betray and lie and massacre," said another voice, this time in unaccented English.

"Voltaire or Montaigne?" asked his fellow passenger, after which the discussion lapsed into French, and he asked them both to turn off the intercom. Whatever they were conversing about did little for his concentration. Any gimbal-eyed Luftwaffe pilot out and about this evening would have little trouble spotting the cumbersome Lizzie lumbering its way towards the coast. Of the three main tasks he had to perform: flying the aircraft, navigating, and keeping a watch out for enemy night fighters, the second posed few problems. He could almost make out the coast, and they were still south of the Mayenne.

Later, as they crossed the river Orne west of Argentan, first searchlights then anti-aircraft fire opened up to his left, beyond Flers. Seconds later an explosion lit up the sky at about the same altitude. Some poor sod had copped it. He hoped it wasn't someone from the squadron. The rest of the flight to the coast was uneventful, although he did see, high above him, a fleet of heavy bombers heading southeast. Were they the new Lancaster, the weapon that would win them the war? They crossed the coast just east of Blonville, as planned. The scattered stratus that had covered the Channel on his way to the target had become almost continuous cover, with only the odd hole through which they caught glimpses of the sea in the moonlight. Halfway across, one of the Joes called out, "Below, Captain. Can you see it?"

"See what?" he replied.

"*Bateau*. A big ship."

He looked first to his right. Nothing. Then to his left. Through a break in the cloud he could see a capital ship of the German Navy, clearly visible in the moonlight and a large luminous swastika painted on the roof of one of its forward gun turrets. It was steaming west, and from the wake it was churning up it was at full speed, no doubt using the low cloud as cover to slip out into the Atlantic. If it were not for the low and almost continuous cloud cover it would be clearly visible from the English south coast. Where was the Royal Navy when you needed them? Was he to break radio silence and inform Tangmere, or wait until he got on the ground, by which time the vessel could be well down the Channel. And what if fog developed? He might have to divert, giving the German ship yet more time to escape. Again that well-worn phrase came back to him: 'It's hard to be decisive in the absence of certainty.' Putting his immediate responsibility first, he reluctantly decided to wait until he was on the ground before reporting the sighting. Instead of flying for range to save fuel, he could increase his air speed, but it would mean that his fuel consumption would escalate, and he might need every drop of fuel, given the possible weather conditions at Tangmere. He would maintain his current engine setting and hope that he would have a clean run into Tangmere.

The homing beacon directed him to the field, but, as he had expected, fog had set in at his destination. The question was, how thick was it and what was the height of the base? A seemingly impenetrable white blanket obscured the landscape. Every minute counted if the battle wagon was to be prevented from breaking out into the Atlantic, and yet the safety of his Joes and that of the aircraft came first. He had no wish to compromise the approach in the interest of expediency. Also, at the back of his mind was the admonishment given to him by his squadron commander: another 'incident' and he was out of the squadron. Again the time-honoured adage came back to haunt him: 'There are old pilots and bold pilots but no old, bold pilots.' Caution would temper his actions. He told the Joes to make sure that they were properly strapped in.

The emergency approach lighting would be activated, pole-mounted funnel lights whose function was to cast a slight glow through the fog. But would it be too thick for the lights to penetrate? Diverting would mean a delay in reporting the German vessel, also he had little fuel to find an alternate, certainly not enough for more than one approach.

Chapter Thirty

Milton Ernest, Bedfordshire

Sergeant Hodges crossed the recently hosed cobblestone courtyard at the Queen's Head, an area that separated his sleeping quarters from the main hotel building, just as the sun was trying its best to appear through a thick layer of fog. A light breeze blew in through the large open gate that led out onto the road.

"Mornin', Sergeant." It was the landlord, wearing his brewer's apron and rolling a barrel out from the cellar. "The inspector's in having his breakfast. He was asking after you. I told him you got in late last night."

"Thanks. For once, it doesn't seem to be raining." With that inane remark he hurried on, not wishing to engage any further with a man who later would be on the receiving end of some embarrassing questions, if he had anything to do with it.

For a hotel that was supposed to be full, few of its guests used the dining room, at least for breakfast. Each morning they had had the room to themselves, more often than not, which this morning was what he wanted. What he had to tell the inspector was not something for general consumption. Whether his boss would be pleased was something he preferred not to speculate on.

"Sergeant. Welcome back. How was the smoke?"

"Much the same, sir. And 'ow was your day?"

"Another one of frustration, I'm afraid. I've set up an appointment at Tempsford for us this morning. We'll have another go at your two smarmy fellows from SIS, who, I have been assured, will be available."

"Right. That should be interestin'."

"But first you must have your breakfast. Today we have been offered eggs, and your friendly landlord has also conjured up some bacon. Let's not concern ourselves as to its origin. Just enjoy it. I've had mine. I hope you don't mind."

"Not at all, sir. Shall I eat first and then tell you what 'appened in the smoke?"

"Absolutely, Sergeant. We should always feed the inner man first. LACW Adler won't be here for another hour."

His body replenished, Sergeant Hodges pushed his plate aside and picked up his second cup of tea for the morning, after which he was prepared to take on whatever the day held for him. How to begin?

"As you know sir, I went down to the smoke to meet with an old acquaintance who claimed to 'ave some information on the case, stuff that he wanted to pass on, face-to-face. If 'e's to be believed, we've found our killer."

"Go on, Sergeant, I'm all ears."

Ten minutes later Sergeant Hodges finished his third cup of tea and studied the man sitting opposite. The inspector sat in deep contemplation, his arms resting on the table, hands clasped. Toast crumbs sat unattended on his bulging waistcoat. He hadn't spoken since Hodges had finished telling him of the previous day's talk with Ashcroft. At last, leaning back in his chair, he said, "And you think we can trust this contact of yours?"

"Why not? 'E may be bent, but why would 'e put across such a story if it weren't true? I did consider the possibility that 'e might, unwittingly, be givin' us a generous slice of codswallop, you might say."

"Codswallop, Sergeant?"

"Yes. Rubbish, sir."

"I'm familiar with the term. In Hindi it would be *bakwas*."

"That's interesting, sir."

"But why? Why would your bent copper dish up such a story if it weren't true?"

"To distract us from the real killer? Without Fred Webster we wouldn't be able to prove or disprove a thing. 'Owever, before leaving the smoke I phoned my own contact in the prison, who 'appens to be a prison inspector, someone I've known for a very long time and would trust with my life."

"A recommendation indeed, Sergeant."

"'E did some quick digging for me, and it's interesting. There's no record of a Fred Webster ever 'aving been at the Ville, which, under the circumstances, doesn't mean 'e wasn't there."

"As you say, interesting."

"But 'e also added that there 'ad been some kind of security blackout imposed on all prison records. As you know, the Scrubs 'as been taken over by the Security Service, so that would seem to go some way to confirming the story, don't you think? Of course, if Webster didn't do it then we're back to square one, so to speak."

"I'm painfully aware of that, Sergeant."

"You may remember, sir, I said at the beginning that it had to be an inside job. Well, if it wasn't the Security Service it could have been SOE, but we've nothin' to suppose that SOE were responsible. Besides, Bonoteaux was not one of theirs, if that means anything. There's always the communists, but we 'ave nothing that says they're involved. I think, sir, we 'ave to accept that my informant was telling the truth, just as 'e was told it. It rather looks as though it was our side who did 'im in."

"Quite." After a pause the inspector patted the side pockets of his jacket pockets, a gesture Hodges had come to recognise as a prelude to a statement of some importance. "Well, that would appear to be that. As you know, Sergeant, I dislike Americanisms, but on this occasion they have one that is particularly apt. We've been played for a couple of suckers."

"Oh, I don't know about that, sir. Don't we 'ave the last laugh? After all, we weren't supposed to find out who killed poor old 'enri, but now we 'ave."

"But without Fred Webster we won't be able to prove anything of what your informant told you. If you're right, the Security Intelligence Service not only disposed of one double agent and a homicidal killer, but also what evidence there was of this criminal who did the deed, along with his stay at Pentonville, not to mention his trip to the Scrubs. It'll all be long gone. Still, it answers a lot of questions. No wonder we weren't getting anywhere with our enquiries. We weren't supposed to. We will, of course, continue with the investigation back in the smoke, but I don't hold out much hope."

"Just as an aside, sir, there is the other matter of our landlord. I'm not concerned with the business 'e's got goin' on between 'im and my acquaintance. I'm 'appy to leave that alone, if that's all right with you, sir?"

"Not our concern, Sergeant."

"Good. But 'ow did 'e know we were from Special Branch? I suppose someone at Tempsford could 'ave spoken out of turn. But what kind of landlord concerns 'imself with such things? That's what I would like to know."

"Ex-copper maybe?"

"I suppose so. Do you agree that we should speak to the man, or should we let sleeping dogs lie?"

"I think our landlord is something of a dark horse, Sergeant. Perhaps we should at least ask him how he knew who we were, if only to make him more circumspect in the future. After all, there's a war on."

"Is that right, sir? I 'adn't 'eard."

"We'll see to our host later, shall we? Let's first do battle with the smarmy gents. I think you've just added some extra spice to our meeting this morning, Sergeant."

"Always 'appy to oblige, sir."

After meeting them at the camp's main gate, Flight Lieutenant Mortlock wasted no time in escorting them to the security area in which SIS conducted its business at Tempsford, Hut B4.

"The person you have come to see, Inspector, has to head back to London just as soon as you have conducted your business. We won't be operational again until tonight. You know where to find me if you need me. I'll leave you to it."

A military policeman, having checked their identifications, showed them into the same spartan room in which they had last met the two smarmy gents from SIS. This time only one was present.

"Good morning. Robert, isn't it?" Inspector Sim enquired. "Mr. Padmore not blessing us with his presence this morning?"

"How can I help you, Inspector," the man said, ignoring the policeman's solicitous remark concerning Adrian J. Padmore. "I'm needed back in London by this afternoon, so I'm afraid our meeting will have to be brief." The velvet condescension of his delivery so upset the sergeant that he was forced to turn away and concentrate on the view that was offered through a cracked windowpane. Beyond a barbed wire fence a cow wandered languidly past the hut. So palpable was his feeling of hostility towards this paragon of elitism that he felt sure the man must be aware of his enmity.

"What I have to say shouldn't take too long. Does the name Fred Webster ring any bells, Robert?"

Hodges had not expected the inspector to be so direct. Clearly he had no intention of beating about the bush. An interesting development. The next few minutes were not without potential.

"It's not a name I'm familiar with. Should I be?" His visage gave nothing away.

"Possibly. In all likelihood it was Fred Webster who murdered Henri Bonoteaux."

"Ah, yes. The Frenchman. That's very informative, Inspector, but what makes you think that I may have heard of this man?"

"Well, that's the interesting bit, you see. If it was Fred Webster who murdered the Frenchman, he was, in all probability, acting on instruction from the Security Intelligence Service." The silence that followed was broken by the sound of a Lizzie being run up on the hard.

"And before you deny any involvement by your organisation, I'm quite willing to believe that you were not personally involved. In all probability it comes as more of a surprise to you than it did to us."

"Really, Inspector! What evidence do you have for making such a preposterous accusation?"

"As I'm sure we both know, whatever evidence there was will have long since disappeared."

"Let me see if I have got this correct. You are accusing the service of having murdered someone, but without any evidence to back it up. Perhaps you should have remained in retirement, Inspector."

"Perhaps you're right, then the sergeant and I wouldn't have wasted so much of our time looking for a murderer who all along was known to the authorities because he was working on their behalf."

"You say you have no evidence to support this ridiculous idea of yours. May I ask on what basis you make such a claim?"

"Information has come to light that, if correct, leaves no doubt as to the complicity of the Security Intelligence Service in the murder of Henri Bonoteaux."

"*Nullius in verba,* Inspector. But, leaving aside for one moment your lack of evidence, why would SIS carry out such an act? Perhaps you can you tell me that?"

"You're better equipped to answer that than either the sergeant or I. But we understand that the man was a double agent, working for both sides. Rather embarrassing, don't you think? Not only for HMG, but for your organization, and, with his return to France cancelled, what do you do with such a person? Maybe he knew too much to be allowed to live."

"Whatever you may think of us, Inspector, we're not in the business of murdering people."

"'Now this is the law of the Jungle, as old and as true as the sky: And the wolf that shall keep it may prosper, but the wolf that shall break it must die.'"

"Very poetic, but hardly relevant. You are barking up the wrong tree, Inspector." With that he stood and started to stuff a number of files into a battered brown leather briefcase. "If, as you say, the service wanted the man put out of the way, wouldn't it have made more sense to have arranged for his despatch in France? I suggest you and your sergeant return to London and put it all behind you. Go back into retirement, Inspector. The death of Henri Bonoteaux was an exigence of war. No doubt you'll write a report on your investigation. It should make for interesting reading, particularly the bit about the lack of evidence to support your outlandish claim. Now I really must go."

The fog had dissipated, allowing the late-morning sun to penetrate the mullion windows of the snug in which the two policemen sat. The landlord, having served them tea, quickly made himself scarce.

"Do you think 'e suspects that we want to 'ave a chat with 'im?"

"Possibly." Pouring two cups of tea from the Brown Betty teapot, he continued. "What did you think of Robert's point about it making more sense for Henri to be dispatched in France?"

"My guess is that they only found out about the double game 'e was playin' after 'e arrives in England. They couldn't very well let 'im return to France, could they? So, what do they do with 'im? It's just as you said, sir. The man 'ad become somethin' of an embarrassment to HMG."

"I agree. Our work is done at Milton Ernest, don't you think, Sergeant?"

"It would seem so, sir. A slightly better outcome than what we 'ad at Bletchley last year, wouldn't you say?"

"I would, Sergeant, and we're not finished yet. You know, I've often wondered since then who it was who murdered that poor girl at the park."

"Sally Evans. I don't suppose we'll ever know. At least we can put a name to Henri's killer."

The thick wooden door to the snug opened, and the head of the innkeeper appeared.

"There's a foreign gent here to see you, Inspector. French, I think. A Colonel Jean-Guy Bernard."

Chapter Thirty-One

<u>Tangmere, West Sussex</u>

He was on his way from Masset back to Vancouver when below and to starboard he saw the sun glinting on the upper fuselage of a brand-new Canso flying boat as it descended into low stratus off the Charlottes, near Jedway. At the time, he remembered thinking that the skipper must have known what lay beneath to be carrying out such a manoeuvre. Why this particular memory should invade his consciousness and distract him at such a critical time he couldn't say. With its rocky coastline and forestry, the Queen Charlottes, the most westerly inhabited islands in BC, were a far cry from the oft-tilled meadows of West Sussex, just as his antediluvian Lizzie was equally as far from the shining new Canso. Was it because he was about to carry out a similar exercise, by descending into an amorphous and threatening environment? The skipper of the Canso would have had foreknowledge of the height of the base below the stratus. There was a possibility that the fog he was about to penetrate was right down on the deck at Tangmere, putting it below minima, although he would shortly speak to the tower and find out the height of the base. Even if it was not right down on the deck before he made visual contact with the ground, how much forward visibility would he have?

Having set the aircraft up for the approach with landing lights on, he reduced power further and allowed the aircraft to slowly sink. He made a double check that he had moved the mixture control from WEAK to NORMAL so as to be able to throttle back completely. The tower had returned his request for a height check with both bad and good news. The fog was in patches right down on the deck, but in some areas as high as a hundred feet. The visibility was a hundred yards in places. On that report he would give it a go. One approach, and if he missed out he would have to find somewhere else to land. His Lizzie became swallowed up by the fog. Ahead the aircraft's landing lights formed a ghostly halo.

With his attention alternating between what was happening outside beyond the Perspex canopy and the indication on his altimeter, he felt that familiar adrenalin rush course through his body. Gone was any doubt as to the wisdom of his decision to try an approach. His focus was on the here and now, winding the tail actuator to such a position that should he have to go-around, the aircraft was properly configured.

Down, down they went. Where were those damn pole-mounted funnel lights? Suddenly a pale orange light appeared ahead and just below them. Then a momentary glimpse of the ground, but then nothing! They were back into the clag. Decision time. Just as he was about to apply power to the engine to overshoot he felt the wheels touch solid ground, but his altimeter was telling him that he should still be in the air. This anomaly had come about due to an erroneous reading on his altimeter.

Bringing the aircraft to a halt and unable to see more than a few feet in front of him, he informed the tower that they had landed and required assistance.

"Welcome to England, gentlemen. We'll taxi to dispersal just as soon as help arrives." In the heat of the moment, with his body winding down from the tension that had built up inside him during the approach, he had forgotten what little French he possessed. But nothing could matter less. They were safely on the ground. Now all they had to do was report the existence of something nasty making its way down the English Channel.

A follow-me jeep appeared out of the fog. Minutes later, at dispersal, they were clambering out of the Lizzie. The reception committee composed of a civilian in a duffle coat and black beret along with an unknown squadron leader who did not hide his surprise at the Lizzie's arrival in such adverse weather conditions.

"We fully expected you to divert, Sergeant. What's the height of this stuff, and how thick is it? We're waiting on a Hudson."

Aware that he had probably burgled his way into Tangmere, albeit inadvertently, Gifford's reply was cautious. 'It's fluctuating, sir. Not all that bad, really."

Later the duty intelligence officer, a young WAAF, took down its position and what little he could tell her of the ship that they had seen less than an hour earlier. In so doing he knew that he would never hear whether or not the Royal Navy was successful in preventing the German vessel from escaping into the Atlantic.

The following afternoon, at Tempsford, Gifford was again on the mat in front of the wing commander and his squadron commander.

"The squadron leader and I have been discussing your position within the squadron, Gifford. You could say we've given the matter some considerable thought. We think the best thing to do is for you to return to Coastal Command. They're crying out for experienced Hudson drivers. Isn't that correct, Squadron Leader?"

"Yes, sir. You may be interested to know why we have come to this decision, Sergeant," Squadron Leader Huntington-Brown commented disdainfully.

For Sergeant Ian Gifford it was something he had been expecting ever since returning the previous day from Tangmere. Had he burgled his way into Tempsford? He didn't think so, at least not intentionally. He had, however, given them the excuse they had been looking for to have him moved from the squadron. Also, he remembered that upon his first meeting with the wing commander he had gained the impression that he was simply filling a gap in the roster until a more suitable pilot could be allocated from OTU.

"Yes, sir." At this stage in the proceedings he had little to gain from antagonising either of the two men who sat opposite while he stood to attention.

"Last night you burgled into Tangmere. It was below minima, Gifford. Shortly after you landed, two other flights, both Hudsons, were forced to divert. Tangmere, Gifford, was below ops. You purposefully put your passengers and the aircraft at risk. You let this matter of the German warship, which you claim to have seen in the Channel, blur your judgement. There's no place in this squadron for pilots whose judgement is blurred. Or maybe you were trying to prove that you were better than the other pilots in the squadron. Either way, you've blotted your copy book, Gifford."

"We also have to take into account the damage you have sustained to two of the squadron's aircraft during your short time with us, one of which was out of the air for a week. Also, one of your passengers was killed while in your care, another severely wounded. You even managed to get one murdered." The wing commander had clearly been keeping score. "I blame myself, Gifford. Do you know that?"

"You do, sir?"

"Yes, Gifford, I do. Bringing you into the squadron was a mistake, something I should never have considered. However, your replacement will be with us just as soon as OTU releases him. Shouldn't be more than a couple of days. Until then, consider yourself grounded."

"You might as well start packing your kit, Gifford. There's nothing more for you to do here. Your new posting will be through any day," his squadron commander added.

Sergeant Gifford returned to his mess not, as both the wing commander and the squadron leader would have supposed, a chastened man, but rather as someone released from a perverse situation over which he had little or no control. All things considered, and in spite of his squadron commander, he had enjoyed his time on the Lizzie. He had nothing to reproach himself for.

He had been granted an insight into a sphere of operations few were ever likely to experience. His war while he was stationed at Tempsford had become more interesting, and he had met people the likes of which would not in the normal course of events ever have crossed his path, among them Simone. The same could not be said for Shirley. Being with ATA, it was possible that their paths could have crossed at any operational unit. That notwithstanding, like Simone, Shirley was a welcome addition to his life. When and where he would again meet either of the two women would depend on his next posting, which, assuming it wasn't overseas, made any possible meeting merely a logistical problem.

What Sergeant Gifford and the other pilots of the Special Squadron did not know was that, for many of their flights into occupied France, collaborators had arranged with both the Luftwaffe and German flack commanders safe conduct to their targets. To the Germans it was the Resistance networks that were of the most interest.

Review Requested:

If you loved this book, would you please provide
a review at Amazon.com?

Lightning Source UK Ltd.
Milton Keynes UK
UKHW01f1754060818
326846UK00001B/208/P